"The only thing you need to understand is that you're assigned to me for a special mission."

Ryder took out a small, bedraggled black notebook. "If you have anything to add to your earlier statement, do it now. Oh, by the way, I don't want you or your dad discussing this with anyone. Is that clear?"

Hope glared across the table. "I brought this to your attention, Colonel. I think I have a right to be apprised."

"On a need-to-know basis, Major. And all you need to know is to do as I say. The first thing I want you to do is introduce me to your dad."

With pleasure! She sprang up and darted around him, cheerfully holding the door open for his departure. The minute he stepped out, she closed it and grinned like a baboon. Her father, a retired major general, would never take orders from an upstart colonel. Lord, but she couldn't wait to introduce those two. Ryder McGrath wouldn't know what hit him.

Dear Reader,

As a rule, my stories come to me first through characters. I was surprised when the setting for this story grabbed me and wouldn't let go. I toured the Titan Missile Museum near Tucson, Arizona, shortly after moving to the city. I never expected to be so chillingly affected. Like me, you may have been blissfully unaware that from 1962 to 1984, fifty-four nuclear missiles were situated throughout the United States, waiting to be programmed for "top secret" targets. All were capable of being launched in less than one minute by order of the president. All but ours have been dismantled. It's been disarmed, but what if…?

That's the question I asked the tour guide. "What if terrorists hijacked this site with its well-oiled doors and highly technical control center?" "Can't happen," he assured me. "Too many safeguards on nuclear fuel." But I write fiction. I concoct fantasy. The next week, I read a news article in the *Arizona Daily Star* that mirrored my uneasy thoughts. Then a writer friend gave me an article from the *Smithsonian Magazine* that insinuated nuclear fuel isn't all that well guarded. Add the fact that a lot of wacky, hate-filled people roam this earth….

But I believe that love conquers hate. It triumphs over evil. I believe that people like Major Hope Evans and Lieutenant Colonel Ryder McGrath exist, people who love family, country and each other enough to go beyond the call of duty. And so this story was born.

I hope you enjoy it—and I love hearing from readers.

Roz Denny Fox
P.O. Box 17480-101
Tucson, Arizona 85731

MAD ABOUT THE MAJOR
Roz Denny Fox

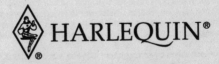

HARLEQUIN®

TORONTO • NEW YORK • LONDON
AMSTERDAM • PARIS • SYDNEY • HAMBURG
STOCKHOLM • ATHENS • TOKYO • MILAN • MADRID
PRAGUE • WARSAW • BUDAPEST • AUCKLAND

ISBN 0-373-70821-1

MAD ABOUT THE MAJOR

Copyright © 1999 by Rosaline Fox.

All rights reserved. Except for use in any review, the reproduction or utilization of this work in whole or in part in any form by any electronic, mechanical or other means, now known or hereafter invented, including xerography, photocopying and recording, or in any information storage or retrieval system, is forbidden without the written permission of the publisher, Harlequin Enterprises Limited, 225 Duncan Mill Road, Don Mills, Ontario, Canada M3B 3K9.

All characters in this book have no existence outside the imagination of the author and have no relation whatsoever to anyone bearing the same name or names. They are not even distantly inspired by any individual known or unknown to the author, and all incidents are pure invention.

This edition published by arrangement with Harlequin Books S.A.

® and TM are trademarks of the publisher. Trademarks indicated with ® are registered in the United States Patent and Trademark Office, the Canadian Trade Marks Office and in other countries.

Printed in U.S.A.

MAD ABOUT
THE MAJOR

CHAPTER ONE

RYDER MCGRATH had surfaced again. Major Hope Evans closed her eyes and dragged a vision from the past of his crooked smile. He didn't smile often, but when he did it was devastating. The man had had the grace of a cheetah, the eyes of a tiger and a mind like a steel trap. He'd been a major when first they'd met. A tactical instructor flying AC-130's for Special Forces. Now a bulletin announcing him as Lieutenant Colonel McGrath, attached to Air Staff in Washington, said he'd come to her Tucson, Arizona, air base to oversee the testing and integration of a new IFF upgrade on the fleet of one hundred and thirty aircraft. Updating codes for electronic Identification of Friend and Foe on the very planes Hope flew. The notice fluttered from her shaking hand. She hadn't seen Ryder, whose buddies called him the Strategist, in five—no, make that six years.

Hope opened pain-filled eyes to stare blankly at the row of gunmetal-gray lockers. A lot had changed in six years. Certainly she'd changed. She'd run from Elmendorf, Alaska, two years ago when sources said Ryder was slated to teach a course there on new battle tactics. She wouldn't let him drive her away again. She had her head on straight and an unbreakable lock on her heart. She loved flying EC-130's out of Monahan. Ryder McGrath be damned. She'd show him she had become as cold and calculating as he.

If he cared to ask about her, which he wouldn't, he'd hear her called the Arctic Fox behind her back. The moniker had followed her to Monahan from her Alaskan duty station. The handle stuck because, while she did her job and did it well, she never dated her fellow male officers. Never. Thanks to Ryder McGrath.

Hope retrieved the bulletin from the floor and round-filed it with a neat flick of her wrist. Luckily no one had been around to witness her initial reaction to the news. Swallowing a sigh, she opened her locker, stripped off her flight suit and stuffed it into her zoom bag, the first step in preparing for a welcome weekend off. After a refreshing shower, she donned a sleeveless tank top and matching knit shorts. At the exit to the building, Hope bumped into another pilot, who was jogging past.

"Hey, Evans." The tall, sandy-haired flyer who'd touched down behind her on the runway, hitched his belt and swaggered closer. Major Lance Denton did everything with a swagger. Quite possibly one of Hope's least favorite people.

"A bunch of us are heading to Rocky Point for a little R and R. We've got room for one more." He braced an arm on the doorjamb above Hope's head.

She telegraphed him her disinterest with a look she'd perfected. "I already have plans," she said coolly, tightening her grip on the handles of the bag.

"You always have plans." Denton crowded her. "I wonder what would happen if I followed you sometime. Would I find tarnish on your pristine image? Is there a hidden kid? A tryst with a married man?"

"Don't judge others by yourself, Denton." Hope batted his arm aside. "And check the ID's on all those little co-eds in Rocky Point this weekend."

"Not everyone believes you're just living up to reputation of the sterling family in blue. Don't forget that I went to the academy with your brother Chris. He's no angel. I've heard stories about your older brother, Rolf, too. I wanna be around when your past surfaces, babe. I have a feeling you won't be so smug.'' His smile resembled a sneer.

She tried for a scowl as she whipped past, taking care not to touch him. Hope prayed the jerk wouldn't notice his threat had made her pulse beat faster. With Ryder McGrath making an appearance, her past *had* surfaced. Surfaced with a vengeance.

Six years ago she'd fallen hard and fast for the handsome major. At twenty-seven, she'd been no dewy-eyed kid. Yet Ryder had been her first—her only—love. Until they'd met at air command school in Alabama, the air force had been her life. As it was now. And that's how it would stay. She should have known better at any age. At thirty-three, she was far too old to cry on anyone's shoulder, yet here she was, headed home to Mom and Dad.

She considered the proximity of her present duty station to the retirement community where Ted and Dory Evans lived a huge perk. While she'd never confided in them about her broken heart, they'd unwittingly helped to heal it. They loved her unconditionally, the way she'd thought Ryder loved her.

Brother, had she been wrong. So very, very wrong.

A SCANT HOUR LATER, Hope swung her sporty, red Chrysler convertible down a street of Santa Fe–style homes in the largely retirement community of Verde Vista. She slowed at a golf-cart crossing outside the private club where her dad played. Apparently not today. Both cars sat in her parents' garage.

"Hel...lo," she yodeled, letting herself into the house with a key. It was shortly after 1300, 1:00 p.m., nonmilitary time. Hope made a flurry of sound in case her folks were in the master suite to the right off the entry hall. She thought it was nice that they loved each other enough after four decades of marriage to enjoy stolen afternoons of lovemaking. Once she'd accidentally interrupted them, and they'd been so embarrassed she now tried to be more discreet.

Today Dory Evans burst from the sunny kitchen, her face wreathed in smiles. "Hope. Thank heavens you're early. Come." She motioned with her hand. "Let your father bend your ear. Mine's ready to fall off." She lowered her voice. "Humor him, dear. The man is certain he's uncovered some horribly subversive plot at the Titan Missile Museum. Between you and me, I think he needs a shrink." Stripping Hope's duffel from her hand, Dory jerked a thumb toward the kitchen as she continued in the direction of the spare bedroom Hope always used.

Hope grinned. Life around the Evans household was never dull. This was exactly what she needed to help her forget Lieutenant Colonel Ryder McGrath's untimely arrival in her orderly life. She pushed through the louvered doors. "Dad. What's got your blood pressure elevated this time? Need I remind you that retirement was designed to help you type-A men relax?"

"Major!" Her steely-haired father, still trim at sixty-five, jumped up from the table and smiled with pride at his only daughter. "You're exactly who I need to see. Sit. I'll pour you a glass of iced tea. It's fresh—your mother just made it. I've got something I want to run by you."

"Mom insinuated something's gone wrong at the museum where you volunteer."

"Used to volunteer," he said, plunking a frosty glass in front of Hope. "Approximately three months ago, the guys in my air force association who acted as tour guides for the museum all received letters stating that someone from the Aerospace Foundation would be arriving to re-structure the volunteer program. A few days later, a man named Patterson showed up. Puffed-up beady-eyed in-tense fellow. Poked into everything. Never asked a sin-gle question of the volunteers. Never said a word, either. But before he left, he handed out an entirely new shift rotation."

Hope watched her dad stir three teaspoons of sugar into his tea. "So," she prompted with an indulgent smile, "he played havoc with your golf foursome?"

"Nope. Hear me out. This is serious. One by one each of us was dropped from the roster, replaced by total strangers. A bunch of young punks."

"All of you?" Hope paused with her glass halfway to her mouth.

"All. Most of the guys didn't balk. Said they were tired of being tied down. Me—" he thumbed his chest "—I want to know why, after all the time we've given them, they phase us out without so much as a thank-you."

"Call and ask the man from Aerospace."

"I did. Didn't turn up anyone who knew about any change—or a man named Patterson."

"What?"

He inched toward her. "My reaction exactly. Last per-son I spoke with said maybe the county or the air force instituted a new procedure. They said there could have been a change in the treaty. So I called the county. They claimed ignorance. And I'd stake my life that that pip-squeak wasn't air force."

Hope quickly ran through what she knew about the Treaty of 1981 that ordered all fifty-four Titan missile sites dismantled, the equipment salvaged and the nuclear warheads destroyed. The site in Verde Vista had been leased to the county by the air force, then, in turn, to the Aerospace Foundation for educational purposes. The missile itself had been totally deactivated and the compound opened to visitors. That was really all she knew, and she'd learned that touring the site with her dad.

"You still have contacts in D.C. Call and see if they've heard of treaty changes," she said, focusing on the ice swirling in her glass.

"Did that last week. Got nothing." He scowled. "Some young, wet-behind-the-ears pup as much as called me paranoid."

Hope hid a grin. Retired or not, Major General Theodore Evans prided himself on staying alert, on keeping up with what was currently happening in the military through his daughter and two sons, all air force officers. "Sorry, Dad, but it sounds like you covered all the bases. I don't know what else to suggest."

"This morning I talked to an old warhorse sidekick of mine, General Pugmire. Pug, we called him. A real bulldog when he gets his teeth into something. He's been kicked upstairs. Shuffles papers at the Pentagon. Told me they've got a man on temporary assignment at Monahan. A colonel. I don't know what all the guy's done, but Pug says he knows his way around the pointy end of a missile. I want you to make an appointment with this colonel and get his take on this situation."

"Me? Monahan hasn't had a connection to missiles since the Titan sites were closed. The people who worked in Strategic Air Command before it disbanded have no authority."

"I tell you, something fishy is going on." Her father thumped the table. "Just talk to this fellow. Lay out my suspicions. He'll know channels to go through to have it investigated. Matter of fact, Pug hemmed and hawed so much, this flyboy colonel may be more than he seems."

"What's his name? It's a big base, you know."

"McGrath. Lieutenant Colonel Ryder McGrath. Know him?"

The glass of half-drunk tea slipped from Hope's fingers and broke on the gleaming Saltillo tile floor. Blindly she mopped up the mess. This couldn't be happening. Her father was suggesting she pay a visit to the very person she never wanted to see again as long as she lived.

"Watch out for slivers of glass, Major. I told your mother these new glasses are slippery as hell. Glad you broke the first of the set. Always figured it'd be me."

Panic set the tea in Hope's stomach churning. Her father didn't know—couldn't know what he'd asked of her. Yet once they'd cleared the remains of the glass and were reseated, he doggedly returned to the subject.

"Dad, I understand, your...feelings are hurt. But I suspect you're making more of this than a few dismissals warrant." She reached across the table and patted his hand.

He snatched his hand away. "Your old man did reconnaissance on subversive activity before you were born. If I say this deserves investigation, it does."

Hope's hands felt clammy. She respected her father and his instincts. But he'd been retired for several years. A new thought popped into her head. She could visit the museum and form her own opinion. After all, she was knowledgeable in surveillance and reconnaissance, too. Her EC-130 flights often patrolled the border.

"Dad, why don't I visit the museum this afternoon? You know…play tourist. I'll borrow Mom's camera and take pictures. If I spot anything unusual, I'll request an appointment with General Pugmire's contact first thing Monday morning."

He flew out of his chair and bellowed for his wife. "Dory, Dory, get the major our pocket camera. Hurry. She'll barely make the last tour, and only if she leaves now." Catching Hope's hand, he dragged her toward the door.

Dory Evans bustled into the room. "Ted, when will you ever call our children by their names? What is it you need in such a rush?"

"The camera, the camera. Hope—" and he enunciated her name as if it were unfamiliar "—had an idea worthy of her old man. I don't know why I didn't think of sending someone to take photos the day after the last of us were fired."

Dory pulled out a kitchen drawer and rummaged through it until she produced the camera. "I don't think *fired* is the proper term for someone who was a volunteer, dear." She rolled her eyes as she handed Hope the case.

Used to her parents' lively banter, Hope merely draped the camera strap around her neck and started for the door. "I expect dinner in exchange for my undercover work, General. I flew a mission this morning before breakfast. Missed lunch to get here early. If I stop to have this film developed on the way home, I'll be surly as a bear."

"Have it developed," Ted ordered. "We'll go out to eat."

"No, we won't," Dory put in quickly. "I'm fixing taco salads. You're mixing strawberry margaritas," she said, linking arms with her husband.

Chuckling, Hope left them planning her favorite evening meal. She'd counted on her mom's intervention. Hope dropped in whenever possible to shed job-related stress, and Dory Evans knew it. She also knew Hope preferred impromptu backyard family get-togethers to eating out.

At one time, Hope might have become a copy of her mother. Hope would have willingly put her career on hold to support Ryder's climb up the military ladder as Dory had done for Hope's father. But once Hope left Alabama, it was as if Ryder had had his fling with her and that was that. He'd never called, written or taken her calls.

For her it had been love at first glance. She thought it had been for him, too. From the minute they'd been introduced at the officers' club, they'd clicked. Rules weren't enforced so vigorously then. They'd spent every minute together that her speaking assignment and his teaching duties allowed. It still hurt to realize he'd played her for a fool.

She prayed her father was wrong about anything untoward going on at this remote missile site. Hope intended to do her level best to avoid Ryder McGrath in and around the squadron office and on the flight line. She wouldn't willingly make an appointment to see him. Not even for her dad.

Hope parked in the gravel lot outside of a heavy-gauge chain-link fence that enclosed the entire museum facility. Just what, she wondered, did Ted Evans think was going on out here? Safeguards under the disarmament treaty made any type of launching impossible, didn't it? Granted, a missile minus its warhead had been reassembled and placed in the silo to simulate realism. But as dictated by treaty, its propellant tanks had been removed and the silo closure doors had been cemented into a half-open position. Could someone be using the site to squirrel away automatic weapons?

She climbed from her car and fell into step with a large group of tourists who had descended from two vans. Good. She could observe without sticking out like a sore thumb. If anything was out of order here, she'd soon find out.

A clean-cut young man who looked as if he worked out regularly with weights escorted the visitors into a darkened room to view an introductory movie. Nothing had been cut from the movie that Hope could see, and the man gave a similar spiel to the one her dad once gave. From there, visitors donned hard hats and crossed the compound.

Hope snapped pictures to her heart's content. Without seeming to, she looked for unauthorized vehicles or added buildings that might indicate a sudden stockpile of weapons. Nothing appeared to be out of the ordinary.

"Have you worked here long?" she asked the guide assigned to take them belowground. He was about the same age as the first fellow, and equally intense. He gazed at her steadily from fathomless black eyes.

"Long enough," he said, stepping to the side, out of the range of her viewfinder.

Hope unwrapped a stick of gum and chewed thoughtfully. "A friend of mine from the U of A who visited here last summer told me all of the guides were old duffers." She wadded another piece of gum into her mouth, taking care to relax her natural military bearing.

"You guys must be independently wealthy," she joked. "Or aren't these jobs still volunteer?"

He shot her a frown. "I work nights at a paying job, and so do some of the others."

"Oh." Hope moved away, feeling like a fool.

Deep in the silo, she expected to be told to not take pictures. If any covert activity was going on, the control room would be the perfect place, but several people in her group took flash shots and no one stopped them. Hope did notice that the volunteers seemed to make a point of avoiding the shutterbugs. That was definitely different. Her dad and his cronies had loved to mug for tourists' pictures.

On the landing that led to the rocket, she fell into step with a third muscle-bound volunteer. "Are you guys all members of some local gym? Or do you stay in shape running up and down nine stories every half hour with tour groups?" Hope puffed purposely lest he wonder and ask how *she* stayed in shape. She routinely ran five miles a day and played racquetball whenever a woman fighter pilot she knew had free time. Hope had about given up on getting an answer to her query when the man spoke.

"Some of us belong to a civil defense unit. Others work part time for border patrol. This site is less than forty miles from Mexico, you know."

Hope chewed on his statement, trying to put it into perspective as he moved ahead and she followed him up the next curl of narrow metal stairs. To her knowledge, though she was by no means an expert on the subject, civil defense had died out after the end of the Second World War. But a resurgence would explain these men's ties to the site and their almost military bearing. If they worked undercover for border patrol, it might even explain their aversion to having their pictures taken.

And by the time Hope followed him topside again, she had no doubt but they were camera shy. As the guide explained to the group about radar-detection equipment so sensitive a jackrabbit on the lower desert floor could set it off, Hope shot her remaining roll of film, always trying to capture one of the volunteers in her lens. Near the display of first-stage rocket engines, she thought she'd succeeded in including a guide who'd stopped to adjust his hard hat.

She took a last look around inside the gift shop before leaving the site. There, as everywhere else, nothing seemed out of place. But like her dad, Hope felt something amiss. A shiver raised the fine hair on her neck when she slipped past the unsmiling young man who held open the door. Maybe that was it. Ted and his friends from the air force association had laughed and joked with tourists. These guys were serious. Dead serious. Every move they made was too pat.

Still, she mused fifteen minutes later as she window-shopped along the plaza and waited for her film to be developed, in all honesty she hadn't noticed one thing to necessitate seeing Ryder McGrath. Hope shrugged off her uneasy feelings. She'd obviously let her good sense be tainted by her father's inflated concerns.

"Everything looked shipshape," she reported to him after returning to her parents' home. "I took thirty-six pictures, and I don't think you'll find any problems."

The crusty retired general got out a magnifying glass and carefully checked each photo. "Where are the 'studly' new guides, as Jace and Mavis Purcell's daughter calls them? Their daughter and a friend from college toured the museum last week. At a barbecue that night, all they could talk about were the muscle-bound hunks who replaced Jace and me."

Hope bent over the table and rifled through the stack of prints. "Um…I was sure I caught one of the guides next to the rocket booster. He must have moved before the shutter clicked. All I got is his hand and arm." She picked up the magnifying glass. "His fingernails are clipped and clean. I can't read the insignia, but it looks like a college class ring he's wearing."

Ted Evans scooted the pictures into a neat pile. "Doesn't it strike you as odd that none of them wanted to be in your pictures? I figure during my ten years of volunteering at the Titan Museum I must be in over a million tourist photographs."

Dory turned from the counter where she stood tossing the salad mixture. "Yes, Ted, but you also drove to Old Tucson and stood in line six hours hoping to be selected as an extra in that last western they shot here on the desert, too." She turned to Hope and arched an eyebrow. "Did you know your father fancies himself the next John Wayne?"

"I do not," Ted said. "Besides, you're the one who pointed out the casting notice in the paper."

Hope laughed at her dad's fast backpedalling.

"Laugh," he said. "All I ask is that you relay this information to Pug's contact. I trust him to do the rest."

Trust Ryder McGrath? Hope had trusted him once. Trusted him to keep the commitments they made to each other during the long nights when he'd initiated her into the wonders of making love. Unfortunately the commitment had been one-sided. All those times they'd shared candlelit meals, danced until dawn, discussed future dreams and made mad passionate love as if there were no tomorrow, Hope hadn't realized that for her and Ryder there'd be no tomorrow.

In all the weeks they'd spent together—his biggest

crime in her estimation—he'd never bothered to tell her
he'd been married once. She found out later, accidentally, through a mutual friend. Who further said that Ryder's wife had died a year or so before he and Hope met.
It just seemed so unlike Ryder to conceal an important
fact like that. But then, he obviously was nothing like
the man she thought she knew and loved. Hope honestly
didn't know how she felt about trusting him.

Not that it mattered now, she reminded herself as she
sat down to the meal her mother had prepared. She was
well and truly over her infatuation with Ryder. She'd cut
her hair and shed ten pounds since Alabama. There was
a good chance he wouldn't recognize her. Or remember
her. Which wasn't to say Hope was eager to present him
with her dad's suspicions. If Ryder did remember her, it
wouldn't be fondly. If she ran to him with spy stories
of a defunct Titan site, he'd laugh her out of the office.
A false allegation could mar her spotless record. Hope
wasn't willing to risk that.

"Dad, I don't believe we have enough to go on. I
think we should wait. McGrath is too new on base. I
only received notice today that he'd come on board."

Ted Evans reared back and glared at his daughter.
"This whole deal has a bad smell. Just tell him, all
right?"

"All right." Hope gave up and poured herself a second margarita. She avoided talking about the situation
for the remainder of the weekend.

SUNDAY AFTERNOON she drove back into Tucson, her
dad's admonition ringing in her ears. "Go see Colonel
McGrath," he'd ordered.

However, throwing herself into the normalcy of everyday activity made the whole notion seem outrageous. By midweek she'd talked herself out of contacting Ryder. Who would be so stupid as to set up subversive activities under the nose of the air force? The answer was, no one.

Wednesday, Hope wandered in off the flight line and nearly tripped over her boots. If that wasn't Ryder McGrath climbing into an outbound plane, her rank wasn't major. God, he looked good. Tall, rangy, suntanned. His black hair gleamed with blue highlights. Unless her eyesight deceived her, there was a touch of frost at his temples that hadn't been there six years ago. Outside of that, barring any change in his honey-gold eyes, which she couldn't see from this distance, Ryder McGrath hadn't gone through any great metamorphosis since dumping her. While her heart had shattered and she had permanent cry lines around her eyes. But why would he look ravaged? He'd never loved her. She'd been too silly-in-love herself to realize he'd never said the magic words.

"Evans, do I detect yearning in those mean green eyes for our new, esteemed IFF ace?" Lance Denton squeezed Hope's shoulder with far too much familiarity.

She shrugged out from beneath his hand. "Is that who's sporting the shiny silver oak leaf? He does project a presence. And he's a rank above you, Denton," she taunted. "Aren't you afraid he'll steal all the girls in your little black book?"

Sandy eyebrows veed over the bridge of Denton's nose. "Guess you haven't heard that he has a reputation as an iceman where women are concerned. So if you've been holding out for a man of rank, pet, don't waste your feminine wiles on McGrath. He won't appreciate the effort. But, hey, you're welcome to try them on me."

It was all Hope could do to cover her astonishment at the news that Ryder apparently hadn't remarried. He'd been attentive, gentle and patient in every aspect of their relationship. Iceman would be the last description with which she'd tag him. On the contrary, Hope would have said Ryder McGrath enjoyed women. She remembered the hours he'd spent going from store to store helping her select a dress to wear for a special evening on the town. She'd gone to Alabama with nothing but her uniforms and knock-around clothes. Ryder had an eye for color and style. She'd never looked better than in the dress he'd spotted on a back rack and insisted she try on. Recalling fond memories brought a raw pain to Hope's throat.

Of all her co-workers, Lance Denton was the one in front of whom she'd never let her guard slip. "Get the message, Denton. I'm an officer in the U.S. Air Force. I don't have feminine wiles." Averting her gaze from Ryder's lean form, she rudely shoved past the obnoxious major.

Not taking the hint, he followed her into Flight Ops. Fortunately a clerk stopped Hope and handed her a message from her father. Muttering that she had a call to return, she excused herself. It didn't surprise Hope that Denton stayed behind to flirt with the pretty airman. Denton was blind to rank when it came to anyone wearing a skirt. Hope didn't understand how he kept from getting reprimanded. Lance, like so many other male officers, had a larger than average supply of Y chromosomes and a small mind. In the case of the airman clerk, Denton had the power to keep her from being promoted, which was why so many women in the military let harassment slide.

The first time Hope met Ryder McGrath, she'd beaten him at darts. Then she'd found out through the men who'd badgered her into challenging him to a game that

Ryder was a strong arm in Special Forces. Some such macho men would have held the win against a woman. They would have humiliated her in front of other flight jockeys. Not Ryder. He had applauded her skill.

Hope grimaced. She'd let Colonel McGrath take up entirely too much of her time and thoughts this week. Finding an empty desk with a modicum of privacy, Hope snatched up the phone and dialed her father.

"Major, thanks for taking time to call." Ted Evans only used his children's birth names when one or more with the same rank visited at the same time. Which didn't happen often. Rolf was on a tour in Ramstein, Germany, and Chris currently flew out of Andrews Air Force Base in Maryland.

"What's up? Mom okay? And you?" Hope could count on one hand the number of times her father had called her at work.

"I went to the grocery store for your mother yesterday. Standing in line I happened to overhear two bird-watchers telling someone about a campout they'd been on over the weekend."

Bird-watchers? Hope's chest constricted. Was something funny going on in her dad's brain? She had friends whose parents had become forgetful or who on occasion spaced out completely. She'd never thought it would happen to either of her parents. They seemed so young and vital. Her heart tripped a mile a minute.

"Are you still on the line, Major?"

Her dad's gruff voice pulled Hope back from the edge of worry. "I'm listening. What do bird-watchers have to do with us?"

"I'm trying to tell you. The two men were camped near the perimeter of the missile site. During my years as a volunteer, we saw a lot of birders on that strip of land. Could tell them by the number of binoculars hanging around their necks.''

"Yes…so?" Hope prompted. "Dad, I have a flight scheduled at 1400. Do you mind getting to the point?''

"The point," he snapped, "is that two tough-looking military types roared up in a jeep, interrupted our birders' evening meal, spouted some official-sounding jargon and escorted them out to the highway. The men in the jeep indicated they had authority to police the area. I just wondered what McGrath thought when you met with him?''

Escorted. At night? Hope fought a knot forming in her stomach. Volunteers—no one worked the museum at night. "I…um…ah…" She cleared her throat. "I've been busy. So has he. I haven't managed an appointment yet.''

"Don't mean to tell you what to do, Major. But could you make this a priority?''

She sighed and raked a hand through her hair. "Yes, sir. I'll do that stat.''

"Ahem," he rumbled. "Call me when you hear something.''

The click in Hope's ear sounded like a death knell. She doodled on a pad lying on the desk. Drew a heart, a bull's-eye and ran an arrow through it. Then she ripped off the page and crumpled it into a tight ball. Stuffing it deep in the pocket of her flight suit, she dialed the squadron office and asked to meet with Lieutenant Colonel Ryder McGrath. It took Hope three tries to get her name out. She jotted the time for tomorrow morning down on the pad—0700. Hope folded the note precisely and tucked it into her breast pocket. She had really prayed Ryder would be too busy to see her this week. And maybe too busy next week. She needed more time to prepare for their first meeting.

Tomorrow. Hope had always known that eventually their paths would cross. It appeared the wait was over. Time had run out. Being an Evans through and through, Hope told herself in no uncertain terms that there was one thing an Evans wasn't—a coward. She'd be in the office they'd assigned Ryder bright and early with bells on.

As she caught a ride to the flight line where her EC-130 had been fueled and made ready for takeoff, she couldn't help wondering what reaction the LC would have when he saw her name on his appointment calendar. She'd never know, of course, but it did her heart good to imagine him suffering a tiny stab of guilt—providing he remembered her at all.

RYDER RETURNED to his desk in the borrowed office after making an air survey of the base's flight line. He'd tried to steer clear of this assignment—which was probably why some demented superior had sent him here. Ryder had a personal reason for avoiding Monahan. His reason had a name. Major Hope Victoria Evans. When she'd transferred from Alaska to Arizona so fast after it appeared he'd be sent to Elmendorf, Ryder knew she didn't want to see him. Which was why he was doubly shocked when he flipped the page on his blotter and saw her name staring back as his first appointment the next morning.

Sweat beaded Ryder's forehead and pooled in his palms. He closed his eyes, tipped back in his chair and recalled the features that had haunted him for six long years. Hope. The golden leggy goddess who'd thrown darts with the precision of a pro. She'd been neither impressed nor intimidated by his status in Special Forces when her so-called friends had tricked them into competing in a darts match.

Captain Evans—she'd been a captain then—possessed a husky sultry laugh that had invaded Ryder's heart and lifted him out of the depths of despair that had claimed him for over a year. Hope exploded into his life the evening of the day he'd finally gotten the courage to clean April's things out of the house. Friends and family had badgered him for months to get on with his life. They said twelve months was too long to grieve for a wife snatched from him precipitously. Sweet waiflike April—the other half of his soul. Ryder thought his grief would never end. And it hadn't until Hope arrived on the scene. Hope, who didn't tiptoe around him like those who knew about his loss. Hope. Her zest for living brought him back from the brink of hopelessness. Her very name made him feel young again.

Ryder covered his face and dragged his hands down over his eyes, his cheeks, his chin. Why was she listed on his blotter? What did she want?

Six years ago she'd wanted something he wanted so badly to give. Something he thought he could give, but in the end discovered he couldn't. Those weeks they'd settled into a comfortable if not clandestine routine, and he'd accepted that Hope had come to love him. She had every right to expect love in return, and Ryder had wanted to commit. He'd wanted to recapture the happy days and loving nights he'd found with April. He *had* recaptured the experience with Hope. Recaptured and surpassed it in a way he'd never dreamed possible.

But when she left for Elmendorf, it was as if their time together had been unreal. What Hope Evans had done was make him forget April. The week after Hope's departure, he couldn't even recall what April looked like. That scared the hell out of him. It made him feel disloyal to the memory of a woman he'd sworn on her deathbed to love forever. The first time he'd heard Hope's lilting voice on his answering machine, Ryder knew he'd been lying to her and to himself. For him it was too soon. His friends and family had been so very wrong. Twelve months wasn't nearly long enough to grieve.

Snapping forward in his chair, Ryder leaned his elbows on the desk and buried his face in his hands. Thanks to time, his grief had eventually lessened. Now he had to face the guilt he felt over having taken the easy way out with Hope. At the time he'd thought it was the best way, letting what could never be fade with time. It hit him now between the eyes what a coward he'd been, never calling to explain. Ryder hadn't considered himself a coward. Looking back he saw that he had needed extra time to deal with April's death, and with the loss of their unborn son. Ryder was as sorry as the devil that his peace of mind had come at Hope's expense.

It had, he knew. Today he'd heard a couple of pilots joking about her frigidity. They'd referred to her as the Arctic Fox. His fault. He'd taken her virginity. Accepted it as a gift at a time when fraternization rules weren't the issue they were now. She'd been a warm, generous lover. So much more giving than April. Another reason he'd felt horribly guilty afterward.

Ryder sat staring at Hope's name until it grew dark and security lights winked on outside his window. He doubted he'd sleep tonight. Quite frankly, he didn't deserve to. He wouldn't blame her if she burst in here and broke a chair over his thick skull tomorrow. A woman capable of the passion he knew her to be capable of would also have a temper. He'd welcome her anger. He owed her the chance to heal, too.

CHAPTER TWO

HOPE DID HER BEST to hide the ravages of a sleepless night. She rarely wore makeup and didn't want to start for Ryder McGrath. However, sometimes a woman had to do what needed to be done to bolster her ego. She had her speech memorized. It was essential that she look calm, cool and collected to deliver it.

An hour later, flight suit freshly pressed, hair washed and brushed to a shine, dark circles covered by a light coating of base makeup, Hope paced outside squadron headquarters, mustering the nerve to go in. She prided herself on always being on time. So with one second to spare, she squared her shoulders, entered the building and announced her presence to the airman clerk who served Ryder's area.

Then she waited. Five minutes. Ten. Fifteen. Twenty. Her assurance began to evaporate. Her patience, as well. Did he think she wouldn't recognize this as a ploy to put him in the driver's seat? After five more minutes of cooling her heels, even the clerk started to glance nervously toward the colonel's door.

"The colonel is on the phone, Major Evans. With the Pentagon," the young man blurted out. "Would you like a cup of coffee?"

Hope relaxed the fingers she'd laced tightly in her lap. She'd say this much for Ryder: when he decided to impress someone by making them wait, he pulled out all the stops. *Pentagon? With General Pugmire?* If so, maybe her task would be easy.

"Coffee would be nice," she said to the youth, who looked so young this could well be his first assignment.

"Cream? Sugar?"

"Black." Hope registered the surprise in the airman's eyes. She knew the brew would be as strong as battery acid. Drinking squadron coffee black was a measure of manliness, a feat that transferred to a high level of bravery in Neanderthal minds. The news of how she took her coffee *would* reach Ryder. She vowed to choke down every last drop even if it ate gaping holes in her stomach. A decision she regretted after one swallow. Because the clerk stopped typing and gazed at her in such awe, Hope kept swallowing.

The cup was barely half-empty when Ryder's office door flew open and he strode out, chin jutted toward the ceiling as he smoothed and adjusted his tie. "Major, sorry for the delay. Unavoidable, I'm afraid. I do apologize."

His gravelly voice still had the power to deliver a quick, hot stab of need. A response Hope checked as she rose automatically and shifted the cup to her left hand in order to snap off a salute. The coffee in her stomach sloshed, then jelled into a knot.

In her brief but thorough assessment of the man she still dreamed about, Hope determined he looked like hell. Ryder hadn't the luxury of using her method to disguise his lack of sleep. Dark circles ringed eyes that could double as a map of Arizona's back roads.

"At ease," he breathed, feigning interest in a spot on the wall beyond Hope's head. "You have an IFF matter to discuss?" he asked in a terse voice.

Hope felt her heels still clicking together from nerves.

She forced her feet apart, set her jaw and gripped her cup with both hands. "Not IFF. No, sir."

Her curt response didn't appear to sit well with Ryder. But rather than take issue, he swept a hand toward his open office door. "I'll have a refill on my coffee, Airman Jackson," he told the clerk. "Then put the phones on hold and take a break. The major and I will be finished by 0800. I'm expecting a call then from General Beemis." He checked his watch against the wall clock and made an adjustment on the timepiece that banded his wrist.

Airman Jackson grabbed the pot and scooted past Ryder and Hope, who'd already stepped into his office. Filling the cup sitting on Ryder's desk, the clerk topped off Hope's drink, too.

She noticed that Ryder was careful not to make any bodily contact as he indicated where Hope should sit before he walked around the desk and took his chair. Ignoring her, he flipped through pages on a yellow legal pad, settling at last on a blank sheet.

Definitely stall tactics. Hope wanted to reach across the desk and rip the tablet out of his strong tanned hands. Clever hands that had taught her to appreciate the power and secrets of her womanhood. The cup she held wavered. She latched on to it with both hands, pretending to study the room while really studying Ryder. Was he really still single? A furtive glance at his left hand revealed only his ring from the academy. A ring she'd touched so many times she knew each raised letter and symbol intimately. The same way she knew his body.

"Now then, Major. What is the nature of your visit?"

His matter-of-fact voice and stiff manner dragged Hope back from dangerous territory. So he hadn't been on the phone with General Pugmire. The slight frown etched between his straight, silky black eyebrows prompted Hope to lay out her father's concerns in the same no-nonsense manner. The facts as she knew them. Ending abruptly after informing him she had only contacted him because General Pugmire suggested it to her father, she drained her cup, leaving Ryder to draw his own conclusions about the matter.

He laid down his pencil and twirled his mug but didn't pick it up. Irritation clung heavily to his next words. "Are you proposing to send me on a wild-goose chase?"

If she lifted an eyebrow, it was minimal. "I'm not proposing…anything, Colonel. I'm relaying information as my father requested. Not that I expect you to remember anything about my family, but Dad's a retired air force major general and not given to flights of fancy. The Titan II's from other dismantled sites are still flyable. I'm sure you know their rockets have been retrofitted to launch weather satellites."

Ryder looked at her—really looked, for the first time. She'd changed. Matured. If anything, she was more classically beautiful. Her cheekbones had sharpened, probably because she'd slimmed down. Her mouth, always generous, still invited kisses. But the laughter he'd loved above all else was missing from her emerald green eyes.

They may well have been two strangers talking, given the perfunctory, emotionless way she filed her report. If it was a report and not a hoax designed to get revenge. His frown deepened, and Ryder glanced over the list he'd jotted as she'd talked. He picked up his pencil again and tapped it on the pad. "I'll do some digging," he said. "See what I turn up. What's your flight schedule for the next few days? Either Airman Jackson or I will be in touch."

"Fine." Rising, Hope reeled off the times this week and next that she was scheduled to fly. Figuring he knew how to find her during off times, she walked out, head high, never once glancing back.

The door shut with what might well be termed a slam. Ryder broke his pencil lead. Sharpening another point brought a return to cool. Hope Evans hadn't risen to the rank of major by indulging in petty acts of vengeance. Her record was exemplary. Ryder knew. He'd spent half the night combing a computer printout of her file. Granted, her story sounded flaky, but few people had any inkling of his real mission at Monahan. General Aloysius Pugmire knew he'd been sent to investigate the consistent disappearance of new airplane parts. Did the general have reason to suspect the two problems were somehow connected?

Ryder rocked back in his chair, his thoughts ping-ponging for a moment between the woman and her il-logical suggestion. Kookier things had happened in the arena of subversive activity. He ought to know. He'd tracked down a few terrorists.

But hell, if Hope *did* want to exact her pound of flesh, she couldn't have dreamed up a scheme more apt to put his ass in a sling. Handling the parts investigation with-out tipping off the thieves would be tricky. If he blew it by going off on a phony-baloney tangent… The screech of tires outside his window brought Ryder up short. He was imagining that Hope was aware he'd volunteered for every dangerous mission that came up after she went back to Elmendorf. Really only a select few knew how near he'd come to letting guilt destroy his life. Guilt for not loving April enough. Guilt for loving Hope too much.

He still owed a couple of higher-ups for recognizing

his death wish and helping to turn him around. Pugmire for one.

Dare he risk losing everything he'd regained by placing his trust in a woman who had every reason in the world to stab him in the back?

Ryder felt a trickle of sweat slide down his spine and lodge against his belt. Honesty and openness had been Hope's way before. As badly as he'd treated her, and Ryder admitted it'd been bad, he just couldn't believe her capable of doing anything sneaky or underhanded to harm his career. If she thought there was validity to her father's tale, then he guessed he could make a few discreet inquiries. Run a few checks. That was, after all, the smartest avenue at this point.

Airman Jackson opened Ryder's door and poked his head inside. "General Roosevelt Beemis is on line one, sir."

Ryder nodded as Jackson withdrew. Beemis was aide to the chairman of the Joint Chiefs of Staff, also a member of the National Security Council. Who would be more interested than those guys if there was any truth to Hope's story? On the other hand, Ryder knew Beemis's reputation for letting subordinates hang for his bad decisions. It might be wise to start his inquiries in a smaller pond.

Undecided as to whether to mention the situation or not, Ryder snatched up the phone and barked, "McGrath here. At your service, sir."

AFTER HOPE LEFT Ryder's office, she dashed off to attend a routine operations briefing with her flight crew. Then, before her training flight, she detoured past a set of pay telephones. Though she had precious little to report, she wanted to call her dad. He wasn't a man to sit idle. Especially if he thought the security of his loved ones or the nation was at risk. Hope didn't want him landing in trouble. But she wasn't at all sure Ryder intended to look into the matter, though she had no concrete reason to believe he'd handed her platitudes, either. If she stretched the truth a teensy bit, she might talk her dad into holding off until Colonel McGrath or his emissary called her back. The way her father answered, before the completion of one full ring, she knew she'd better sound convincing.

"Dad, I met with McGrath this morning. The colonel said he'd do some digging." *That wasn't a lie. Those were Ryder's exact words....* "He indicated he'd be in touch again soon." *So she'd taken a little liberty with the projected time frame.*

Hope held the phone away from her ear as her father thundered questions at her.

"How soon?" she said. "Tomorrow? I…uh…doubt it'd be that quick. Takes longer than that to fill out a request in triplicate." She laughed and waited for a like response. Hearing what might pass for a chuckle, she plunged ahead. "I expect McGrath will call Aerospace. With luck, he'll get answers at that level. A colonel on active duty has more clout than a retiree." Darn! Why had she said that? She knew his philosophy—once a military man, always a military man. To Hope's surprise, he let her comment go and asked an unrelated question concerning Ryder.

"Did he strike me as reliable?" Hope repeated almost hysterically. *How to answer? Probably in military matters. Certainly not on a personal level.* It was past time to ring off. "I don't see that we have any choice but to wait. I hate to rush, Dad, but I have a recon flight scheduled to take off at 0900. Tell Mom I said hi." Hope hung up right after he wished her a good flight and headed for the locker room.

Her thoughts flipped back to Ryder the minute she'd replaced the receiver. When she'd first seen him today, she'd fantasized that she'd been the cause of his puffy, bloodshot eyes. Or rather, she'd imagined him seeing her name on his schedule and walking the floor all night. She'd dropped that notion before two words left his lips. He was all business. You would have thought they'd never met before, let alone shared a scorching love affair.

Now her steps slowed. Why had Ryder been on the phone to the Pentagon? Who was General Beemis? Oh, well, probably a lot of issues she knew nothing about fell under the heading of changing IFF codes. She hadn't paid any attention to that arena before Ryder showed up. Why involve herself now? He'd made it plenty plain that he didn't want to rekindle dead flames.

"Forget Ryder McGrath," she ordered herself as she slammed out of the women's locker room—and smacked Major Lance Denton against the side wall.

He straightened, looking rather dazed. "Forget who?" His eyes suddenly glittered with interest. "Don't tell me someone has finally melted the ice from the fur of our Arctic Fox."

Few people called Hope that to her face. A testament to what a jerk Lance Denton was. Hope sidestepped him. "She boils. She melts. She's human. And right now she's very late. I never forget to set my alarm. Last night I did. So shoot me, Denton. Is my bird ready to fly?"

He hooked a thumb in the corner of his flight-suit pocket and trailed her to the jeep waiting to take her to her plane. At the moment it was driverless. Denton leaned a shoulder negligently against the windshield.

"This is a momentous first. Major Evans flapped over a little thing like tardiness? Where's a witness? Nobody will believe it."

"Believe it. And get out of my face." Hope smiled gratefully at the driver who raced toward the jeep. Swinging her door wide, she whapped Denton again. "Oops! Sorry."

"Ow! Hey, watch it." He jumped back, holding his stomach.

"I did warn you." Honey dripped from her smile. "You really ought to learn to stand out of the way of doors, Major. What label do you suppose our flight psychologist would attach to that repetitive behavior? Early-stage sadomasochism perhaps?" Hope signaled her driver to take off. Oh, how she loved besting Denton. She wasn't alone in that respect. She'd caught the driver's smile. Denton was such a loudmouth. He'd needled Hope almost from the day she set foot on Monahan soil.

Not today, but more often than not, he brought her brother Chris's name under fire, too. Hope kept forgetting to ask Chris if he'd aced Denton out on some important level at the academy. Chris had graduated in the top one percent of his class, and he was a superb athlete. Hope was well aware by now, though, that some men needed no excuse to be miserable human beings. In some squadrons, they outnumbered the good. Thankfully that wasn't the case at Monahan.

Here, her copilot, flight crew and engineers were decent men. They respected her professionalism and appreciated her attention to detail. Right now they had a training mission to fly. It felt good to lose herself in the familiar system checks, and in so doing, flush Ryder and Denton from her mind. Hope succeeded in keeping thoughts of Ryder in abeyance only until she touched down at Edwards AFB for lunch. As was her habit, she left the men to congregate together while she found a quiet, empty corner of the officers' mess.

Gazing out the window at the palm-studded greenbelt surrounding Edwards, she watched an officer walk by. His broad shoulders and slim hips reminded her with a painful jolt of Ryder. Looks hadn't been the first thing that attracted her to Ryder, but certainly came in a close second. Initially, however, she'd been impressed by his sensitivity mixed with a hint of mystery.

She grinned at nothing. In other words, Ryder hadn't hit on her like two out of three other officers playing darts at the O-club that night. Of course she'd learned much later—too late—that the mysterious reticence had come from grief. Why hadn't he told her? What in heaven's name had prompted him to have a fling with her of all people? She was no femme fatale in any sense of the word.

Sadness overcame her as she realized she'd never truly gotten Ryder out of her system. Apparently she'd only suppressed memories of those wonderful weeks they'd spent together and the hurtful time after. Oh, God. Did dredging up the past mean she was going to have to transfer bases again?

"Ahem." A man cleared his throat and Hope's head shot up. She blinked uncertainly at her copilot, a lieutenant with shiny new wings and a serious nature.

"Are you okay, Major?" He gazed down at her in concern. "We're ready to go, but it doesn't look as if you've touched your meal."

She blinked at her plate, then at her watch, surprised to see that she'd been sitting in this catatonic state for nearly two hours. "Too much late-night TV," she lied, forcing a yawn as she stood. "How would you like to fly our sweep down the Baja?" Hope enjoyed the fact that he barely contained his delight.

"I'll do it, sir. Uh...Major. If that's your preference, of course."

"It is. You'll be looking out for any suspicious civilian aircraft that might not want to identify themselves or boats anchored in otherwise untraveled waterways. Double back along the border. I'll keep an eye peeled for foot traffic."

He stood straighter. "I'll file our return flight plan if you'd like to take a minute and eat that salad."

Hope's lips twitched. "Thank you, Lieutenant. Maybe I will." As he strode off, Hope thought about his eagerness. She used to be like that. Ready to fly off to the ends of the earth at the drop of a hat. After meeting Ryder, she'd thought more of taking a desk job and settling down. Her mother had dropped hints about that, too. Dory Evans teased Hope, saying she needed to find a househusband. A man willing to stay home and see to matters while she flew off into the wild blue yonder.

Frankly, Hope couldn't imagine marrying a man she had to support. Or rather, someone who'd let her support him. And what man would put his career on hold to follow her from base to base? From the time Hope first noticed boys, she'd been most attracted to the rogues. Guys with an edge. Her brothers always ran them off. Where had Rolf and Chris been when she'd met Ryder?

That line of thought was nonproductive. Hope pushed her salad away and stood. May as well give this meal up as a lost cause. All the way out to the plane she lectured herself on forgetting Ryder. Once he called, or had his clerk call to clear up what had really happened to change the volunteer program at the Titan site, there'd be no reason to deal with him ever again.

The idea both elated and depressed her.

Nor did her mood change when she returned to base and stopped by her in-basket to see what awaited her attention. The week after she'd transferred to Monahan, Hope had been handed the duty of morale officer in addition to flying spook and spy missions three days a week. As morale officer, it fell to her to set up social functions the commander's wife didn't handle. Not a difficult task, just tedious and time-consuming. Today the secretary had left a typed list of cards and flowers needing to be sent to squadron family members. Some had had surgery. Two had had babies.

Babies. Hope had imagined she'd start her family before this age. Before thirty. But even when they'd made plans, Ryder never wanted to discuss having children. Well, she thought wryly, it was fortunate they hadn't had an accident. And as they hadn't, she'd put aside plans for marriage and babies. When she'd moved nearer to her parents, the yearning had surfaced again. She had loosely set a new goal of thirty-five. That seemed unrealistic now. But forty? The barefaced truth was that at this point forty wasn't a good prospect. As Lissa, her former roommate had pointed out, you had to mingle with men to meet them. Meet them to date them. Date them to get a marriage proposal. Hope did none of those things.

She stabbed out the number to the flower shop with the eraser end of a pencil. So for her, even forty was unrealistic. The first flowers she ordered were for Lieutenant Baker's wife. Pink flowers for a baby girl. Hope had seen Pam Baker at the commissary last week. Pregnant. Glowing. Bubbly. Twenty-three years old, max.

A vase with a blue lamb would celebrate Captain Stevenson's boy. His second son. The older one was two. Hope added cheery words of encouragement to the message. Stevenson had been sent to Italy last month to fly EC-130 E air control radar support. His wife was a tiny, quiet woman. She also had a four-year-old girl at home.

Hope made a snap decision. "Don't send that bouquet. I'll pick it up in an hour and deliver it myself."

She did, then felt foolish for taking her job as morale officer so seriously. Trisha Stevenson's hospital room overflowed with family. Both beaming grandmothers, two aunts and an uncle. They were all impressed that the air force cared enough to hand-deliver flowers. Of course one of the proud grandmas insisted on escorting Hope to the nursery to properly admire the nine-pound boy. *Nine pounds.* Hope pressed her nose to the glass and wiggled her fingers. He had a pudgy face, a shock of dark hair and a yawn that sneaked through the bulwark guarding Hope's heart.

She left the hospital feeling twice as melancholy. Everyone she passed seemed to be rushing places in twos. If she wasn't so hungry and still in her flight suit, she'd stop at the O-club for a drink. No, she wouldn't. She never went there alone. Only with other women officers. And she'd be sure to run into Lance Denton, who'd make a big deal out of it. Or worse, Ryder. Vulnerable as she felt this minute, that would never do. Instead, she made her way to her car. But because she couldn't face going home to an apartment that seemed more empty since Lissa had transferred to Langley, Hope stopped off at the gym. She always kept a gym bag packed with workout clothes in her car trunk.

It was dark when she finished. The air had grown humid. Thunder rumbled in the distance and lightning danced over the Catalina Mountains. Even after a brisk workout with weights, Hope felt oddly keyed up. She'd heard plenty about Arizona's monsoons. Flyers, especially, didn't like the unpredictability of the electrical storms that frequently blew up from Mexico in the fall. Hope was no stranger to flying in storms, though, and this disturbance probably wouldn't amount to anything. They had another week left of summer for pity's sake.

Wrong. Five minutes later the wind blew in a heavy rainstorm. Hope had to pull over and raise the top on her convertible. She was drenched before she finished.

The storm was raging by the time she reached her apartment complex. She had covered parking, but a distance away from her building. Already water ran ankle deep in the street. Though the temperature had cooled considerably from the hundred and six it'd been when she flew in at three, it was still warm enough to go wading.

She pulled off her boots, her socks and rolled her pant legs up to her knees. Hope hunched over to keep the items dry while she made a mad dash to her apartment on the second floor. Drawing near the door, Hope realized she should have dug her key from her fanny pack before she left the shelter of the car. Slowing, she began to fumble the zipper open. She didn't see the dark form huddled in her doorway until she ran headlong into a solid wall of flesh.

"Eeee-yike!" She screamed and dropped her belongings. One boot hit her bare wet toe, another bounced on the slick concrete and fell over the railing into the courtyard below. Her socks plopped soggily on the shoes of her foe. A man. She kicked out blindly.

Ryder McGrath gripped Hope tightly by both arms. He gave her a little shake to get her to look at him. He'd been pacing outside her apartment wondering where in hell she was at such a late hour when the storm struck with a vengeance. He decided he wouldn't get any wetter waiting here than if he tromped back to his car parked a block away. He'd been sadly mistaken. By the time he figured that out, however, it was too late.

Hope stared at him through spikes of wet hair plastered to her forehead. She reached out a tentative hand to see if he was real or if she'd conjured him up. Ryder McGrath, here on her doorstep, didn't compute. The shirt stuck to his steamy chest felt pretty darned real. Her mouth worked to form a question but failed to do much more than pucker.

"Do you have a key to that door?"

She patted him again.

"Playing touchy-feely in the middle of a damn cloudburst isn't my idea of fun," he snapped. "I stopped by to discuss the complaint you filed. Would it be too much to ask that we do it inside and away from prying ears? As I should have called out instead of scaring you to death, I'll retrieve your boot while you open up." Bending, he scooped up her socks and the boot that lay outlined in the dim light shining from her neighbor's lamp. Without ceremony, he shoved them into her arms.

His snappish tone brought Hope back to earth with a crash. Clutching the wet things in one hand, she unzipped her fanny pack and unearthed her house key. "Forgive me for not being here to roll out the welcome mat, Colonel. I was under the impression that I'd hear back by phone, if at all."

A flash of lightning lit the porch jaggedly. Ryder identified the glitter of anger in Hope's eyes. He couldn't very well tell her his harshness had stemmed from worry over her being out so late in a bad storm. He'd given up the right to worry about her six years ago. Unfortunately, old habits died hard.

He pushed her gently into the alcove. "If you're going to take a swing at me, Hope, do it inside. Much as you'd like to see me in hell, I don't think you want to deal with filing the report if I get struck by lightning on your balcony."

Standing out here sniping at each other was pretty dumb, Hope admitted grudgingly. Inasmuch as she'd recovered from the fright of having an apparition jump out from her doorway, she was supremely curious as to what message he'd come to deliver. Now that she had a clearer head, Hope didn't, by any stretch of the imagination, kid herself that Ryder had made the trek from the base in the rain due to any great urgency to see her again.

She opened the door and flipped on some lights but the instant she heard his footfalls, she yanked open the door and offered him shelter from the pounding rain.

He puffed in exertion from the dash down and up the stairs. They each shook like wet dogs, then glanced at each other and laughed.

"Let me get you some towels," she said, shoving the hair out of her eyes. "I'm afraid I don't have anything you'd be able to wear. I'll put coffee on if you'd like to wait out the storm."

"That'd hit the spot. Please…you go on and change into dry things. What I have to say will keep that long."

She edged away, suddenly self-conscious about standing so close to him. "I'll listen now if you'd rather. I'm sure you have other things to do."

"Yeah, like eat." He screwed up his face. "If I weren't so wet and if the roads weren't rivers of mud, I'd suggest we discuss this over dinner."

"I haven't eaten, either. How does tomato soup and smoked-turkey sandwiches sound?"

"Good. Real good." He shifted from one foot to the other and rolled his shoulders forward, attempting to pull the wet shirt away from his skin.

Hope shivered unconsciously. "Honestly, we're two adults here, McGrath. I have a huge beach towel you can wear. Strip in the second bathroom…right through there." She pointed. "Then toss your shirt and pants into the dryer." She indicated the laundry room.

Ryder gazed at her. He fingered the middle button on his cotton shirt. "Makes sense," he said, all the while knowing that the lustful thoughts streaking through his mind made no sense at all. And if Hope had the slightest inkling of the nature of those thoughts, she'd throw him out on his ear. He hadn't come here to take up where they'd left off. He was here on official business. And only then because he'd had his arm twisted by the powers that be in the Pentagon. A group no career officer in his right mind would refuse.

As Ryder accepted the towels from Hope, his gaze strayed to her lush curves, outlined too provocatively by her wet clothing. He wondered if he might not have been smarter to have disobeyed orders.

Obviously he was the only one in the room who was bothered by the situation. Hope marched across the living room and disappeared through another door. He heard the lock engage with a snap and was stunned to discover how much it hurt that she didn't trust him anymore.

Yet how could he blame her? It'd been his fault she'd lost her trusting innocence. She had matured. He saw it in her carriage, in her eyes. And in the cool detachment she threw up at a moment's notice. Once they'd been comfortable with each other's nakedness. It startled Ryder now to realize how much he missed the closeness they'd shared, but he'd be damned if he'd sit naked in this chilly atmosphere. Not even if he got pneumonia from wearing soaking-wet clothes. He only rubbed his hair dry with the towel and draped it around his shoulders.

When Hope reappeared, fully covered by gray sweats, Ryder had the coffee made and the soup heating in a pan.

She didn't appear to waste a glance on his attire. Nevertheless, Ryder knew she'd taken in every last wet inch of him. He knew something else—that she'd steeled herself to see him in much less. And she'd visibly relaxed seconds after stepping into the room. That told Ryder she wasn't nearly as self-possessed around him as she'd like him to believe. In spite of the reasons he'd come and the miserable state he was in, Ryder's mood took a decided upswing.

They were seated at the table behind steaming mugs of coffee and soup and within reach of fat sandwiches when Hope decided she'd waited long enough. "I take it you found out why the missile museum dropped air force association retirees from their volunteer roster."

"No." Ryder bit into a sandwich.

"No?" Hope gasped. "Then why are you here?" She scooted forward on her chair, ready to strangle Ryder as he chewed every last morsel to death.

Still not saying anything, he dug in his back pocket and extracted a much-folded set of orders. Orders Hope saw had been signed by her wing commander releasing her temporarily to Colonel McGrath. "Why? What? I...I don't understand."

He hefted his mug. "The only thing you need to understand is that you're assigned to me for a special mission.'' From the other pocket he dragged out a small, dry but bedraggled black notebook. In it, he'd precisely printed all of the facts Hope had given him earlier. "If you have anything to add to your earlier statement, do it now. Oh, by the way, I don't want you or your dad discussing this with anyone. No one. Is that clear?''

"But…''

"That's an order, Major.''

Hope dropped her spoon in her bowl of soup and glared across the table. "I brought this to your attention, Colonel. I think I have a right to be apprised.''

"On a need-to-know basis, Major, all you need to know is to do as I say.''

It crossed Hope's mind to upend her tomato soup on the bastard's head. If only looking at him didn't cause her to breathe erratically. It wasn't fair that she had to work with him. And one on one. Not fair at all. Hope wiped a sweat-slicked hand down her thigh and picked up her cup. She was as determined to appear as detached and impersonal as Ryder.

"Good,'' he said. "The first thing I want is for you to introduce me to your dad. Rain or shine, I'll pick you up at 0800 tomorrow.'' Ryder polished off his sandwich, totally unaware that his first order had brought a smug smile to Hope's face.

With pleasure! She repeated the two words in her head like a mantra until Ryder pushed his empty dishes aside, rose and said, "0800, Major. Be ready on time.''

She sprang up and darted around him, cheerfully holding the door open for his departure. The minute he stepped out, she closed it. Sagging against it, she continued to grin like a baboon. Her father would never take orders from an upstart colonel. Lord, but she couldn't wait to introduce those two. Ryder McGrath wouldn't know what hit him.

CHAPTER THREE

HOPE HAD FORGOTTEN to ask if he planned a day trip or more. And she'd be damned if she'd track down Ryder's home number to ask for clarification. Neither did she know if he expected her to dress in uniform. After some deliberation, she packed a flight bag with bare essentials for three days. If he'd only intended one, Ryder never need know she'd packed for more.

She laid out jeans, a sleeveless blouse and a light denim jacket to wear. At the very least, he'd probably tramp around the desert to get a look at the missile site. Adding boots and sneakers, she called her parents to warn them. Hope's mother answered. Ted, who'd recently started bowling in a league, was at the alley.

"I don't know any more, Mom. Tell Dad we're driving to Verde Vista at 0800. Colonel McGrath wants to speak with Dad. Tell him not to expect too much," Hope drawled. "McGrath is being extremely secretive."

Hope listened to Dory plan aloud what she'd serve for lunch and dinner. "Keep it simple," Hope said. "This is work, remember." She clicked off after another brief exchange and got ready for bed, fighting the sinking feeling that her mother had read more into the planned visit than Hope intended.

Vigorously plumping her pillow, Hope shut off the light. What had tipped her mother off? Or was it nothing but her own jumpy nerves? A fear that she wouldn't be able to pull off the same degree of detachment Ryder managed with ease? Maybe her mother didn't suspect anything at all.

HOPE HAD HER MOUTH full of toothpaste when her phone rang the next morning. "'Lo," she garbled, assuming it was her father.

"I'm calling for Major Evans. This is Colonel Mc-Grath."

Shifting the toothbrush, Hope gagged on the toothpaste. "This is Hope," she said. "I'm brushing my teeth. Hold on." She quickly rinsed her mouth. "Sorry. What's up? Is the mission scrubbed?"

"I hate to ask, but if you have wheels, could you drive? I'm driving a Hum-V, on loan from security. You know, with the top bar of flashing lights. If you don't want to play chauffeur, say so. I'll rent a car."

She shifted the phone to her other ear. "I...ah...don't mind driving..."

"Is that a but I hear?"

"Well, I'm not in the habit of picking up men on base."

Ryder bit his tongue to keep from saying *good.* "I leased a house from a colonel I know who hasn't been able to sell." He rattled off an address.

"I know approximately where that is. All those houses look alike. Watch for me. I've got a bright red convertible."

He laughed. "So much for thinking my Hum-V would stand out."

"If your agenda includes a trip to the missile site, you can drive my mother's car. She has a nondescript, perfectly respectable sedan. You ought to go alone, since I was just at the museum last week."

"I'll decide what to do after I talk to your dad. Do you have room in your trunk for a bag of binoculars and some special equipment?"

"There's room. You didn't say if we were staying over, but I packed a bag."

"Um. I should have told you to figure on at least two days. Three max. Once I make an assessment, I'll come back to Monahan and file a report."

"To whom?"

The telephone line crackled. "Nice try, Evans. Shouldn't you be leaving home? I did say we'd start at 0800."

"Yes, sir." Hope clicked off, not even bothering to say goodbye. She gnashed her teeth over being left dangling. Who'd brought the situation to his attention in the first place? Oh, but he probably thought she'd try to take some of the credit. Hope had never considered Ryder to be a glory hog. Ha! When would she get it through her thick skull that she didn't know Ryder McGrath at all? She knew only the man she'd sculpted in her mind. A fetish that had toppled and cracked apart as easily as a porcelain figurine.

Hope had her protective bulwark fully restored and in place by the time Ryder flagged her down outside his Mediterranean-style house. She climbed from the car and briskly opened the Chrysler's trunk so he could toss in his duffel. She gave only a cursory glance at a row of cookie-cutter dwellings when he returned to his porch for a second, larger bag. Hope did think the two-story home looked awfully big for a bachelor. Then a thought curdled her morning coffee. *Maybe he lived with someone.* He might be married, too. Married men didn't all wear wedding bands. Some went out of their way to avoid the attached look. That way when they went TDY, temporary duty out of town, they could play the field. In all fairness, it wasn't just males who seemed to forget their vows. Hope tried not to judge anyone too harshly. Look how quickly her affair with Ryder had come about.

Fool.

Ryder placed one last bulky bag in the trunk and slammed the lid. He walked around the car as if inspecting it. "Pretty nifty. But it has *ticket me* written all over it."

"Really? Not if you don't speed."

"How can you not? The power plant in this baby turns an easy hundred in a quarter mile."

"Not with me at the wheel." Hope opened the driver's door and sank into the leather seat. Ryder did the same on the passenger side, only more slowly. Hope thought he seemed disappointed. Surely he hadn't expected to drive?

"I don't even let my brothers drive my car," she said in case he had. She started the engine and pulled into the traffic.

Ryder rubbed a hand over the dash. "I'm not surprised after the stories you told me about those two." He laughed, then slanted Hope an unreadable look.

Hope, shaken by the notion he remembered silly tales about her brothers she'd relayed one rainy night when the two of them cuddled on the couch in front of a roaring fire, abruptly changed the subject. "Verde Vista is largely a retirement community. It's about a twenty-minute drive."

"That close to Tucson?" he asked sharply. "What are we talking in terms of total population within a fifty-mile radius of the missile museum?"

Her heart jammed for no real reason. "I don't know. There's reservation land between here and there that's sparsely settled. Played-out copper mines on both sides of the highway for quite some distance. You'll see the mounds of tailings soon. Visitors assume they're foothills of the Sierrita Mountains. Are you, by chance, trying to scare me?''

He glanced over in surprise. ''Scare you?''

She shrugged. ''The question about the population. Are you thinking of evacuation?''

''Evac...? You're reading too many spy thrillers. Hope, you came to me with concerns. I'm conducting a routine investigation. Don't blow this out of proportion.''

''I'd feel a lot better if you were up front with me about what suddenly made this a priority. When I left you, I had the impression that it'd be a cold day in hell before you even made any inquiries into the matter.''

Frown lines marred his forehead, yet sunglasses hid any irritation that might be in his eyes.

Hope speeded up on the straight stretch of road.

Ryder's words were torn away and tossed over his shoulder. ''The catalyst was your flawless record, Major. I doubt that you got such a clean slate by bullying superiors.''

''Bullying...?'' Her jaw tightened and she clamped her teeth closed. She'd been out of line. He wasn't friend, good buddy or lover. This was a different man. One definitely in command of his mission. In command of her. Hope decided she'd better watch herself.

Silence took over. Several minutes went by while Ryder tapped his fingers on his knee. Suddenly he turned in his seat and faced Hope. ''It's clear that you want to erase our past. Before we hit your parents' house, just tell me, do they know about our...uh...about us?''

Her arms tensed and her foot let up on the gas. Tromping hard again, she said between her teeth, "No. And there is no us."

Put in his place, Ryder sat back. He wanted to ask about the lace-leaf trees they were flying past. He wanted to ask her to pull over underneath one. To stop and have this out. The fact that he couldn't deny her the right to her fury kept him staring mutely at the blur of flora and fauna sliding past his window.

Ryder crossed his fingers that Hope's parents weren't astute people, otherwise they'd see right through him. Too bad he was such a poor actor. Maybe if Hope had changed her perfume, the good memories wouldn't keep flooding back. Then again, he realized, that wouldn't help. That would have meant that everything that'd been so right and good between them was superficial. Which wasn't how Ryder remembered their time together at all.

Hope slowed the car, and he was jolted back to the present.

"This is the golf course where my dad spends a large percent of his day."

"Do you play?"

"I like something faster. Are you into golf?" Her stomach balled. She should know if he was a golfer.

"I play. I try to get in one game a week. But I'm probably still better at darts."

She smiled. "That's not much of a recommendation, since I creamed you royally."

"You did," he admitted. "But I've been practicing."

Their timely arrival at the Evans' home made an answer unnecessary.

"This is it," Hope announced, waving to her folks, who came out of the house. To keep Ryder from opening her door, a gentlemanly act he never failed to perform, Hope scrambled out on her own. She hugged her parents before introducing them to Ryder. First her mother, whom she called Dory. Then her dad. "Major General, Theodore Evans, retired," she crooned. "Lieutenant Colonel, Ryder McGrath. The colonel has some pointed questions, Dad. I get the impression he expects your tale to differ from mine." Hope used a teasing note with her father. She waited patiently for him to set Ryder straight.

Ted Evans shook hands with Ryder, then clapped him on the shoulder. "Best place I know to discuss business is on the golf course, my boy. I trust you play?" When Ryder nodded, Ted whooped. "Dory, grab us a cold six-pack while I unhook the golf cart from the battery charger. Hope, your mother's clubs will be too short for Ryder. I'm going to lend him yours."

"But…but…but…" Hope continued to sputter even after her mom hurried back into the house and Ted led Ryder around to the side door of the garage. When it appeared they weren't going to pay her the least attention, she followed. Hands on hips, she demanded, "Just what do you expect me to do while you play eighteen holes?"

Ted chucked her under the chin, something he hadn't done since she was ten. "Oh, thanks, honey," he said as his wife slipped a six-pack inside the cooler attached to the cart. "Dory, the major feels shut out. I'm sure you can keep her occupied helping you prepare dinner or something while I brief Colonel McGrath."

Dory looped a plump arm around Hope's tense elbow. "Don't worry about us, Ted. You men go and do your thing. Hope hasn't seen the pictures Rolf sent of the new baby. Or—" she winked "—we may go spend your money." Letting go of Hope, she rose on tiptoe to brush a kiss on her husband's lips.

"Do that, hon. Ask the major's opinion on that black

dress I tried to get you to buy last week. But don't mess with the barbecue. The colonel and I'll do the dirty work when we return.''

Hope seethed as her dad backed the blue cart into the street and her mother stood beside her waving at them as if they were going to be gone a month. She waited to explode until the men disappeared from sight. ''Mother, I swear. Has Dad forgotten I went to the air force academy because I hated domestic folderol? How you've lived with his condescension all these years is beyond me.''

Dory laughed as she closed the garage door and led Hope inside the house. ''You, of all people, should recognize the air force attitude, dear. It's a mind-set I assumed they taught in the academy. I recognized the hierarchy of leaders and followers only days into our marriage. Fewer decisions get made if you have too many leaders and not enough followers. I'm wonderfully happy being a follower.''

''Well, I'm not a follower,'' Hope said as they walked into the kitchen.

Dory sighed. ''I know. I wish you'd pretend for your dad's sake. He's really upset over this deal at the museum. Acted like a new man when I relayed that you were bringing the colonel. What's the harm in letting him bend your young man's ear for a while?''

Hope, who'd reached for a mug and the coffeepot simultaneously, almost dropped them both. ''Ryder McGrath is *not* my young man.''

Dory held up a hand. ''You don't have to confide in me, Hope. I've never pried into my children's lives and I'm not about to start. Given today's military climate, it's better not to know who's dating whom. Have a seat at the table to drink your coffee. I'll run get the brag book Rolf and Krista sent. Krista sent a long, newsy letter, too. She's so good about writing.''

Hope had time to collect her frayed nerves while her mother went to find the items. Was Dory's radar working or had news of Hope's ill-fated affair somehow reached Rolf or Chris? Realistically she didn't think that was the case. Her brothers would have been all over her for her stupidity. Those two—one older than she, and one younger—had always considered themselves her protectors.

Knowing her mom and how badly Dory wanted all three of her children settled into happy marriages, it was probably nothing more than wishful thinking on her part. After all, Hope hadn't brought a man home for any reason since her high-school senior prom. A date that warranted the dud-of-the-year award.

''Here.'' Dory bustled into the room. ''Meet Justine, your new niece.'' She plopped an open picture album in front of Hope. ''Have you ever seen such a little beauty in your life?''

''Mother, she's bald. Her eyes are closed and...'' Hope leaned closer and squinted at the picture. ''Is she blowing bubbles?''

Dory snatched the album back and turned the page. ''Hope, you are so unsentimental. Where is your biological clock?''

''The sand shifted to the bottom,'' Hope said dryly. The flat truth was, she envied Rolf and Krista their solid marriage and their beautiful family. Rolf was only two years her senior. He'd dated Krista all through high school. They'd married a week after Rolf graduated from the academy. Ten months later they'd had Amy. Two years later, Michael, and now when Amy and Michael were well in school, Justine.

"Here, read Krista's letter. She and Rolf think Chris may have a special girlfriend."

"Chris? My - brother - the - professional - bachelor Chris?"

Dory refilled her own coffee mug then took a seat across the table from Hope. "I knew if he ever found the right lady, our Chris would tumble hard. It's about time. He's thirty-two."

Hope ducked her head and skimmed the first paragraphs of her sister-in-law's letter. But her mind wouldn't stay focused. All Hope saw was the blaze of thirty-three candles on her own birthday cake last month. Where had the years gone? Until she saw Ryder yesterday, Hope had believed she was content to put all her energy into a fast-track career. Ryder's appearance, combined with this immersion in reality, served to remind Hope that almost everyone she knew in her age group was married. For all she knew, that included Ryder.

As she read more of Krista's precise writing, Hope found herself speculating on Ryder's life since they'd parted. His love life, to be more specific. She could ask him outright if he'd remarried. Then he'd know she'd found out about his lie. Not a lie, she admitted reluctantly. Omission. No huge technicality from her perspective, but she supposed others who were more magnanimous might be more lenient. Of course she wouldn't ask him anything personal. He might get the idea she cared. Dammit, she didn't care. At least she didn't want to.

Hope blinked several times and saw her mother watching her. "I envy Rolf getting to see so much of Europe," she said quickly. "Maybe I'll put in for a transfer. England would be nice. Or Spain. I liked the four years we all spent there."

"I enjoyed our tours abroad. But then, Ted and I didn't leave unsolved problems behind." Dory drew the album to her and leafed through it page by page. "Shall we go shopping, Hope? Now that I've seen this little rascal, I know exactly the frilly pink dress I'm going to buy. It comes with one of those headbands. The kind with a pretty bow. That way her baldness won't be as noticeable."

Hope didn't miss Dory's sly remark, she just decided to let it go. She knew exactly what her mom, the matchmaker, had in mind and it wasn't going to work. "Shopping sounds okay. You take care of frilly and I'll buy the same practical gift Aunt Hope always gives. A hundred-dollar savings bond. Start the kid on the road to independent wealth in case she wants to follow in Aunt Hope's footsteps and be an old maid." She made the statement a challenge.

"To each his own, but in my estimation cash makes a pretty poor bed partner on cold, lonely nights."

Hope knew she should let well enough alone, but it seemed important to have the last word. "Then maybe I'll stay in Arizona. The nights are plenty warm."

Her mother took the hint. The subject of men and marriage never surfaced again even though they spent two hours in a baby boutique. The store stocked so many precious outfits that Hope bought a soft yellow sweater with white angora kittens on the collar and matching booties to go with her practical gift.

They reached home a scant five minutes before the men returned. Dory dragged out the presents immediately to show them.

Hope didn't expect any reaction from her dad or Ryder. Her dad slipped his arms around his wife and said he could hardly remember a child tiny enough to wear those itsy-bitsy things. Ryder didn't comment. But he couldn't seem to stop touching the sweater. Talking about babies had a way of reducing adults to mush, but she never would have expected that reaction from Ryder. Hope had no recollection of him ever commenting one way or the other on babies.

She didn't have time to ruminate long. Her mother asked for her help fixing a salad. Ted dragged Ryder into his study to look at the pictures Hope had taken at the missile site. Not before Hope noticed Ryder had filled additional sheets in his little black notebook. He was nothing if not thorough. She felt an unaccountable sense of pride.

A short while later Hope lamented not having been invited to join the men in the office. Cooking was her least favorite chore. Well, it ranked right up there with cleaning the bathroom and doing laundry. Maybe she wasn't as cut out for marriage as she'd thought. If she *did* marry, her mate would have to cook. Otherwise they'd go broke eating out. She could get by with deli salads, but men required a whole lot more sustenance to keep them happy.

Dory asked Hope to call the men just as they emerged from the study.

"Do you still have the negative of this photo?" Ryder asked Hope, handing her the one where she'd captured the hand and arm of the elusive volunteer.

"Yes. But I already checked. The developer didn't crop any of the shot. The man's hand and forearm is all I got."

"I don't doubt it." Ryder frowned. "He's wearing a signet ring of some type. I'd like to blow it up. It may prove to be a dead end, or the blowup might provide a college or university name. We have damn little to go on, but it's all we have."

"I have a friend who has a darkroom at home. That way we'd avoid questions," Hope said.

Ryder hooked a thumb over his belt. "Air force?"

Hope looked puzzled.

"Your friend. Is he air force?"

"It's a she, and no. She lives downstairs from me. Does sex matter?"

Ryder turned that statement over in his mind several times before he considered the fact that her parents were there and gave her a straight answer. "Until we know what we're chasing down, I'd just as soon not have any speculation connecting this to the squadron. You know how scuttlebutt travels."

"I do indeed. Shelly photographs models. She does their portfolios. Her boyfriend tends bar. He's more interested in the models than in a possible crime, I can assure you."

"Oh, and I suppose you can tell that by looking at a man," Ryder said brusquely.

"In Joe's case, yes."

Dory clapped her hands as Ryder snorted. "Dinner is going to get cold. I'll give you two seconds to wash up."

Hope's dad peered at the neatly set table out on the patio. "Ready? Dinner? I never lit the barbecue."

"I know, dear. You were busy. It isn't a big deal, you know. What do you men want to drink?" She rattled off a list.

"Raspberry iced tea sounds good to me," Ryder said. "I had more than enough beer playing golf."

"Who won?" Hope queried lightly.

Ryder wrinkled his nose. "Ted. No one told me he

played on the Senior-Am circuit.'' Hope received the brunt of his accusing stare.

She snapped her fingers. ''Darn. Slipped my mind.''

''I'll bet.'' He turned toward the bathroom. ''I should have realized competitiveness runs in the family,'' he said over his shoulder.

Dory polled Hope silently, then stared curiously at Ryder's back.

''SO WHAT DO YOU THINK?'' she asked Ryder a short while later after they'd all loaded their plates.

''About what?'' He bit into a juicy piece of chicken, his strong teeth a flash of white.

''About what's happening at the missile site!''

Ryder set his piece of meat aside and blotted his lips with his napkin. ''Dinner is super, Mrs. E. It's been months since I've had home cooking. I'd almost forgotten how great it is.''

''Why, thank you, Ryder.'' Dory smiled her appreciation.

Hope thumped down her fork in disgust. ''Fine. If you men choose to treat this as some big secret, deal me out. Release me, Colonel. I'll gladly go back to flying.''

''Are you this impatient when you fly?'' Ryder said. ''Investigations take time. I started my inquiries at the top, but no one at Aerospace seemed concerned, although they couldn't document a policy change that shuffled personnel. I felt they should have a record of a shift of that magnitude so I'm digging deeper. How about cutting me some slack here? Rome wasn't built in a day.''

''I'm not building in Rome,'' Hope snorted.

Her mother nudged the salad bowl toward Hope. ''Business talk hurts digestion. You three can gather in the den and rehash old ground while I do dishes.'' She changed the subject. "Ryder, where do your parents live?''

"In Alabama. So does my sister. Her husband is a doctor. I haven't made it home this past year. Too busy hopping from point A to point B.'' He shrugged.

That news surprised Hope. His family had been close-knit.

"I take it you're not married,'' Dory continued in the same tone. "Otherwise home cooking wouldn't be such a novelty.''

Hope held her breath. Would Ryder answer?

He glanced uneasily at her, then lowered his gaze to the roll he'd more or less shredded. "I was married, Mrs. Evans. Three years. I'd known April all my life. Her family lived next door to mine.''

April. Hope had a name to put with the faceless person. A pretty, feminine name. Hope concentrated on pouring dressing on her salad. Did her mother hear the pain in Ryder's voice?

"I'm sorry, Colonel,'' Dory said softly. "You don't owe us any explanation.''

"That's all right. It's been seven years. April miscarried in the sixth month of pregnancy. I…she…we… wanted a big family. She was sick from day one and didn't bounce back after the miscarriage. During an exam, her OB discovered a fast-growing ovarian cancer. April never fully recovered. Blood loss, chemo…it proved too much for her…'' His voice trailed off, but he caught and held Hope's gaze until she looked away.

A few simple sentences explained a lot. Ryder had entered the relationship with her carrying a ton of emotional baggage. If the tremor in his voice was any indication, he carried it still. If she'd been vacillating about whether or not to keep Ryder McGrath off limits, she had her answer in neon lights. To save her heart from being mangled a second time, it was necessary to keep things strictly professional between them. Ryder had never recovered from losing his wife.

She was grateful when her father drew everyone's attention to the glorious sunset. "I keep trying to describe those colors in my journal. Words are inadequate. Times like this, I wish I was an artist."

"You have time to take lessons now, Dad," Hope said.

"Me?" He laughed. "Pretty late to try to teach this old dog new tricks. I can engineer anything and do slide-rule calculations in my head, but I can't lay a straight bead of paint between a wall and a cupboard. Just ask your mother."

"Alas, it's true." Dory rolled her eyes. "If everyone's finished, I'll clear the table. Since the sunset is so spectacular, why not stay and talk shop here on the patio?"

"Suits me," said Ryder.

Ted scooted his chair back. "Or we can all pitch in with the dishes, and that way Dory can join us."

"No, thanks. I'll use the time to whip up a little dessert."

Rising, Hope collected a stack of plates.

"Where are you going?" asked Ted.

"Am I invited into the inner sanctum?"

"Be serious, Major. Quit clowning and bring those pictures on your way back from the kitchen. I left them on the dining-room table."

"Yes, sir." She turned her back to the men and waggled her eyebrows so that only Dory saw.

Ryder and her father were deep in conversation when

Hope returned. Ryder had his notebook out. The page Hope could see looked like an outline. Such strong hands for such tiny and precise writing.

Ryder reached over, and without interrupting what he was saying to Ted, pulled out a chair for Hope.

She gave a start. It was another thing she'd forgotten about him. His ability to keep track of five things at one time. She'd hate to think he'd known she was admiring his hands. Hope slipped quietly into the chair as Ryder sat back. "The next step, as I see it, is for me to visit the museum."

"I'll drive you first thing in the morning," Hope offered, forgetting she'd cautioned against that earlier.

"Better not," he said swiftly. "You were just there, taking pictures, asking questions. If they're up to mischief, we don't want to tip them off."

"Tip *who* off? What kind of mischief?" Her exasperation showed plainly.

Ryder drummed his fingers on the table for several seconds. "Will you excuse us, Ted? Hope has been assigned to my team. We'll take a walk and I'll brief her."

Ted's eyes glittered with interest, but he said nothing, just motioned them out.

They wandered some distance down a winding path that led through cholla and prickly pear cactus. Finally Hope stopped. "What team? What's going on?"

"Everything I'm telling you is classified. The first feelers I put out in D.C. rattled a few cages. It seems our trusty CIA watchdogs have lost track of a couple of well-known international terrorists. Missiles are their specialty. We've been ordered to check this out on the q.t."

"Us? *Who* are *we?* Shouldn't they send in someone who's trained?"

A muscle at the base of Ryder's jaw jumped. "I am trained, Hope. And that's not for publication, either."

She felt panic rise in her throat, sapping her breath. Not for herself. Hope knew instinctively Ryder would die to protect her. Her fear was for him. If a man felt he'd lost everything, he might be reckless with his own life. Could Ryder McGrath be bent on self-destruction?

CHAPTER FOUR

"I KNEW I SHOULDN'T have briefed you," he said, raking a hand through his hair. "You're already blowing this out of proportion. We don't know that terrorists have taken over the missile site. This is nothing more than a routine investigation."

"You must think it's a possibility."

"These guys have dropped out of sight. But they're hit-and-run types. The people I spoke with say in-depth infiltration isn't their style."

"What people?"

"Men whose business it is to know these things. Who isn't important. Now that you understand our mission, I'm sure you'll follow my orders."

"What precisely do those entail?" She knew that her eyes, her tone, her body language were all edgy.

"Maybe nothing. Maybe a lot. At this point there isn't much sense involving local law enforcement. Tomorrow I'll join one of the site tours. Afterward we'll compare notes. Then I'll touch base with my source and make plans accordingly. If the terrorists have turned up and nothing else looks off-kilter, our investigation ends." He put a finger to his lips as they neared the patio where Hope's dad sat smoking a pipe. Just then Dory Evans stepped from the house carrying a tray of iced drinks.

"Good timing," she said. "I told Ted we'd save dessert for tomorrow. These iced lattes sit better after a heavy meal.''

"Thanks, but none for me." Ryder smiled at Hope's mother. "The dinner was more than enough. But if Hope wants one, I'll wait." He glanced at his watch. "Point me toward a phone book. I'll reserve a room at the closest motel. When you finish," he told Hope, "I'd appreciate your giving me a lift."

Dory set the tray on the glass-topped table as she looked in turn at her husband and her daughter. "But...I assumed you were staying here, Colonel. I made up the second guest room."

"I couldn't," Ryder protested. "It was never my intention to put you out."

Hope panicked at the thought of him sleeping across the hall from her. "Colonel McGrath probably feels awkward bunking with strangers."

"Nonsense." Ted gestured at Ryder with his pipe. "We bought this house with four bedrooms so that all our kids could converge at one time. Besides, Dory planted sofa beds all over the place to accommodate grandkids. So far, the major—" he smiled at Hope "—is the only one who's managed a visit. That means I'm always outnumbered by women. I'll be put out if you don't stay, my boy."

The corners of Ryder's eyes crinkled as he dipped his chin and lazily tugged at one ear. "Couched in those terms, how can I refuse, sir?"

"You can't. That's the whole idea of intimidation," Ted responded gruffly. "Grab us a couple of those sissy drinks. Come sit a spell and we'll swap stories."

"Sissy drinks?" Hope paused in the process of taking one of the tall, frosty glasses.

"What else do you call whipped cream on top of cold

coffee?'' Ted grumbled. "I only drink 'em because your mother goes to all the trouble of dragging out that cappuccino machine Rolf sent her from Italy when he was on a tour of duty there. I accuse her of trying to show off. She says they have less calories than real dessert."

Dory didn't seem the least bit perturbed by his grousing. "I use skim milk and fake whipped cream. Ted doesn't understand that at our age we have to cut out fat."

"Mother, why don't you just tell him to make dessert himself instead of complaining?"

"I don't need rescuing, Hope. Your dad gave orders for so many years it's second nature. When the boys are home, they do the same thing. Even you at times. I figure it's because I'm the only one in this family without rank. Food is the only area where I'm captain of the ship...to borrow a navy phrase. If you'll notice, I fix what pleases me."

"Your mother is being modest," Ted said, gazing on her lovingly. "Not nearly enough credit is given to those who keep the home fires burning."

Dory shrugged off his praise. "Hope," she instructed, "bring your drink and come help me wrap the baby gifts."

"When you ladies finish, come back," Ted said. "We'll badger the colonel into a game of cards."

"What kind?" asked Ryder.

"Bridge?" Dory said hopefully.

"I play." Ryder paused to lick a dollop of cream that slid over the edge of the glass Ted had thrust into his hand in spite of his protest. "I'm probably rusty."

"It's like riding a bicycle," Ted told him. "Once you learn, you never forget. We'll take it easy on you until you get the hang of it again."

"If you believe that, I have a plot of land in the middle of a ghost town for sale," Hope drawled from the doorway. "Dad likes to win."

"So it runs in the family," Ryder said to Hope.

"Hope held her own with Chris and Rolf," Dory said. "You'd think one in three would be a graceful loser."

Hope flushed. "Mother, I'm sure the colonel doesn't want to hear about family squabbles."

"Actually, I find it fascinating. Tell me, Mrs. Evans, did she beat her brothers at darts?"

"Darts, Ping-Pong, Monopoly. Swimming, badminton."

Hope focused on her dribbling whipped cream. Once she finished catching all the runs with her tongue, she said sassily, "By all means let's not forget racquetball and the hundred-yard dash."

Ryder laughed. "Did you let your brothers win at anything?"

Ted set his pipe aside. "Football, because Rolf was built like a steamroller. Maybe basketball. At age fourteen, Chris stood six-two in his stocking feet. Me, I'm smart enough not to get drawn into athletics with any of them. Games that take strategy...now that's a different matter."

"Then it's only fair to tell you, Dad. Men who've served under the colonel refer to him as the Strategist. You may not want to brag too loudly."

Dory Evans gave their guest a long assessing look. She conducted a similar survey of her daughter. "I didn't realize you knew Colonel McGrath before calling on him about the incident at the missile site, Hope."

Hope choked on a mouthful of latte.

"Didn't she tell you we'd met once when she was a guest lecturer at air command school?" Ryder asked mildly. "It was several years back. She'd just made captain, I believe."

Hope could kick herself for opening her big mouth. If her mother hadn't already suspected there was past history between Ryder and her, Dory would beat the bushes now until she satisfied her curiosity.

"It's later than I thought," Hope said, taking a closer look at her watch. "Let's just deal the cards. We can wrap Justine's gifts tomorrow while the colonel visits the museum."

"Fine with me." Dory opened a drawer in the sideboard and removed a deck.

Hope knew from the look her mother gave her the issue was far from dead. Tomorrow she'd have to be on her toes, or else talk her dad into a game of golf to avoid her mother's interrogation. Rolf and Chris would agree that Dory's inquisitions had a military precision that would put air force techniques to shame. None of them ever wanted to be on the receiving end.

After one rubber of bridge where she sat knee to knee with Ryder, Hope almost wished she'd taken her chances with Dory. Looking in Ryder's eyes, feeling their legs brush all too often, was pure torture, and Hope fumbled easy plays.

Rarely critical, at one point Dory folded her cards and tossed them at her partner in exasperation. "Hope, I'm going to have to eat what I said about your inborn drive to win. Give me one good reason why we're handing them this game."

"I'm sorry. I can't seem to concentrate. My mind must be working overtime trying to figure out what could be going on at the missile site."

Ted yawned. "We're so far ahead of you ladies now that you can't possibly resurrect yourselves." He nudged his daughter, and in a rare admission, he said, "I don't have to worry anymore now that I've dumped it on you young pups. Dory's been hounding me to relax and keep my nose out of it. By Jove, I am, and it's a relief."

Dory reached across the table and placed a palm on his forehead. "Call a doctor, Hope. He's sick, I'm sure."

That dragged a laugh from everyone at the table. Banter continued as they sorted out the cards and stored them neatly in the teak case Ted had bought during his last tour in Asia. Hope collected the dirty glasses. "Mom, why don't you show Colonel McGrath to his quarters while I rinse these and stick them in the dishwasher?" Hope congratulated herself on quick thinking. Dory had no doubt planned for *her* to attend to Ryder.

"Quarters?" Ryder lifted an eyebrow. "Someone's overdue for R and R. In your parents' home we could probably call it a bedroom. Away from base you have my permission to use my first name, Hope. If we carry on with this investigation, we'll conceal the fact that we're military."

Somehow, calling him colonel allowed Hope to distance herself from him. Not a lot, given their sudden close working relationship. But any distance was welcome. And she dare not think of Ryder and bedroom in the same context. "I'm comfortable using rank until we know more. Surely you've noticed even Dad calls me major?"

The ice that overlay Hope's message irked Ryder into responding with equal frost. "I'll make it perfectly clear when and if it becomes an order, then."

Facing Hope's parents, he again thanked them for their hospitality. "I'm an early riser," he added. "So I believe I'll turn in, too."

Dory, whose faintly puzzled glance rested on her

daughter, turned and gave Ryder a broad smile. "I've given you a bedroom with a private bath. Make yourself at home, please. We're an early-to-bed, early-to-rise family. I'm sure there'll be coffee ready when you get up. Hope generally runs first thing, and Ted swims laps in the pool at the club. Take your pick."

"Or the club has a well-equipped weight room," Ted said.

Ryder studied Hope's jerky movements as she went about her tasks in the kitchen. She didn't want him intruding on her morning run. For some perverse reason, he was tempted to do it anyway. But because he understood the history behind her strong negative feelings, he backed off. "I enjoy swimming and rarely have the chance to indulge, but I'm afraid I didn't bring a suit."

"No problem," Dory said. "You and Chris are about the same size. I bought extra for the boys for whenever they visit. The suits are new. You're welcome to use one."

"Then if you don't mind, General, maybe I'll tag along."

Ted Evans clapped Ryder on the back. "Love to have you, my boy. These old geezers who live around here are going soft. They think eighteen holes of golf a day will keep them fit. I guarantee we'll have the pool to ourselves. Is 0530 too early?"

"Not at all." Ryder wished he hadn't seen Hope grow less tense when he chose to join her dad. Righting the wrong he'd done her wasn't going to be easy. On the one hand, he almost wished this investigation would continue. On the other hand, that would mean the terrorists were still on the loose. There was no question in Ryder's mind that he didn't want Hope to get within a hundred miles of terrorist activity.

As he followed Dory down a wide hall into a bedroom that had a masculine southwest motif, Ryder knew that should the investigation go forward, he'd request that Hope be replaced. Any discussions or explanations of a personal nature would take a back seat to keeping her safe.

"This is more than comfortable," he responded to Dory's question. "I'm not used to such luxury. I've made do in bachelor quarters since I sold my home in Alabama. A place to go home to on leave is nice. But…" He swallowed several times and spun away toward the bed.

"Did Hope know your wife?" Dory asked unexpectedly.

Ryder dropped his duffel bag on the comforter. His shoulders tensed involuntarily. "No. No, she didn't meet April. Did I give you reason to think she had?"

"Um, I guess not. Well," she said briskly, "I won't detain you. The bath is fully stocked. If you want something to read and can't find what you'd like on these shelves, there are more books in the living room, as well as a magazine rack."

Ryder looked at the rows of built-ins displaying neat lines of books on diverse subject matter. "I can't imagine that I wouldn't find something to suit me here. You and Ted must be voracious readers."

"Not me." Dory laughed. "Ted and Hope. Especially Hope. She reads more than one book at a time and leaves them lying in every room in the house. Wherever she sits down, that's the book she picks up and starts reading. I'd think she'd get so confused she wouldn't know the gist of any of them."

That tidbit of information rattled Ryder. He didn't know Hope's reading habits. He couldn't say why, but it bothered him. In the time they'd spent together, she'd been open about her life. He was the one who'd kept secrets. Not that reading habits compared to what he'd withheld from her. What it did point out was that he hadn't known her quite as well as he thought.

"Good night, Colonel. If you need anything, anything at all, feel free to rummage."

"Only if you call me Ryder. You and I can use first names, even if Hope and Ted prefer ritual."

"Indeed we can. See you in the morning, Ryder. Sleep well."

But he didn't. Shortly after he showered and climbed into bed, he heard Hope's unmistakable tread in the hall. Her footsteps paused right outside his door, and he held his breath. Surely she wasn't going to pay him a visit. Ryder scrambled to find the sheet he'd thrown off. He wanted them to talk, but didn't want her waltzing in on him when he was naked as a jaybird. Even as he drew the sheet up to his chest, the door directly across from his opened quietly and closed.

Disappointment held a tug-of-war with relief. Eventually Ryder called it a draw between the two. However, the noises Hope made moving around—noises that provoked images of her undressing, drove him crazy. And drove away any possibility of sleep.

He snapped on the light, swore under his breath and searched the shelves until he found a book on military strategy guaranteed to send him into snoozeville. Still, night flirted with dawn before Ryder drifted off.

RYDER GROANED as he opened one eye to invasive shafts of sunlight peeking through the shutters. Determined to hide his restless night from his hosts, Ryder forced himself to get up and dress. He opened the bedroom door and almost tripped over Hope, who was kneeling there. As he flailed his arms to keep from going sprawling and taking her with him, Ryder realized he'd interrupted her in the act of placing the swimsuit and a bath towel at his door.

"Sorry." She rose quickly to steady him. "I didn't hear you. The pool doesn't have a place to change. You'll want to wear your suit and leave your jeans here."

Once Ryder grasped the door frame and managed to slow his racing heart, he saw that Hope wore skintight bike shorts and a tank top. Why couldn't she wear baggy running gear? The outfit molded to her slender figure like a suntan and sent his pulse skyrocketing again. "Thanks," he managed to mumble gruffly. "Don't let me keep you from your run. Tell your dad I'll be along shortly." Ryder backed inside the bedroom and started to shut the door.

Hope's hand shot out, preventing him from closing it. "Wait. Do you know more about what's happening at the missile site than you've let on?"

He stopped his backward progression. "No. I told you everything. Why?"

"I…I noticed your light was still on after I shut mine off. I think that was sometime after 0100," she admitted.

Again Ryder wanted to put her at ease. He pointed to his nightstand and the open book on military strategy. "Afraid I got so engrossed in that book, I forgot the time."

"That book?" Hope wrinkled her nose. "That book is drier than the desert in July." She shook her head. "A spy thriller I could understand."

"I'm sure you could, given the number of thrillers on the shelves."

Hope failed to mask her shock. "I guess your choice of reading matter changed, too. I picked up the habit of reading spy novels from you."

As she primly marched down the hall, Ryder smacked himself in the head with the heel of one hand. A window cracked, shedding more light on his past. Last night he'd been mistaken. He'd had a hand in molding and shaping a number of Hope's tastes. Reading material being only one. How convenient of him to have pushed that fact out of his mind. No wonder she looked at him as if he'd lost his mind. He had, a little, after she left. He'd tried to forget everything. Obviously he had succeeded in some areas.

The big question now as he saw it was, was he up to the task of repairing the damage?

Not a question destined to be answered soon. Hope had gone on her run by the time he changed into the suit and tracked the sound of Dory's and Ted's voices to the patio.

"Are you ready for some fast laps?" Ted boomed when he glanced up and saw Ryder stepping through the doorway.

"Ready as I'll ever be. Is there a reason to rush?"

"Dory just read in the local newspaper that a group of college kids are set to tour the missile site at 0800 today. That'll be a perfect cover for you. If you mix in and act like you belong, the volunteers will assume you're a professor."

Ryder dashed a hand through his shaggy hair. "Luckily I need a haircut. Otherwise I'd stick out like a beacon."

"I've got a pair of cheaters you can wear."

"Cheaters? Wading boots?"

Ted guffawed. "Glasses. The magnifying kind you

buy at the pharmacy. I don't tell many people, but a month ago I decided to try them. Dory can hunt 'em up while we're at the pool.''

Dory did. She had them waiting, along with two or three pens and a pen guard to wear in his breast pocket, when he returned from his swim.

"You have a notebook.'' She pointed to the black book in which he'd logged all the information he'd gathered to this point.

"If you have another,'' he said, "I'll take it instead. I'd hate to accidentally drop this one at the museum.''

"Will a small spiral one do?'' Dory asked. She quit pawing through a drawer and held it aloft.

"Great. While I dress, I need someone to sketch me a map. Oh, and Mrs. Evans…is it all right if I use your car? They know Ted's and maybe even Hope's. Is Hope back?'' he asked.

"Yes. No. And I thought you were going to call me Dory,'' the older woman said with a laugh.

Ryder grinned. "Touché.'' He touched a hand to his forehead in salute and smiled as he made his way back to his room. Ryder liked Hope's folks. He didn't feel like an interloper here. He wondered if they were aware that Hope had once chosen him to be their son-in-law. No, he decided. They never would have welcomed him so warmly, if at all.

Ryder backed from the garage, pulled into the street, slowing as he adjusted the rearview mirror. He caught a glimpse of Hope loping toward the house. She was maybe two blocks away. He touched the brakes, enjoying the sight of her long lithe strides. Her short blond hair was plastered to her head; she'd worked up a sweat on her run. In Alabama, her hair had been long. Mostly she'd worn it secured in something she'd called a scrunchie or clipped high on her head in a metal-toothed clip. He'd liked to watch it tumble over his wrists in honey-gold waves when he took it down. It always smelled of flowers.

The memory jabbed him in the groin. The pain. Oh, so sweet. A horn honked behind him, and Ryder realized he'd gotten lost in nostalgia. Dawdling wouldn't bring them answers. Nor did he want Hope to catch him gawking. Still, he couldn't resist taking one last lingering look at her as he drove off.

THE EVANS FAMILY had gathered in the den to eat lunch while they watched a special news broadcast on a new skirmish along the Gaza Strip when Ryder sauntered in again.

"We were debating earlier on whether or not someone had kidnapped you," Hope said lightly to hide the fact that she'd been worried about him.

Ted motioned Ryder in as he picked up the TV remote and turned down the sound.

"I made a tuna sandwich for you, Ryder. I hope you like wheat bread." Dory rose from her chair.

"Anything is fine. I didn't realize it was so late. A couple of the volunteers actually tried to hustle us through, but the college prof who'd booked this particular tour wouldn't be rushed."

"Did you see anything suspicious?" Hope set her plate on an end table and poured a glassful of lemonade from a pitcher that sat on a silver tray. Getting to her feet, she carried the drink to Ryder.

"Thanks." He was surprised by her gesture. "I saw nothing outwardly suspicious other than stuff you already mentioned. The guides work like robots and skip out of camera range. The professor complained about them. He said on all the tours he'd scheduled in the past, his students had received the red-carpet treatment. I gather the old volunteers gave added information. Especially those who'd been attached to SAC.''

"They did," said Ted. "We were all old air force cats. People often asked questions that weren't covered in our canned babble, and most of us had interesting side stories to tell."

"Hmm. I'd bet my bottom dollar these guides give the same speech to every tour group—without the added information. I can't prove it, but it's a strong hunch."

"Is that significant?" Hope walked over and sat again as her mother handed Ryder his plate.

"Maybe, maybe not." Ryder selected a seat. "They're a young bunch. More brawn than brain is my guess. I bought one of the books they sell in the gift shop and looked it over. Far as I can tell, they covered the facts. Which isn't a crime."

Ted set an uneaten portion of his sandwich back on his plate. "So, are you calling off your investigation?"

Hope glanced at Ryder and held her breath. She'd thought nothing would make her happier than to end this charade and get back to regular duties. Now she wasn't so sure.

"I'm not quite ready to pack it in," Ryder told Ted. Everyone waited while he ate a bite of sandwich. "In view of the conversation you overhead between those birders, Ted, I think I'd like to get a look at the area after dark."

"You mean go over the fence?" Hope gasped. "Isn't that dangerous?"

"Dangerous and illegal," Ryder supplied. "I was thinking of starting with long-range surveillance."

Hope relaxed. "Eat first, then we'll talk."

Dory Evans gathered the plates of those who'd finished. "Ted, if we don't hurry, we'll miss our tee time."

"I'll take care of the dishes." Hope took the stack from Dory's hands. "I didn't know you were playing golf with Dad's group."

"Not his regular foursome. He and I play with the Rasmussens on Tuesday and Thursday afternoons. Generally we all have dinner at the club. We'll skip that tonight since you two are here."

Before Hope could urge her parents to keep their dinner date, Ryder spoke, "Don't let us disrupt your routine, Mrs. Evans. The major and I have plenty to do. I've worked out a plan for setting up surveillance, and we'll need to buy some camping gear, for one thing."

Dory touched her husband's sleeve. "We still have Chris's tent, don't we, dear?" She turned back to Ryder. "I'm just not sure what you expect to find."

"It's true I didn't see anything out of whack at the museum," Ryder said, "but can any of us swear someone isn't working on the missile? I had a very uneasy feeling when I looked into the launch duct. There were some pretty usable tools at the feet of the mannequins they've set up to simulate mechanics."

"Every time I visit the place it gives me a chill." Dory shuddered. "It boggles my mind to think a nut could have destroyed someplace the size of London or Moscow with the flick of a switch."

"World tension ran high during the Cold War, Dory," Ted chided her. "The Titan sites had checks and balances. Safeguards. Launching required two people to punch two buttons simultaneously. Great engineering minds designed those features to keep some zealot from jumping the gun."

Hope paused at the kitchen door, juggling plates in

both hands. "That's the part that's scary to me. If, and I'm still saying *if,* dad has stumbled onto some organized takeover attempt, ramifications might not be so far-reaching as foreign cities."

Ryder, who'd polished off his sandwich, got up and paced the room. "You mean someone could be planning to level…say, New York City?"

She rolled a shoulder slightly. "It seems inconceivable, I know, but…"

"No." Ryder slowly massaged his chin. "There's no underestimating the minds of the truly evil." He turned suddenly to Ted. "Do you believe that rocket is launchable?"

Air whooshed from the older man's barrel chest. "I'd say no. Question is, would that stop a real fanatic from trying?"

"Hush, you two," Hope said. "Look at Mom. All this speculation is frightening her. She's as white as a ghost."

"You're absolutely right." Ted drew himself up taller. "Launching is at the farthest end of the spectrum. More than likely, if anything underhanded is going on, it's punks who plan to use the silo as a dump site for drugs smuggled across the border. Forget it, hon. Let's go play golf."

Nodding, Dory offered him a thin smile. "Hope, honey…Chris's camping equipment is in the garage. In the cupboard nearest the back door. No sense buying a lot of stuff you and Ryder will never need again. I'll wager Chris has forgotten we're still storing all that junk. If you can use anything, you're welcome to it."

"Thanks, Mom. You two have fun. And don't rush home on our account. I'm perfectly capable of grilling cheese sandwiches or something."

"Ahem..." Ted cleared his throat. "Take pity on your stomach, son. Eat out."

Ryder watched Hope puff up like a cobra ready to strike. Wisely, he held his tongue. After the elder Evanses left, he trailed her into the kitchen.

"I'm sorry we involved your mother in that discussion."

"Not to worry. She's tough."

Ryder ran water over his plate and placed it in the open dishwasher. "She is. But still we let talk get pretty intense for a civilian."

Hope arched an eyebrow. "For a civilian or for a *woman?*"

"Don't twist my words. Wouldn't you agree that we military personnel sometimes strip off other people's rose-colored glasses when we discuss national security?"

"In some cases we do," Hope admitted. "I just don't happen to think that military spouses hold too many illusions." She opened the fridge and replaced the pitcher of lemonade. "Oh. Did you want another glass?"

He shook his head. "So you weren't holding back in there? You laid out all your concerns?"

"Not all," she said with some reluctance. "My concerns built as we talked. That particular Titan has been out of service a long time. Plus, the two-stage propellant needed to launch is volatile at best. Extremely toxic. Even a reckless on-site accident could endanger the lives of everyone living in this valley."

"That's what ran through my mind when D.C. mentioned terrorists. I don't mind if subversives kill themselves messing with toxic fuel. The problem is, people like that have no morals or conscience. They couldn't care less who they take with them."

"Now you're scaring *me,* Colonel." Indeed, a shiver had Hope briskly massaging her arms. "I'll be the first to admit I'm out of my depth here. Maybe we should turn this over to Special Forces."

Ryder gazed long and hard at her.

"I see," she said, slowly releasing a pent-up breath. But, in fact, she was more confused. If Ryder was still in Special Forces, why was he at Monahan briefing pilots on routine changes to IFF codes?

"At the moment I don't want to alert a Special Forces team for nothing," he said. "They may be needed elsewhere. We have some potential hot spots brewing. I'm not forcing you to stick if you'd rather not. You're hereby relieved of special duty, Major."

"No...I...ah." Hope stroked her throat, then waved her hand ineffectually. "I didn't mean I wanted to bail out. I'm in...so what's your plan?"

"Reconnaissance. At night, from a distance. If that doesn't net us added evidence, I propose moving closer to the compound. Press those robots a bit and see if they'll show their hand. All fairly routine."

"And if they show their hand, how will we explain being out there?"

"I hit on an idea when I tagged along with that college bunch. Tonight I'll rough out some credentials making us entomologists attached to the local university. All we have to do to look legit is to collect a few prize specimens."

"Specimens?" Hope wrinkled her nose. "What exactly does an entomologist do?"

"Insects."

"Pardon me?" Hope sagged against the kitchen's center island.

"You know…scorpions, arachnids, beetles. Entomologists collect and study them."

"No." She shook her head so fast that everything in her line of sight, including Ryder McGrath, became a blur. "Arachnids as in spiders? No way, Jose. I'll be something else. A…a…botanist. The desert has hundreds of different cacti. I do not do creepy-crawlies in any shape or form. Period!"

"Our cover has to look good," Ryder warned. "How much do you know about cactus? Can you spout off their Latin names?"

"Are you such an authority on bugs?"

"I had a pretty fair collection as a kid. In high school I helped a professor who lived next door with his field studies. Not desert insects, of course, but the collection process is the same. I'll manage."

"Bully for you. What will I be doing? I will *not* be doing collection."

Ryder slanted her a rakish grin. "Is that any way to talk to a superior officer? What happened to 'I have but one life to give for my country'?"

Hope looked uncomfortable.

"Just kidding. I'd never have guessed you'd be squeamish."

"I'm not…normally. Blood and gore doesn't bother me. I wish I hadn't said anything. All I need is for this to get blabbed all over the base."

He sobered immediately. "Surely you know I wouldn't do that."

She held his gaze. "I don't know you at all, Colonel. Getting back to business, what *is* my role in this camping charade?"

Ryder absorbed the sting of her words. He wanted to deny them, to protest, but how could he? He deserved all she dished out and more. He pulled out a chair, spun it around and straddled it. "If it's not too late, I'd like to explain. Six years ago—''

"There's no need." Hope stopped him curtly. "We're both here because a special assignment requires it. Is there more to this briefing, or may I be dismissed?"

Ryder felt his back teeth grind. He might deserve her anger, but he also deserved a hearing. At least he was trying to make amends. But if the tension radiating from her slim form was a true indication of the depth to which he'd hurt her, then he had some heavy groundwork to lay first. And lay it he would. Brick by brick. She might not know what a rare framework of love they'd constructed back then but he did. He'd foolishly let it slip through his hands, and now he wanted it back. He'd only just realized how badly.

"Have a seat." Stone-faced, Ryder dug the black notebook out of his back pocket. "All research scientists, regardless of field, need an assistant to take notes. That will be your official capacity." He flipped to the back of the pad and ripped out a page, and passed it to her. "Now then," he murmured as Hope stiffly pulled out a chair across from him and picked up a pen. "Let's list what we'll need to make our cover appear real."

CHAPTER FIVE

AN HOUR LATER, the list was as complete as Ryder and Hope could make it.

"Okay." Ryder stood. "Shall we see what equipment your brother has? We'll check each piece off this list, then shop for the rest. Will we have to go all the way back to Tucson to find a recreational-equipment store?"

"It's not all that far." Once the focus returned to the mission, Hope had begun to relax. "I know of a huge store that'll have everything we could possibly want."

"Good. Before we leave, I'll get authorization to rent an off-road vehicle in our phony professor's name."

"You can do that?" Her forehead puckered in consternation.

"Hope, if by some remote chance these men we're dealing with are our misplaced terrorists, they play for keeps. We need to get our cover story down pat. Even if, as your dad suspects, it's a bunch of drug thugs, they've built an elaborate network. One they won't let go willingly. Either way it's doubtful they'll stumble into our camp and divulge big secrets."

"I know that." Hope stood and opened the door leading into the garage. "I have a top-level security clearance with special background in investigation. And while you played with bugs in high school, I spent summers doing little theater. Give me the part you want me to play and I'll play it."

"Mmm," he mused. "Odd that we both ended up in the air force."

"Given my family history, my choice isn't hard to understand. What prompted you to deviate from entomology?"

"I listened to a recruiter's speech at our senior class career day. To a kid who'd never been out of Alabama," he said with a laugh, "they were offering the moon. A paid college degree and a chance to see the world."

Hope opened the cabinet doors and dragged out a box marked with her brother's name. "How many starry-eyed kids do they sucker in with *that* old promise? And what did they do? Base you at Maxwell in your old hometown."

He hauled a neatly folded canvas tent out of the box and set it aside while he rummaged for the poles. "I'd asked to be stationed at Maxwell. My dad had had two heart attacks. April...my wife was a cardiac nurse."

"Oh." Hope swallowed a rock-size lump that had risen in her throat. More things she hadn't known about Ryder. When it came down to it, she hadn't known any of the things that counted.

He straightened, placing his hands on his hips. "You want to ask something, Hope, so ask it."

"Really, it's none of my business."

"You're dying to know why I never said anything to you about April."

Of course she was. The need to know why he'd kept such an important aspect of his life from her hurt badly. She'd die before she'd let him see how it ate at her. "N-n-no," she stuttered. "I never thought your father looked ill."

"Ultimately he had a quadruple bypass. He had a second surgery three years ago. I was on a mission out of the country and didn't get stateside for that. Claims he feels on top of the world now.''

"I'm glad he's better. The few times I met him, I enjoyed our conversations. He impressed me as a real Southern gentleman. But you do get around. A couple of years ago I recall hearing you might be transferred to Alaska."

It was on the tip of his tongue to say he knew that was why she'd transferred out so abruptly, but he didn't want her to ice up again. "I'm fairly mobile. Guess you could say I'm finally getting to see the world."

Hope turned and pulled a two-burner camp stove from the box. In addition to a tent, the carton held a lantern, assorted flashlights and a full set of aluminum cookware. Ryder whistled. "Well, will you look here." He set out a series of various glass jars of different sizes. All had aerated lids.

Hope glanced over from where she stacked tent poles atop the canvas. "Canning jars? Er...jam jars?"

"Bug jars, my lady. Your brother must have been a collector, too."

"No, no. Chris only collected hearts. He left a score of broken ones in his wake, but to my knowledge, he never held on to any this permanently."

Ryder tapped the array of lids with his thumbs as if playing bongo drums. "How old is this stuff? Maybe in high school there was a girl he tried to impress."

"With bugs?" she snorted.

"A teacher. He had a crush on a science teacher? Or maybe he dated a zoologist. Could be he's not as shallow as you think."

"I'm not saying Chris is shallow. He's just very good-looking and he knows it. Women have always fallen at his feet. And he makes the most of it."

"Makes sense to me."

"Hmmph. It would. Men are all alike."

"I beg to differ. There are some who are one-woman men." His dad. Hers.

Hope clammed up. When had he discovered he was a one-woman man? Before or after Hope had made a damn fool of herself?

Still unaware she'd withdrawn fully, Ryder pawed through the items a second time and checked them off the list. "If this is everything, I guess we're ready to find that camping-supply store."

"Fine." She headed for the house.

"Hey, shouldn't we box this stuff again? It's taking up space where your dad parks his golf cart."

Scowling, Hope balanced half in, half out of the house. "Go ahead."

"Is something wrong?" he asked, puzzled by her prickly tone.

"Nothing." She sighed. "I thought I'd better leave the folks a note. Knowing them, they may not stay at the club for dinner. When shall I say to expect us back?"

"Twenty-one hundred or later. By the time we shop, rent a vehicle and eat, it'll be at least that."

"If you're planning to eat at the officers' mess, would you drop me at my place? I have plants to water. I also have hiking boots and appropriate camp-out clothing I may as well use. No sense spending taxpayers' money unnecessarily."

"I thought we'd eat in a restaurant," he said, realizing his irritation was showing. "My treat," he added. "Can't have you worrying that we'd be ripping off taxpayers."

She took his words as a rebuke. Or maybe he'd seen through her ploy to ditch him. Hope was only prepared to provoke a superior officer so far. "As you wish, Colonel."

"That wasn't an order," he snapped. "If you'd rather not eat with me, say so in plain English. Don't beat around the bush."

Surprised, she said, "All right. I'd rather not eat with you where there's a chance we may be seen by anyone in my squadron."

"That's plain enough. Do you mind if I ask why?"

She hesitated and worried her lower lip with her teeth. Releasing it, she stared at a spot over his left shoulder. "I have a reputation to uphold."

"So I heard." Ryder didn't mean to snarl, but it sounded that way even to his ears. "Strike that." Looking away, he brushed at a stubborn lock of hair that had flopped over his forehead when he'd bent to empty the box. "I'd prefer we not be seen together, too. We'll want to discuss our plans, and the last thing we need is even friendly speculation as to our sudden fraternization."

"Out of curiosity, how is my absence from the squadron being handled?"

"For now Colonel Bradley shows you on a week-long training assignment at Holloman."

"I'm glad you told me. Fortunately I've flown into Holloman before. I won't have to bone up if people ask questions. And I know Lance Denton will."

The ferocity with which she said the name piqued Ryder's interest. He shouldn't have let her see his curiosity. The question just slipped out. "Is Denton someone special?"

"He's a jerk. The flight-line Romeo." Hope's lip curled.

"Enough said. I'll stack this in a neat pile while you

go write a note. I'll lock the garage and meet you at your car.''

''My car. That's another red flag. It's so distinctive I'll probably be paranoid until you rent something else. Oh, Ryder…if I'd really flown out to Holloman, my car would be parked at the base.''

''If the subject comes up, and it may not, say your folks came up to shop at the BX and dropped you off,'' he said, referring to the Base Exchange where even retired military shopped. ''Then make up a plausible story as to how you got home again.''

''I guess I'm not as adept at lying as you are.''

Hope disappeared into the house before Ryder could collect his wits enough to respond. After mulling things over, he decided not to open that can of worms yet. If she considered omission lying, then he was guilty. His only excuse was that he had compartmentalized the joy he'd found with Hope and kept it separate from the painful memories of April's tragic fight with cancer. And, yes, he'd asked his parents not to mention April, as well. They'd been only too happy to comply. They'd been relieved to see him out among the living again, but now they blamed him for Hope's sudden disappearance. Although they did their best to understand, Ryder knew they'd taken Hope deep into their hearts.

He had a lot of wrongs to right and was prepared to spend the rest of his life paying if need be.

They reached the car at approximately the same time. ''Do you want the top down or up?'' she asked as she unlocked the passenger door.

''Your call.'' Pulling sunglasses from his breast pocket, he put them on, then glanced at the sky. ''It's a beautiful day, and I guess it won't get much hotter?''

She squinted at the sun. A shimmering red ball already

arced in its western descent. "I've found once the mercury goes over one hundred, it doesn't make a heck of a lot of difference."

"You're probably right. Is it really over a hundred? Somehow it doesn't seem as hot as ninety does in Alabama."

She nodded. "The difference is humidity. Today it's eight."

He smiled as he watched her walk around the car. "Yeah, I've seen the cartoon of the skeleton lying on the desert. The caption reads, 'Hot? Maybe. But it's the lowest humidity on record.'"

"I should know better than to discuss weather with a flatland furriner."

Her laughter rolled over him, low and melodious. It caught Ryder off guard like a punch to the stomach.

Hope saw his features soften. Though his eyes were hidden from her view, she felt a tug in her abdomen that pinched off her breath. It struck so swiftly and unexpectedly that she fumbled her keys, dropped them and bent from his sight to retrieve them. When she rose and glanced in his direction, his jaw had tightened again. "Well," she said. "No sense standing here trading jokes all afternoon. Let's just leave the top up." She drummed her fingers on the canvas.

"Suits me. Makes it harder to identify the occupants. We've both been out to the missile museum and probably asked enough questions to stand out in those jokers' minds. I'm not saying any of them will be driving into town, but if they do, as you said earlier, this car sticks out."

Once they'd both climbed in and buckled their seat belts, Hope asked, "If there's a chance they'll remember us, are you thinking we should don some sort of disguise?''

Ryder chewed on the idea while she got under way. ''You'd probably be easier to spot than me.'' He started to lift a hand, but when it hovered near a tuft of hair that sprang softly over her ears, he curled his fingers inward and dropped his hand back into his lap. ''When your hair was longer you had more faces. One time you'd wear it in two tails like a kid. The next knotted in a bun like a corporate exec. I liked it best hanging loose around your shoulders.''

Hope felt blood surge into her cheeks. It was odd that he remembered her hairstyles so vividly.

''Sorry,'' he said quietly. ''I didn't mean to embarrass you. I was trying to show how little it takes to alter a person's appearance. A new setting, for instance. Those guys from the museum won't expect to see us in the roles I've manufactured. We'll buy hats, wear different clothes and drive a new vehicle.''

''But you made specific reference to my hair. You think it's identifiable because I cut it short?''

He turned sideways and looked her over carefully. ''Blond hair, green eyes, turned-up freckled nose. The whole package is memorable.''

Hope gasped. ''I do not have a turned-up freckled nose.''

''You do, too.''

''Do not.''

A grin quirked one corner of his lips. ''Listen to us. We sound like my sister's kids.''

His grin was infectious. Laughter bubbled from Hope's throat. ''I agree. But the freckles are a touchy area, so back off, McGrath.''

''Ouch. Your disposition used to be so sunny.''

"I never look backward. Only toward the future. It'd be better if we declare observations of a personal nature off limits, Colonel."

"I don't believe in making promises I'm not sure I can keep."

Don't I know it. Hope clamped her mouth shut, ignoring his comment. If she made any reference to what they'd once meant to each other, she'd be violating her own edict.

Ryder had been sure Hope was on the verge of spilling the anger she held so tightly in check. Against the backdrop of a fading sun streaming in the window, her face seemed chiseled from one of the red rocks that dotted the landscape. Ryder saw no sense in provoking an argument. He swore to himself that when this mission ended, they'd sit down face-to-face, and whether or not she wanted to, she'd hear his reasons for letting her go. Then it would be up to her to accept or reject his apology.

She'd turned off the highway onto a road angling toward the Rincon Mountains—one of several ranges that ringed the city of Tucson. After five minutes on the back road, they'd left all pretense of civilization behind.

"Should I worry?" Ryder joked. "Will they find my body picked clean by buzzards in the morning?"

"A friend of mine rented a car at the place I'm thinking of. By taking this road, I'll miss the downtown traffic."

Ryder settled back. "You're in the driver's seat."

She said nothing as she slowed for a turn.

"Did we have a compass on our list?" He rummaged in his pocket for the paper. "I'd hate to get lost in the desert. One desolate area bleeds into another, and pretty soon they all look alike."

"If you learn the mountain ranges, you can generally get your bearings. Water is the biggest problem. We'll need to pack all we think we'll use. Right after I came here, a couple of airmen died on a weekend outing. They apparently got turned around. Neither had taken a canteen. During the day heat in the open desert often climbs to one hundred twenty degrees. Dehydration occurs rapidly."

"You went from one extreme in Alaska to another. How long did it take you to acclimate?"

She thought a minute. "Temperature shifts must not bother me. I loved the cold winters in Alaska. The air, the sky. Everything is crisp. But I also love the sun. The desert has a haunting beauty."

Ryder smiled. "I thought you'd lost that wonderful streak of optimism, Hope. I'm glad to see you didn't."

She was genuinely surprised by his comment. And pleased to realize she hadn't lost an outlook that she herself had thought gone. "I wish I were more optimistic about this mission. What do you think is going on at the missile museum, really?"

"I haven't the foggiest. A gut feeling tells me something is. On the surface everything looks fine. Pulling off something like a launch under the noses of retired military personnel takes brains and money. That's why I keep thinking we must be off track. That whatever's going on is on the up-and-up."

"I know." She sighed. "We're probably barking up the wrong tree."

"Speaking of trees, what are the ones with the green limbs and sort of feather-duster foliage?"

"Paloverde. Earlier this year they were covered with yellow blossoms. Next spring you'll see how beautiful the desert can really be. There's a tram that'll take you to the top of Sabino Canyon. In late March or early April you'll have to ride up and hike down.''

''If I'm still here,'' he said, hating to put a damper on her enthusiasm. Ryder loved to see the sparkle back in her eyes. He, however, had promised himself to be honest in all dealings with her from here on out.

''That's right,'' she murmured. ''You're only at Monahan temporarily. How long?''

''I don't know.'' His tone said, *Don't ask.*

Hope asked anyway as a new idea suddenly struck her. ''There's one thing *I* know. You're not an IFF inspector at all. You came to Monahan to investigate the loss of airplane parts and equipment, I'll bet.''

''What do you know about that?'' he asked sharply.

''Nothing.'' Her breath came out on a puff, and the shoulder nearest Ryder rose and fell negligently. ''Then again, maybe that's not true. I've heard gossip regarding cases of missing spare parts, like everyone else on the flight line. I heard the parts were stored in secured hangars. There's talk of it being an inside job. Maybe even a ring of black marketers within our own security forces. You have too much authority and freedom to just be here updating IFF codes, so I'd say that's your real assignment.''

A deep chuckle rumbled from Ryder's chest. ''So much for my top-secret briefing with your base commander. *He* didn't know that much.''

''So it's more than penny-ante theft?''

''When it comes to the price the air force pays for even the smallest wrench, no theft is penny-ante.''

''Is it possible the robberies at the base are connected to whatever's going on in Verde Vista? I only now thought to connect the two.''

''I'd like to say yes. But late last week we traced a

shipment of electronic parts from Monahan and a shipment of radar instruments stolen from the base in Phoenix to a leased warehouse in Mesa. The warehouse was clean as a whistle, but I don't think they moved anything here. From all indications, they made a sale." He held up a hand. "And don't ask me where. That's classified. Everything I've said is classified, and I've already told you more about this case than I should."

She assumed a pained expression. "I listen. I don't usually repeat. I'd have never brought it up now except I thought there might be a connection."

"That's okay, Hope. After we wrap this up I may ask you to keep an ear to the ground along the flight line. It's doubtful that pilots are involved, but I've been surprised before."

"So our theft isn't a rare, isolated instance?"

"Unfortunately, no."

She took her eyes off the road a moment as she pulled up to a stoplight and glanced at Ryder. "I'll never understand how someone can jeopardize national security for a few bucks."

"It's quite a few bucks. In most cases I doubt if the culprits look beyond the dollars and cents that end up in their pockets."

"Still... Oh, hey. There's the car-rental agency. Shall I go in with you?" Hope pulled into the lot and parked next to the flagpole. "Do you need my home address? What will you use for ID?"

"You wait here and I'll go." Ryder pulled out his billfold and rifled through a compartment. "Ah, here. I have a New York driver's license for a Rhys Jones. A professorial name, don't you think? I doubt anyone is following, but we can't have them tracing us back to your place or mine. I'll pick an address out of the phone book and transpose a number or two. Do the same with a phone number. They never check. They just want their money and all the blanks filled out on their form.''

Hope gaped at him. "They should call you the Chameleon rather than the Strategist." She snapped her fingers. "You lie just like that."

"I prefer to think I'm leaving dead ends in an intricate maze. If you aren't sure you can carry this off, say so. I'll hold off a day and call for an operative."

"An operative? I can do it," Hope said, gritting her teeth. "Honestly, it's just that this all sounds so Clancyesque."

"His stories aren't so far-fetched. The world is full of crazies. If I thought there was any real danger, Hope, you'd be out of this already. If it goes beyond the simple observation stage, you'll be back to your old job in a flash."

"Let me say again, Colonel, I'm no stranger to spook and spy. I've never had to change my name and become Anna Agent, but I'm certainly capable."

"I never doubted it for a minute. All the same, I want you to wait in the car. And don't let the clerk at the desk get a good look at you. Together we'd be much easier to identify."

Hope watched him climb from the car and walk inside the building. Her heart revved on its own. When the pretty clerk glanced up and flashed him a brilliant smile, Hope tucked her head down. She didn't blame the reservationist. Ryder's cocky grin had a lasting effect on women. Hope busied herself straightening maps and insurance information in the glove compartment. Her heart rate gradually slowed to normal, only to escalate again when Ryder rapped on her window and dangled the keys to a black GMC Yukon with smoked side and back windows.

She leaned out her window. "Looks sort of James Bondish. Too bad it doesn't have all the special effects."

"You've got to stop reading those spy thrillers. Just hush and lead out. I'll follow. I've decided to drop your car in an all-night grocery-store parking lot. I'll drive to the camping-supply store. A quick run by your place, then dinner." He rubbed a hand over his stomach. "By then I'll be famished."

Her gaze tracked the circular path of his hand. Feeling her palms grow decidedly damp, Hope mumbled agreement.

"Do you still like Chinese food?"

His query hit her unexpectedly and brought visions of shared meals in front of his fireplace and in his bed. Hope's head whipped around fast. "I...uh...yes."

"If you know of someplace good, we could order takeout and eat back at your condo. I need to make a few phone calls, and I'd just as soon not use my cell phone."

"There's a great place not far from my house. Food'll still be hot when we get home."

He smacked her door with the flat of his hand. "Okay. So that's settled. Move out."

Hope started the engine, but instead of pulling into the exit leading to the thoroughfare, she studied the rise and fall of Ryder's back jeans pockets as he swung toward the Yukon. His wide shoulders tapered to narrow hips. His gait was easy on the eyes and defied description. He had to honk at her twice before she put her tongue back into her mouth and drove off in a squeal of tires.

THE STORE, a smorgasbord of sporting and camping folderol, wasn't overly busy. A few teens with their dads
checked out fishing poles, and a couple of muscle men
tried a weight bench. Ryder unfolded the list and hunted
up the aisle with meals-in-a-pouch.

Hope stood by while he selected ten or so and dropped
them in the basket. "These look only marginally more
appetizing than MREs."

"Freeze-dried food is pretty tasteless no matter who
produces it," Ryder said, "but we don't dare get caught
carrying anything that smacks of air force issue."

"I know. Where to next?"

"You said you have boots and appropriate clothing.
I'd better buy boots and some sort of lightweight pants
and shirts."

"And hats," she reminded him. Rounding the corner,
they faced an entire rack of hats. Hope had a great time
selecting one for herself and helping Ryder choose. She
talked him into regalia more suited to an African safari
or the Australian outback. The brim of his khaki twill
hat was clipped rakishly up on one side. Hers, of olive
felt, sported a wider brim that fell sort of willy-nilly over
her face and hair.

"Good for hiding those memorable eyes," Ryder told
her when she started to protest that she couldn't see.

He purchased boots, then walked around the store to
break them in while they picked out sunblock and other
incidentals. They worked well jointly. Sales staff smiled
at them in a way that told Hope they thought she and
Ryder looked good together. Like they belonged. Like
they were married. A sobering thought. One that gave
Hope pause and made her hang back while Ryder got
into line to pay the bill.

He set everything on the counter, then handed the

clerk at the register the tag for his boots. He glanced over the head of the next man in line in search of Hope. Finding her, and noting a slight frown on her forehead, he quickly scanned the list. "Did we forget something?"

She smoothed a lock of hair behind her ear. "No. I see a pay phone over there. I'll call and order our food. That way it'll be ready about the time we drive by."

"Fine." He smiled one of his crooked, devastating smiles, and Hope wished he hadn't. It gave her butterflies.

I just need to eat, she told herself.

It wasn't until after they loaded all the bags into the Yukon and Ryder asked what they were having for dinner that it dawned on Hope she'd ordered their favorites of six years ago.

"I...uh...I ordered mu shu pork for two and steamed rice. Two egg rolls with double hot mustard for you." She climbed into the passenger seat and buckled up without looking at him. He remained still, a hand cupping her elbow even after he'd given her a boost up.

She tossed her head and pulled loose from his grip. "If you'd prefer something different, we can eat at the restaurant. I give them enough business, so I'm sure they won't mind switching."

"It's perfect. Old habits die hard, don't they?" he said quietly.

"Don't make a big deal of it, McGrath. Ask them and they'll tell you it's what I always order."

He closed her door softly, walked around the front of the vehicle and climbed in. "When did you start eating hot mustard?" he asked casually as the engine roared to life.

"I don't. I hate hot mus...tard."

He licked his index finger and slashed it through the air. "My point, I believe."

Hope rolled her eyes. "Oh, for Pete's sake. I didn't realize we were keeping score. So we had a few laughs together once and I happened to remember your preference for Chinese. I have a mind for detail. The restaurant's in the middle of the next block. Pull over and stop. I'll run in."

He started to reach for his wallet, but Hope stopped him. "My treat for old—"

"So help me, if you say for old times' sake like we're long-lost pals, I'll park right here and we'll duke it out. We were more than pals. A lot more, Hope. I hurt you badly and I'm sorry. I get the message that you don't want to talk about the past. You're off the hook tonight because we have other fish to fry. But we *will* discuss it fully before I leave Monahan. Bank on it."

Her temper flared instantly, then mellowed again as she wrenched open the door and slid out. He'd certainly become more hardheaded in the intervening years. But so had she. "You'll pardon me, McGrath," she said, turning to him, "if I don't hold my breath waiting to see if your promises mean more now than they did six years ago."

Ryder jerked as her door slammed. She had a right to take that potshot. On the other hand, he was getting damn tired of turning the other cheek.

CHAPTER SIX

THE SACK WITH THE FOOD radiated heat and a tantalizing scent that left Hope and Ryder drooling.

"I actually didn't know I was so hungry," she said as Ryder pulled into her complex and parked. "I'll race you to the condo."

"You'd lose. How fast can we set the table?"

"I'll stick this in the warming oven, set the table and fix a pitcher of iced tea. Why don't you start making your calls?"

"Such a deal. But I'm not averse to helping in the kitchen."

Hope remembered clearly the evenings they'd fixed dinner together. Sometimes they finished and it got on the table. Sometimes not. "My kitchen isn't really big enough for two people," she said tersely.

As she opened the door to her unit, Hope snapped on the living-room light and pointed to the phone on the end table near the chintz couch. "If you need privacy, there's an extension in the bedroom." She motioned down the hall. "My room is the first door on the left."

"You have two bedrooms?"

"Yes." She proceeded into the kitchen.

"But you live here alone?" Last time he'd been here it'd never entered his mind that she might not live alone. He scowled.

Her head bobbed up and she stared at him across the

breakfast island. "Now I do. Since my friend transferred last month." Let him make what he would of that information. If he chose to think she'd been living with a man, all the better. He'd seemed a little too amenable to taking up where they'd left off. At least it sounded to Hope as if he wanted to explore options.

Ryder waited a minute for her to elaborate. When she set her purse on the counter and poured water in the iced-tea maker, he said, "I'll use the phone out here. I wouldn't want you to worry that I'm doing anything behind your back." He thought perhaps his statement would tweak her conscience. She merely glanced up and smiled. Ryder had an inkling that she was playing cat-and-mouse. He decided to let it go. He had ways of finding out if her roomie had been male or female. If she'd been living with a man, that threw a whole different light on the subject.

He sat, took a small address book out of his wallet and punched in the direct link to General Beemis.

"General, this is Colonel Ryder McGrath. Sorry to bother you so late, but I wanted to bring you up to speed. So far I've nothing to go on but gut instinct. Thought I'd give it a couple more days. No word on the two men we've lost?" He listened, interjecting noncommittal grunts here and there. Then he explained their cover and asked the general to pull strings and get him on the phone roster at the university. "Thank you, sir. We'll try and smoke them out. Two days tops. I'll phone again then. Oh, say, General. Do you have Joe Striker's number handy? Thought I'd see if he's tracking any propellant." Taking a pen from his shirt pocket, Ryder scribbled a number on his hand. He thanked Beemis again, then pressed the button with his thumb.

A glance toward Hope showed her still bustling

around the kitchen setting plates and silverware on opposite sides of the breakfast island. He recalled a time the two of them would have sat side by side. A sadness invaded his heart and left him feeling disconnected.

In an effort to shake the feeling, Ryder lifted his thumb from the phone button, listened for a dial tone and quickly punched in another string of numbers. The phone rang three times, then cut to an answering machine. Ryder started to hang up, then decided to leave a message. "Joe, Ryder McGrath. I wonder if there's been any report of strayed nitrogen tetroxide or any components of Aerozene? If you get in, I'll be at this number forty-five minutes or so." Placing his hand over the mouthpiece, he asked Hope for her number and repeated it into the phone. Then he hung up. The enticing odor of food permeated the air.

"Finished your calls?" Hope asked as Ryder stood. "If so, I'll put our food on the table. If you're not ready, I won't be responsible for my actions. I'm starving."

"Me, too. Just let me wash up."

He knew the way to the bathroom already, so Hope didn't bother directing him.

Ryder washed quickly, dried his hands, then tiptoed out and down the hall. Quietly opening the door to the second bedroom, he peeked inside to see if he could get a feel as to whether the decor was masculine or feminine. Bare white stucco walls, the same as the ones in the living room, stared back. The beige berber carpet matched that in the rest of the apartment. Softly closing the door, Ryder still had no clue as to the sex of Hope's former roommate.

"There you are," she said inanely as he reappeared. "I thought for a minute that maybe you'd decided to take a bath."

"I wasn't gone that long. You could have started without me."

"I considered it," she said, placing the open, steaming cartons on bright pads she'd set on the Formica counter. "I'm so hungry I could eat a bear. Maybe I should have ordered for three."

"If this isn't enough, we can raid your folks' refrigerator later." Ryder spooned a portion of white rice onto Hope's plate, then did the same with his.

"Dessert. Mom will have fixed dessert and she'll have saved us some."

"Are you sure? Or should we stop at the store and buy a carton of frozen yogurt? Last night your mother said your dad needed to cut down on desserts."

"She always says that. Then Dad goes around looking like a lost pup and she gives in and bakes something. His favorite is chocolate-chip cookies."

"Um. Mine, too. If they're made from scratch. The store-bought ones are too sweet for my taste."

Hope stopped filling her thin pancake with the mixture of pork. "According to your mother, oatmeal-raisin cookies were your favorite. Why else would I have baked them three times a week for eight weeks?" She busied herself folding the ends of her pancake.

Putting down his chopsticks, Ryder gazed at the top of her head. The play of the overhead lights across her blond curls formed a soft halo. Ryder suffered a stab of need so fierce he reached for her without thinking. He slid off the stool and pulled her off hers and into his arms. He registered the shocked look in her eyes and the muffled squeak of protest as she dropped the roll she'd so carefully fashioned mere seconds before his lips crashed down on hers.

She gurgled briefly. Then, as Ryder's lips softened,

Hope's fingers inched up the front of his shirt. She clasped the points of his collar, and little by little her body sagged against him.

When the phone shrilled they broke apart, both breathing raggedly. Hope had done her fair share of returning Ryder's kisses, yet he needed only one glimpse at the fire replacing the dreamy love-light in her eyes to see she didn't count herself a willing partner. It didn't matter that his heart still brimmed with feelings of love for Hope, Ryder knew he'd pushed too fast. He'd also overstepped his bounds. He never should have put them in this situation. *Damn!*

Since Hope didn't make a move to answer the phone, even though his knees wobbled like sponge rubber, he dived for the receiver and barked, "Hello.

"Joe? Yeah, I called. I'm not onto anything for sure," Ryder said, leaning his still-trembling body against the overstuffed arm of Hope's couch. "At this point we're more or less shooting in the dark. Just need to know if any illegal liquid propellants in sufficient proportions to lift a Titan II have made their way into the southwest U.S. recently."

Ryder shifted the phone and rubbed his neck. "From anywhere, buddy. And I don't know the shot range we're talking. Or even if we're talking. Hypothetically speaking, the target might be anywhere in the world. If I knew who we were dealing with, I'd have a better idea of a possible target. Or maybe not. Hell, Striker, all I've got now is a hunch." Ryder rotated his head full circle, massaging his flesh harder.

"Great. You set your team to digging. I'll call back in a couple of days. No. No, I won't be at this number. Let me phone you. I have a cell unit, but if these guys are sophisticated and I arouse their suspicions, they may be able to snag the airwaves. I'll call when I feel it's safe. Hey, thanks, Joe. I owe you one.''

Out of the corner of his eye, Ryder noted that Hope had taken her plate of food to the dining-room table, leaving his on the island counter. He almost begged Joe not to hang up just so he didn't have to face her. Not that he blamed Hope for being upset. Kissing her had been a dumb move on his part. Deciding it was time to face her anger, Ryder dropped the receiver back into the cradle and sighed.

A sigh Hope heard across the room. She'd intended to set him straight in no uncertain terms. He looked so genuinely undone when he got off the phone, she scratched her original plan. ''Who's Joe Striker?''

''What?'' Ryder had been busily combing his mind for excuses as to why he'd grabbed and kissed her. He wasn't prepared for her to ask a normal question.

''Joe Striker,'' she repeated. ''Who is he?''

''He's former military. Now a bird dog at the Center for Nonproliferation Studies.''

Hope waved her chopsticks in the air. ''At the risk of sounding obtuse, I don't know what that center is.''

''Mainly it maintains a database that tracks worldwide movement of nuclear materials both legal and illegal. They do a phenomenal job.''

''Don't those involved in the arms-control agreements police the program?''

''Unfortunately, no. Frankly, most ranchers around here probably guard their cattle closer than anyone guards dismantled nuclear equipment. For people who move in the right circles, there are always buyers who have questionable ambitions.''

''You mean...ambitions to rule the world?''

"Some aren't even that lofty. Some only want to over-run a neighboring country. And there're always terror-ists. Their agendas are often less clear."

"Less clear and scarier." Hope picked up a piece of pork with her chopsticks. "It's sobering to think those might be the nuts we're dealing with. You'd better eat up. The sooner we get on with this job, the better."

"No need to get hyper. As I told Joe, we don't know for sure if there's even anything wrong at the missile site."

"*Something's* going on. Aerospace said they didn't order a change in personnel at the museum. The county disavowed knowledge. D.C. suggested my dad's getting senile. The guys manning the place all look like clones of Arnold Schwarzenegger, except we know Hollywood isn't shooting a movie there, because every last one of them hides from the camera. If not an act of terror-ism…what?"

Ryder returned to his now-cold food. He pushed it around and made furrows in the clumps of rice but didn't take a bite. "I don't know what. General Beemis said they've had people who know these terrorists checking footage of all incoming passenger flights. None of their known aliases have turned up on any manifest."

Hope snorted. "This from a man who pulls a sheaf of fake ID's out of his wallet."

"I'm not saying our sources are infallible, but they're pretty damn good. Until something more jumps out and hits us, we're going to proceed with caution. That's an order, Major."

She rose, picked up her plate, and with eyes little more than narrow slits, glided into the kitchen and dumped her remaining food in the trash. "I get the message, sir!

Now you get this. My person is off limits. Is that clear, Colonel McGrath?''

Before Ryder could draw a breath, she'd stomped down the hall and slammed into her room. ''Hell!'' he exclaimed. Following her lead, he also scraped his plate. He, however, looked forlornly at what remained in the cartons. Judging it cold, he pitched them, too. Then, because he needed a breath of fresh air, he tied the garbage bag and went in search of the complex's Dumpster. It wasn't hard to find. And the jaunt made him less tense. He returned to the apartment, rinsed the plates and tucked them into the dishwasher before Hope emerged carrying her hiking boots and an overnight bag.

''I'm ready to leave,'' she said, brushing past him, headed for the door.

Ryder didn't move from his seat at the counter. At the risk of irritating her further, he raised a question. ''Weren't you going to water your plants?''

Balanced on the balls of her feet at the door, Hope almost denied the truth. But as he looked so truly contrite and uncomfortable over having to bring it to her attention, she shook her head and chuckled.

''Watering my poor plants was the purpose of our making a side trip to my condo. Thanks for reminding me. You saved me buying new ones.'' She left her things beside the door and went to fill a watering can and a misting wand. ''Although,'' she continued as if there hadn't been a spate of silence between them, ''My choice would have been silk plants. There's not a hint of chlorophyll in my thumb. If Lissa hadn't willed me these, the place wouldn't look half so homey.''

''Who's Lissa?'' Ryder asked, not because he cared but because he loved the low, husky tone of her voice.

He had an elbow propped on the counter, his chin

resting in his palm. Nothing threatening or devious about his relaxed stance. Hope's answer was equally cavalier. "Lissa was my roommate." The minute the information left her lips, Hope knew what she'd done. Ryder's satisfied grin said *gotcha* as plainly as if he'd spoken aloud.

Maintaining a straight face, Hope pretended not to notice her slip or his claim to victory. She watered the plants in the stand below the pass-through. Then, with the ease born of long years getting even with two rotten brothers, she casually swung the misting wand over Ryder's head and turned on the spigot.

"Hey!" He few off the chair, knocking it over in his haste to escape. If he'd harbored doubts as to whether the wetting had been accidental, they fled when Hope convulsed in laughter.

Ryder laughed, too, as he shook water from his hair and face. This was the Hope he remembered. The side of her he liked best. Mischievous and full of the Old Nick.

"Score is even up," she crowed, blowing on her fingers and scraping them lightly on her blouse above the breast pocket.

He rocked back on his heels and pretended to look stern. "Ah, but you said we weren't keeping score."

"Well, I changed my mind," she said cheekily. "A woman's prerogative."

"*It is that,*" Ryder said under his breath as she went into the kitchen to put away the can and wand. If he had his way, she'd do a complete about-face. She'd go back to loving him the way she had six years ago.

SOME HALF HOUR LATER, after Ryder and Hope returned to Verde Vista, Hope's parents greeted them warmly.

Ted Evans pulled Ryder aside. "I drew some detailed

maps of the museum's fenced and unfenced perimeters. According to the lease, they comprise approximately ten acres. Three of which are inside chain link. On one map I've sketched the Doppler radar motion-detection system and the TPS-39, commonly called Tipsies. There are both UHF and VHF antennae at all four corners of the property. If you intersect the beam, anyone below will know. The stuff's so sensitive it beeps if a crow flies across the perimeter.''

Ryder looked smug. ''Then they'll know we're camping on the desert. It remains to be seen how close we get to the property before whoever's in charge sics the goons on us.''

Ted stroked his chin. ''It'll be interesting to see if they check you out during the day or if they wait until night. My theory is that people are jumpier and more easily intimidated after dark.''

''I know I am,'' Hope put in.

''You won't have to worry,'' her dad said. ''Just let Ryder do all the talking.''

Hope failed to block a sound of disgust, but the men paid no attention. Her father rubbed his hands together gleefully and beckoned Ryder to the table.

''Come on, son. I'm ready to brief you on landmarks.''

Ryder didn't follow. Instead, he aimed Hope a hesitant glance. ''I need to run my new clothes through a couple of washes so they don't look so new. I should also scuff up my boots. And I still have to pack the Yukon.''

Ted turned back. ''Delegate, son. Let the major take care of the small stuff.''

Hope whipped around to stare openmouthed.

''Do you mind?'' Ryder's eyes settled on her worriedly.

"Uh...no." She managed to get the word out without too much insincerity. After all, he'd asked, not ordered. She couldn't blame her dad for his attitude. He came from the old school—before the concept of teamwork and partnership came into play. Leaders were doing better now involving junior officers in the decision-making process.

Ryder smiled his thanks. Stripping off his new boots, he handed them to Hope, along with the keys to the rented Yukon.

The smile lit his face, darkened his eyes and knocked the pins out from under her. Though Hope dropped the keys and fumbled picking them up, she knew then she'd walk over hot coals barefoot for Colonel Ryder McGrath if he asked with a smile.

Darn. How could she still be so susceptible to his smile? Nerves on edge, she felt a frantic need to get out of his sight—to let her pulse return to normal.

Outside, the night was warm, the stars bright. She listened to the low call of night birds that nested beneath the sage. By tomorrow night, when she and Ryder were camping far from the glow of city lights, the moon would be full. To avoid thinking about how she'd handle being alone with him throughout a long moonlit night, Hope opened the double doors of the Yukon's tail compartment and began dumping shopping bags.

Dory Evans joined her about the time Hope had price tags removed and everything separated into neat piles. "Looks like you have enough stuff here to camp out for a month. Aren't you only planning on spending one night out there?"

"One or two. It depends on whether anyone makes contact and asks us to leave."

"You will do as they say, won't you?"

Hope glanced up sharply. "Why, Mom, you sound worried. I always thought you were a pillar of strength. That you had nerves of steel."

The older woman looked abashed. "Then I did a better job of acting than I gave myself credit for. Ted did Korea and Vietnam. Rolf, Panama and Bosnia. You sat up there at Elmendorf within a stone's throw of the USSR. Chris doesn't say, but he was suspiciously silent during the trouble in Panama. I understand fighting for peace. Oh, it doesn't mean my stomach is less jumpy, but I do understand. This..." She waved a hand in the direction of the museum. "Ted's sure it's a drug cartel. Those men have no conscience. They kill for the sake of killing. I mean...maybe you shouldn't get involved, Hope. It might not have anything to do with the military."

Hope hugged the distraught woman, unable to keep her own voice steady. "We don't know that they're drug runners. Even if they are, it's still a military concern. Part of our job is to track suspected shipments into the country. Surely you didn't think our government was kidding about waging war on drugs?"

"N...no." Dory dabbed at her eyes. "I'm sorry, Hope. Of course drug transfer is a world issue. Don't pay any attention to me. Give me the things Ryder needs washed. I'll go throw them in the washer."

"I'm afraid, I've been assigned that duty." She screwed up her face.

"Give them to me," Dory demanded. "I'd hate for you to kill that nice Colonel McGrath over a little thing like a load of laundry."

"Are you okay, Mom? You're never this cranky."

"I'm fine. Chalk it up to the odd letter I got from Chris today."

"Odd? How so?" Hope chewed at her lower lip as Dory filled her arms with Ryder's shirts and pants.

"You'll have to read it when you're finished here. He sounded…homesick or something."

"Chris? Homesick?" Hope broke into peals of laughter.

"No one in this family gives Chris credit for being sensitive. He has a tender heart, Hope."

"Yeah. And he wears it on his sleeve."

"So, he needs the love of a good woman. Maybe unconsciously he's missing balance in his life. Instead of making fun, pray he's found himself a bride."

"Mom, Chris won't quit playing the field until the air force issues him a wife. He's a typical fighter pilot. Pure alpha jock, and proud of it."

Dory sniffed. "You sound like your father. When did you get so cynical?"

Hope's lingering laughter died a sudden death. Luckily her mother stepped into the house with Ryder's stack of clothes or Hope's face would have given her away. She'd turned cynic six years ago. And the man responsible for her cynicism was seated inside at her mother's antique table. Hope knew she'd have to take greater care not to let conversations like this ramble out of hand. If Dory, who was the intuitive one in their family, picked apart Chris's letter looking for nuances that indicated he needed a wife, she'd pounce on the slightest aberration in Hope's behavior. Dory Evans rarely missed a chance to stress how her two youngest offspring would be happier if they found suitable mates.

As Hope scuffed Ryder's boots along the concrete driveway, she daydreamed about how life might be if she'd married him six years ago. Meshing two military careers worked for some people. But six years ago she'd been a mere captain, and therefore had less options. Their duty assignments might have been split. For reasons more obvious now, Ryder never mentioned having kids. Hope had assumed he would want them when the time came—because she did. Frankly she'd always thought of marriage and kids as a package deal.

Obviously Ryder had once, too. Cruel, how the timing for their involvement had been all wrong. Although Hope's former roommate, Lissa, insisted stuff like that was preordained.

Her mind was definitely elsewhere as Hope started methodically loading their gear into the Yukon. She struggled to pick up the tent and yelped when two hands reached around her and gave the heavy canvas a boost.

"Whoa. I'm just trying to help."

"You scared the crap out of me," Hope said, wrestling the awkward bundle out of Ryder's grip and over to the vehicle's open back door. "What are you doing, sneaking up on me that way?"

"I can't believe you didn't hear me. I walked right around the house to see what was taking you so long."

"Long? Look at that pile of price tags I scraped off."

Ryder picked up a black duffel bag that sat at his feet and heaved it into the Yukon. In so doing, he toppled two of Hope's even stacks.

"Stop! What are you doing? You told me to organize, and now that I have, you go and mess it up. Uh, mess it up…sir," she added belatedly when she saw Ryder's eyes narrow.

"Don't call me sir," he snapped. "We already discussed the need to drop all trace of the military for this operation. From here on, until I say otherwise, you are Teri Harris, my assistant. I'm sorry if you feel this assignment is beneath you, but it's what assistants to professors do during field studies. They assist.''

"Do tell.'' Hope crossed her arms. "I wasn't asking for a pat on the back…just for a little consideration in keeping straight what I've already done…Professor Jones.''

"If this surly attitude is all because I kissed you earlier, Hope, then we'd better take a walk right now and straighten this out. We both know I was out of line. We need to at least give the appearance of working together cohesively if those jerks show up tomorrow.''

Hope peered around uneasily. She didn't relax until it became apparent that neither her mom nor her dad was within earshot. "If you think my attitude is surly now,'' she said in a voice dripping honey, "wait until you see how much worse I can be if my mom gets the slightest hint that you kissed me. Or figures out we have a history. My mother may look sweet, but when it comes to getting Chris and me married off, she has the mentality of a pitbull. Unless you want to end up at the altar, I suggest you zip your lip. And zip it tight.''

"Who says I don't want to end up at the altar?'' Ryder spaced his feet apart, hooked his thumbs in the corners of his pants pockets and gave Hope an assessing look.

"Wh…a…at?''

"I said—''

"I know what you said,'' Hope said through gritted teeth. "Stop it, Ryder. Just stop playing games. I wasn't the one who ended our relationship. You did. At one time I did want to know why. I no longer care. Fate has thrown us together to do this job. I'm not sure how, or why. But it did. We're both highly trained intelligent adults, so let's stop acting like kids.''

"Quite a speech." His hands came out of his pockets. Ryder crossed his arms and rocked back on his heels.

"Don't. Don't lecture me. It's been a long day. I'll set my alarm for daybreak and finish this tomorrow. What time do you want to get under way?"

Ryder could tell by the slight tremor in Hope's hands and lips that she was seconds from shattering. Forcing her to break down was the last thing he wanted. If she really no longer cared about the good things they'd experienced in the past, there probably wasn't any use in rashing out old hurts. He happened to think she was lying. He'd tasted it in her kiss, and every so often he'd caught a glimpse of yearning in her eyes. No, he didn't believe for a minute that the love they'd shared was completely dead. Only napping. Unlike the fairy tale, it obviously took more than one kiss to awaken his sleeping princess. He was no prince, but his day would come.

"Go on to bed, Hope," he said gently. "I'll finish here. I don't sleep well before a mission, anyway. According to your dad, we'll be smart to go early and start collecting specimens while it's still cool. If it's okay with you, I'd like to leave here at 0500."

She inclined her head. Wasting no time, she disappeared into the house. Her dad sat in the living room viewing the late news on TV. Hope saw her mom in the laundry room folding Ryder's clothes. Preferring not to offer explanations for leaving Ryder to finish packing the equipment alone, Hope scooted into her room.

A hot shower soothed her rattled nerves. By the time she stowed the few personal essentials she planned to take, her control was firmly in place again and her sense of well-being back on an even keel.

She'd just crawled into bed when she heard Ryder come down the hall. Hope held her breath, expecting him to pass. But there came a light tap. She hastily pulled the sheet up to her chin. She wore a sleeveless batiste gown that was very thin. Her summer-weight boxer pj's were packed for the trip. Although she just might sleep in her clothes.

"Come in," she called, doing her best to keep her voice steady.

Ryder pushed the door open a crack and peered around the edge. "I didn't wake you, did I?" He sounded contrite. "I thought your light was on."

"I was awake. Is there something you need?"

Seeing her in bed, even though she was fully covered, built a hunger in Ryder like nothing he'd experienced in years. Somehow he doubted Hope wanted to hear about that particular need.

"I figured you'd go to bed immediately when you came in. The light threw me. It's been almost two hours. I decided to check and see if you were all right."

"I showered and packed a duffel." She yawned. "Two hours. No wonder I'm so sleepy."

He smiled. "I have to pack yet. I see a good elf left a stack of clean clothes outside my door."

"My mother. She always did that for us kids. We cleaned our own rooms, but she never went in. Said she respected our right to privacy."

"Boy, not my mom. Nothing was sacred. She used to say if my sister or I had anything in our rooms that she couldn't see, we shouldn't have it, period."

"I suspect I'd be more like your mom. Today parents have to be alert to so many things."

"Yeah. Nobody ever said parenting was easy. You sound as if you're planning on having kids."

"Um. Someday. Well, good night, Ryder. See you at 0500."

"Right. I'm sure we'll have time on our stakeout to finish comparing life stories. G'night, Hope." He shut the door without a sound.

Hope stared at the spot where he'd stood. Did it show on her face how badly she wanted to get married and have a baby? No. Their conversation had been happenstance. Ryder wasn't interested in her plans for the future. Nor she in his. Above all else, she planned to avoid heart-to-heart chats with him from now on.

Reaching up, she snapped off the light. It took her forever to drop off to sleep. When she finally did, she was plagued by dreams. Of a ranch-style house with a fenced yard. A swing set. Childish laughter wafting on a fall breeze.

Even though Hope awakened with a start several times and tried to force her dream down an alternate path, she slid right back into the same scene. And always the man of the house looked exactly like Ryder McGrath.

CHAPTER SEVEN

THE SMELL OF CINNAMON enticed Hope out from beneath her pillow. She waved a hand toward her nightstand several times and finally connected with her clock, which she dragged close to her face. "Yikes! It's 0450," she gasped sleepily. Her feet hit the floor with a thud. She hurriedly stripped off her nightgown and began to throw on the clothes she'd had the good sense to lay out the night before.

Too bad about her puffy eyes. She stuck her tongue out at the image looking back from the mirror. *Ghastly.* Tossing and turning did that to a body. But Hope would be darned if she was going to try to disguise the telltale signs with makeup. Pancake makeup would turn to concrete after a few hours in the desert. She gave herself five minutes with a cool pack fashioned from a washcloth and brushed the sleep snarls from her hair.

With two minutes to spare, she snagged her duffel and yanked open the door. She and Ryder almost collided in the hall.

He glanced at the watch strapped to his wrist, then at her. First his shoulders started to shake, then hers. Soon they both erupted in laughter.

"I forgot to set my alarm. What's your excuse?" he probed after sobering.

"Normally I'm out running by now. I trusted my inside alarm, and it failed miserably."

Dory Evans bustled out of the kitchen. She stopped in the living room when she saw the two of them walking down the hall. "There you are. I know you're running late, but I fixed granola cereal, juice, coffee and cinnamon rolls. It's all on the table. You eat while I fill your canteens."

"Mom," Hope protested. "You shouldn't have gone to all that trouble."

Unexpectedly, Ryder leaned over and kissed the older woman on the cheek. "Since you have, Dory, we'll spare the time to chow down. I've been salivating half an hour over the smell of those cinnamon rolls. I'm darned sure not running off until I sample them."

Hope heaved a sigh. "You're the leader."

A grin creased the hollows of Ryder's clean-shaven cheeks. "Finally we agree on something."

Without thinking, Hope slugged him on the arm.

Dory's eyebrow rose ever so slightly. She said nothing as she led the way back to the patio where Ted sat reading the morning paper. He wasn't as tactful as his wife.

"Beautiful morning. Too bad you missed it."

Hope dropped her duffel and sat in the chair Ryder had already pulled out for her. She made a face at her father. "If God had wanted humans to see the sun rise, he'd have made it come up at 1200 hours." With a flick of her wrist, she spread her napkin.

"I won't be able to start collecting specimens until sundown," Ryder said.

Hope shot him a dirty look. "As far as I'm concerned, you don't have to collect them at all."

Ryder opened his mouth to respond, but Ted interrupted. "That reminds me, son, I found a different pair of glasses. These are wire-rimmed. Ought to make you look scholarly."

"Thank you, sir." Ryder accepted the case. Opening it, he took out the glasses, perched them low on his nose and peered over the lenses at Hope.

She laughed, spewing orange juice over her plate. He looked pained, but put the glasses away while she cleaned up.

"I think they're a nice touch," he informed her. "All dedicated scientists wear specs."

"Did I say you didn't look bookish?" she asked, feigning innocence.

The way her lips still twitched devilishly caused Ryder to ignore her and dig into his cereal.

Following his lead, they all ate. Talk diminished.

Hope pushed away from the table first. "That was good, Mom. Except now I need to brush my teeth again. I'll only be a minute," she said to Ryder.

"Ditto for me." Ryder stretched then patted his full stomach.

Dory beamed. "I'll wrap the rest of the rolls. You can eat them tomorrow."

He stayed her with a hand. "I'm afraid the sugar and cinnamon will attract ants."

Hope grinned wolfishly. "This from the avowed entomologist. Why not collect ants? They're less offensive, to my way of thinking."

"Except they come in armies," he said dryly. "And if you've ever run into desert fire ants, I guarantee you'd find them offensive. They sting like hell."

She supposed he wasn't just pulling her leg. "That's okay," she interjected smoothly. "Dad's eyeing the leftover rolls, anyway. I'd hate to deprive him of one of the only sweets Mom lets him have. Poor fellow."

"Thank you, Major," Ted said stiffly, though behind his wife's back, he gave Hope a quick wink.

She grinned and continued to her room. Ryder trailed more slowly. They emerged again within seconds of each other.

"We're only an hour late," Ryder said, setting his watch to match the digital clock on the microwave. "I have the maps your dad drew committed to memory. We'll reach our destination in nothing flat."

Ted slapped Ryder on the back and walked with him out to the vehicle. "You have a cell phone, right? You'll buzz me if you need anything?"

"Yes, sir." Ryder shook the older man's hand. He started around the front of the Yukon to help Hope in. Seeing that she'd done without his aid, he backtracked and slid beneath the wheel.

When at last they backed out of the driveway, the sun loomed high over the desert, bathing the landscape below a molten gold.

Ryder settled comfortably against the leather seat. Obeying the speed limit, he drifted in behind a line of cars headed out of town.

Hope fiddled with the radio. She ran through several stations before locking on to one playing old tunes. Mellow rock. She plumped the pillow she'd brought into the corner, lay her head on it and closed her eyes.

Ryder had a difficult time keeping his eyes on the road. During their brief time together, he'd made it a point to wake up early so he could steal a few minutes to watch her sleep. Her thick eyelashes fluttered softly on pale cheeks. Her lashes and eyebrows were dark for a blonde. A contrast Ryder found intriguing. Her lips were plump. The bottom one pouted slightly when she slept, as if begging to be kissed.

Ryder's hands tightened on the wheel.

Damn, he'd almost missed the spot where Ted had

said to turn off the highway. He swung the wheel hard
bouncing Hope out of her snug corner. Her head hit the
padded roof seconds before the right wheel hit a rut that
flung her sideways across the seat.

She scraped a mass of curls out of her eyes, blinking
like a mole emerging into daylight. "Wh…hat happened?"

Ryder eased up on the pedal, which in turn slowed
the wildly bucking Yukon. "Are you hurt, Hope?" He
almost came to a full stop. "Your dad didn't warn me
that this road-of-sorts was so rough. Ted said the trail
was packed solid because the local saddle club ride
horses here."

Hope rubbed her head. She thought she might have a
lump. "We're driving on horse trails?"

"Better than blazing our own, wouldn't you say?"

"I don't know," she said ruefully.

His eyes narrowed. "Why aren't you buckled in?"

Hope grabbed for the seat belt. "I thought I was. It
must not have engaged fully. Or it popped loose when
you hit that chuckhole." She swiftly connected the two
pieces, and none too soon. As the Yukon topped a rise,
it immediately plunged into a cactus-strewn arroyo and
struck something that lay across the track. Wham! They
heard the left front tire blow.

"Dammit!" Ryder smacked both palms on the steer-
ing wheel. "I never thought to check and see if we have
a spare."

"Who would?" Hope said, looking worried. "What
did we hit?"

Ryder disconnected his seat belt and opened his door
a crack. "I can't tell. Be careful if you get out. We're
sitting in a forest of cactus."

She chuckled at that. "That's probably what you hit."

He climbed out gingerly. Hope slid across the seat and jumped down beside him. "Looks like a dead cholla," he muttered, hunkering down beside him.

"From the size of the hole it blew in our tire, it must be petrified cholla." He pronounced it *choy-ya*, as did he.

"You should throw a fit when you take this back to the rental place. It's an off-road vehicle, but these aren't off-road tires." Standing, Hope kicked the flattened tire with the steel toe of her boot.

"You're right." Ryder rose, then walked all the way around the Yukon. "I didn't even notice." He swore softly. "Providing we have a spare, we'll have to put it on and go back to town. I'll buy a set of off-road tires and let D.C. fight it out with the rental agency."

"This ground is pure sand. It's not going to be easy changing a tire here."

He scoffed, but her words turned out to be prophetic. It took them ten minutes to shift the load and get to the spare—which ended up to be much smaller than the other tires. An hour and a half later, under a blistering sun, Ryder finally managed to brace the jack solidly enough to keep it from sliding out on the slick, glassy sand. Sweat stained his new khaki shirt.

Hope said very little. She fancied she saw smoke coming out of Ryder's ears. Her watch said 1100 by the time they limped back into town.

At 1300 they headed out again. Ryder wasn't in any mood to discuss stopping for lunch. Hope bought two bags of peanuts and two sodas out of a machine at the tire shop. Though why she worried about feeding a man too surly to talk, she couldn't say.

The ride wasn't any smoother with the bigger tires, but the tread was so deep, Hope didn't think they need

worry about punctures from even the longest cactu
thorns.

Another bit of trivia Hope pulled from her memor
about Ryder—his propensity for buying top-of-the-lin
She'd met women who married men only to find ou
later they were miserly. Ryder's wife would have th
best. If he ever remarried, that is.

She mused about that so deeply she didn't realize ju
how long they'd been driving across the bumpy dese
until she glanced up and saw they were in the middle o
nowhere. "Hey, are you going all the way to Mexico
I thought the birders were only a mile or so from th
museum."

"I want to see how far the surveillance rang
stretches." He pointed to a flat plateau ahead. "We'
start there and inch our way toward the compound. Th
plateau puts us above their radar towers. Tonight I'
going to do some spying of my own."

An hour later they were both hot, dirty and shor
tempered after raising the tent at the top.

"It's smaller than it looked all folded up," Hope sai
eyeing the squat igloo with misgiving.

"Two-man," Ryder grunted. "Let's don't waste tim
jawing. We'll put the canteens, sleeping bags, a chang
of clothes and the collection containers in the tent. Ev
erything else, except for the black bag, we'll leave i
the rig."

"Wait a darned minute. You're not bringing creepy
crawlies into the tent where I'm sleeping."

"Most of what I plan to collect are night hunters
Leave them out here and they'll draw a crowd o
friends."

"I don't care. No way."

"Hope, you aren't being reasonable. If the jeepster

show up, they won't buy a scientist leaving his collection out where any Tom, Dick or Harry can steal it.''

"Like we're in an overpopulated metropolis here," she fumed. Snatching a canteen from the six her mother had filled, Hope unscrewed the top and splashed water over her hot, sticky face.

Ryder jerked the canvas container out of her hand. "Hold it. That's drinking water. All we have for whatever time we spend in this heat. Starting now, we ration what we use." He pulled a spiral notebook from one of the bags. With a red ballpoint pen he wrote his name on one side, hers on the other. "In this book we jot the time and amount every time we use a drop of water. I have another notebook to categorize the specimens."

Hope shoved the canteen at him and strode to the tent. She was forced to crawl inside on her hands and knees, but at least the tent caught the minimal breeze and seemed to breathe through the canvas pores.

Ryder threw a duffel inside, then crawled in to sit beside her. "I'm sorry we didn't talk more about what this vigil would be like. Surveillance is never fun."

His gentle chiding made Hope feel about as small as one of his specimens. "I wasn't expecting a carnival, Ryder. I'll be fine. You do your thing and I'll do mine. Give me the notebook you want me to use as a log."

Eyes still dark with concern, he found the book and handed it to her. He scuffed the back of two fingers along her jaw, making her shiver.

"No touching, Ryder," she said sternly, edging away. "Don't make this outing any harder than it already is."

"That wasn't a pass, dammit. I just wish you'd stop gritting your teeth." But Ryder knew his action could be misconstrued. Around Hope, he found it difficult to remember the rules.

Of course it wasn't a pass. Did he have to shred her pride? Hope scooted out of the tent and busied herself straightening items in the back of the Yukon. She dug a fire pit and ringed it with rocks. Climbing down the slope of the plateau, she wandered to a stand of mesquite trees and began collecting dead branches.

Ryder sat inside the tent and watched her frantic efforts to avoid him. His ingrained chivalry didn't allow him to sit idle while Hope did chores, so he, too, emerged, then paused to tie down the tent flaps to keep out pesky predators like pack rats and chipmunks.

He skidded down the slope and promptly got into a tug-of-war with Hope over her burden of branches. "Your face looks like a tomato. Go take two swallows of water and sit in the shade."

"Is that an order?"

Ryder completed the transfer of the armload of wood. "If need be, yes."

She inhaled and wiped a hand across her forehead. Accepting defeat, Hope waded up the wall of sand and flung herself into a band of shade created by the tent.

Dumping the wood beside the fire ring, Ryder walked the perimeter of the plateau. Once he had the lay of the land and had set down the coordinates, he knew exactly where to place the night-observation scope—the newest technology the air force had to offer. Given the list of equipment that had disappeared from Monahan recently, it was conceivable the people they were dealing with, whoever they were, had equipment almost as sophisticated.

What if they had better? Ryder didn't fool himself that there weren't some high-tech devices in the hands of unsavory people. Had he been foolish to involve Hope in this venture? He'd never forgive himself if his selfishness in wanting to see more of her caused her harm in any way.

It wouldn't. He'd make damn sure.

THEY WHILED AWAY the afternoon lazing. Reading. Both were grateful when the fiery sun sank and cool shadows danced across their tent.

"I'll let it get a little darker before hunting specimens," Ryder said.

"Shall I fix dinner first, or after you finish?"

"Either. But, Hope, I'll need your assistance with the collection."

She froze as, in a panic, she stared at the empty jars. Her tongue wet her dry bottom lip. "I only agreed to catalog them in a notebook, Ryder."

"We may have to walk quite a ways. I can't carry the pack, the empty jars and the flashlight and handle the scoop, too."

Ryder thought she was going to bolt. Then she drew herself tall and regally inclined her head. "I'm yours to command."

Ryder ground his teeth, but he let the comment pass. Frankly, he found Hope's distaste for insects at odds with her spunky spirit. Had something happened in her childhood? Ryder supposed her brothers may have taunted her with bugs. Now he wished they'd explored other possibilities for a cover. This one had seemed so convenient and logical.

"How many jars do you want?" she asked, loading two into a day pack as he readied a net, a scoop and a good-size flashlight.

"Three ought to do us for tonight. Morning brings out different species. We'll want to look busy as we break camp and move closer to our target's operation."

Her body cringed in denial, but she said nothing, only rucked the pack higher on her shoulders.

"I doubt we'll find much of interest on this plateau. Let's forage out on the desert floor. With the air cooling and the humidity rising, several species should come out to water and feed."

Her answer was to fall into step behind him. Very close behind him, so that they both walked in the beam cast by the flashlight. They wandered for some half hour without collecting a thing. One by one stars winked on. The moon rose slowly over a copse of mesquite. Full and translucent, big as a platter, it cast a shimmering blue light across the night desert.

"There." Hope shuddered and aimed a shaky finger off to Ryder's immediate left. "Ugh. A tarantula."

He shone the light in a wide arc. "It's nothing. A rock, maybe."

She stood stock-still. "A spider, I tell you. I can spot those hairy uglies a mile away. But if you don't want it that's A-OK with me."

Ryder made a slower sweep with the light. "Since you're so sure, you take the flashlight and hand me a jar."

Hope gladly made the exchange. She just couldn't hold the plastic barrel still, and dropped the light altogether as Ryder pulled a jar from the pack.

What Ryder thought was a rock rose on eight legs and skittered out of the arrow of light.

"Hot damn," he said. "You were right. And he's a beauty. A granddaddy by the size of him."

"Won...der...ful." Hope clamped her teeth tight.

Despite the wavering beam as she highlighted sky, trees and about everything but the spider he was after, Ryder scooped up the nasty-looking, virtually harmless creature. He screwed the lid on the jar as he ran back to her.

"Wow, this is great! My old neighbor, the one who taught me about bugs, would have walked a hundred miles for a treat like this. Do you have the notebook?"

Backing well out of his reach, she nodded.

"Okay. List him as number 001, and in the next column print Theraphosidae."

She gaped. The pen poised over the paper wavered. "You actually know the Latin name, or are you making this up as you go?"

He quit smiling at the creature in the jar and glanced up, looking more than a little offended. "I told you I was good at this."

"Uh…well, yes. Could you spell it, please?"

She was on the last letter when Ryder circled behind her and raised the flap on her backpack. Hope shot away like a lightning bolt. "What do you think you're doing?"

"Storing our first find in the pack."

"Think again, buster. I will not mule tarantulas, centipedes or anything that looks like them. Not even if it's a direct order. Report me as over the hill."

"Don't be silly, Hope. The lid is on tight. Honestly, he's more afraid of you than you are of him."

"So you say. The answer is still no. Capital N, capital O."

"This is going to be a long night if I have to haul every find back to the tent one at a time."

"I don't care. Take it or leave it."

"All right. We may as well eat while we're there. My stomach is rumbling. I just realized we missed lunch."

"I'm not hungry," Hope said, being very careful to keep her distance from Ryder.

"Don't tell me you're going to let something like a measly spider steal your appetite."

"All right, I won't tell you."

They'd rambled farther than either of them realized. Clouds drifting out of the southwest occluded the moon before they reached the tent.

Hope almost stepped square on a huge, grotesque beetle ambling slowly across the sand. *"Aiyee!"* She hopped over it in a giant leap.

"What?" Ryder, who'd been trudging ahead with the light, turned. All Hope could do was point.

He set the spider down and ran back to see what had caused the fuss. "You did good!" he exclaimed, rubbing his hands together excitedly. "You've found a Hercules beetle, a collector's prize. Quick, give me a jar."

She managed that—barely. This time she gripped the flashlight harder, aiming a steadier light. Proud of herself, Hope decided maybe she had gotten the hang of it.

Ryder trapped the insect without effort, took the flashlight from Hope and strode off to retrieve his first find.

"Hey, wait." Plunged into darkness, Hope paused with her pen over the notebook. "I can't see to log that bug in. Ah…or don't you know the technical name?"

"The Coleoptera family." He didn't wait for her to ask; he just spelled it. "In lay terms it's known as the nightmare bug."

"If there's anything I hate," she mumbled, "it's a know-it-all."

Because lightning forked across the sky ahead of them, followed seconds later by a roll of thunder, they quickened their pace. Even Ryder was breathing hard when they reached the campsite.

He grumbled, but he set the specimen jars outside the tent as Hope insisted. Muttering about how they were contained, Ryder knelt and struck a match to the fire he'd prepared earlier. Thunder cracked, rumbled and broke apart close by.

"Wow! I've never seen a storm roll in so fast," he remarked, casting an eye toward the ribbons of lightning.

"Welcome to Arizona, Rhys." Hope practiced using the name as she ripped open a packet of freeze-dried stew and guessed at the amount of water to pour from the canteen. She logged one cup on his list and one on hers.

He scanned the sky. "Will it rain?"

"Maybe. Maybe not."

"You're a fountain of knowledge. How long have you been stationed here?"

"Stationed? Tut-tut. Am I *stationed* at the university?"

"So I goofed. Throw me in irons. About the storm—are we in danger? Should we take cover under the trees down on the desert floor?"

"Really, it's hard to tell. I've flown through some real bang clankers. A couple of times planes were grounded. Most storms pass quickly. I'd say monitor it for now."

"Awesome sky," he mused, sitting cross-legged on a quilt she'd spread near the fire. "Our own private laser show."

"Yeah." Hope stirred the stew. "As long as a person doesn't get carried away with the show and forget the danger. Dry riverbeds fill up fast when these seemingly minor storms turn into gully washers."

"No washes on this plateau. I'll enjoy it while I can." Ryder stretched out on the blanket, propped up on an elbow, watching the lightning leap-frog through the clouds.

''I thought you brought equipment to do some spying.''

''I did. It'll keep till after we eat.''

She handed him the pan. The mixture bubbled merrily, beginning to emit an enticing aroma. ''There are crackers in the green tin. I'm going to turn in. Do you have a preference for which side of the tent you get?''

''You really aren't going to eat?''

''Worried about my health, Ryder? It's not your concern.''

Her tone implied it might once have been his concern, but he'd forfeited the right. Ryder chose not to comment. ''I'll cook in the morning,'' he said instead. ''I don't expect you to do all the KP.''

''Fine. So…do you have a preference or not?''

His eyes darkened wickedly. ''I'm sure if you think hard enough, you can remember which side of the bed I slept on.''

Hope sucked in a harsh breath that threatened to sear her lungs. ''In that case you'll take what I leave. I don't remember.'' She grabbed a lantern and marched over to the tent to light it. Which was a good thing, because if he'd seen the way her hands shook, her bravado would have been for naught.

Ryder sat still, watching her shadow move around inside the tent as she spread the sleeping bags. When she stripped off her blouse he nearly choked to death on some unnamed vegetable. ''Ah…'' He breathed easier when she donned another top. *He* would have slept in the Yukon if she'd climbed naked into that sleeping bag. Some temptations went beyond what mortal man could bear. Even supposing they were both fully clothed, the tent had suddenly shrunk in size. The longer Ryder sat, the less sure he was that this stakeout had been a good idea.

He polished off the stew, measured out a small amount of water and washed the pan clean. Ignoring the woman in the tent and the thunder rumbling overhead, Ryder hauled a pair of long-range night binoculars from the black bag and studied the lay of the land. He traded the binoculars for a scope that allowed him to see the chain-link fence clearly. The radar scanners quivered in the wind. If there was any activity at the museum site tonight, it was all underground. The place looked dead.

Ever thorough, Ryder spent a good half hour examining every inch of the desert floor from Duval Mine Road to I-19 and back again. He picked out a few jackrabbits and a pack of six mangy coyotes, their yips sounding faint as they started to work their prey. Ryder rooted for the jack and let out a pent-up breath when he saw the rabbit streak into an almost hidden hole.

Intermittent rain had started to splatter and sizzle in the fire. Soon drops fell fast enough to convince Ryder to call it quits. The rain had cooled everything off by the time he hid the black bag under the back seat of the Yukon and made a dash for the tent.

Hope wasn't going to like it, but he had to bring the jars inside to save them from filling up with rainwater.

She sat upright the minute Ryder's light illuminated the interior. "It's raining pretty hard, isn't i...t? Oh... what are you doing?" She scooted, bag and all, as far to the right as she could get. "Get those awful things out of here. Ryder, I swear..."

"Would you rather I let them drown out there?"

She huddled in her bag. Wide, unfocused eyes stared at him over green fabric she had snugged around her throat. She remained remarkably silent.

"I'm sure you don't mean what's running through your head." Ryder tucked the two jars close to the foot of his bag, near the tent opening. "It's not like you to hurt any living creature, Hope. That I do know." He remembered how she'd rescued a bird with a broken wing outside his home in Alabama. The vet said she was wasting her time and money, that the bird would die when she released it into the wild. Hope didn't care. She took care of the warbler. She built a cage on the porch and a feeding trough for his friends so he could keep in touch. Six weeks later, when the vet pronounced her patient healed, she set the bird free. Each morning when the little warbler and his pals came to feed, Ryder had seen tears of joy run down Hope's cheeks.

"I don't want the specimens to die," she said at last. "But I can't help wishing they were field mice or plain old plants."

Ryder sat on his bag and pulled off his boots. "You're a good sport, Hope. It won't be for long. I have a gut feeling those ol' boys will show themselves the minute we intersect their space."

Hope yawned and curled into a fetal ball. "I vote we intersect it tomorrow."

Eyeing her, Ryder undid his belt and stretched out atop his bag. He remained fully clothed. Which didn't help much. The strain worsened after he doused the light.

"Ryder," Hope whispered. "What are you going to do with the specimens after those guys make contact?"

Relieved to have something else to think about, Ryder rambled at length about the types he aimed to add to the collection tomorrow.

The butterflies in Hope's stomach settled, too. He sure knew how to kill a woman's passion. "Good night, Ryder,'' she said abruptly. ''If you don't want to end up buried in some remote part of the desert with your damn bugs, have them out of the tent before I wake up in the morning.''

HE DID. Ryder hadn't slept much. He knew Hope didn't fall asleep until nearly dawn, either. Neither had said a word after her curt speech, but they both remained awake and aware. That he knew.

Because the rain had passed sometime in the night, leaving a layer of clouds behind to cool the morning, Ryder elected to let Hope sleep in.

He added several species to his assortment, including a couple of the two hundred or so variety of scorpions. He was back, seated by the fire, enjoying his first cup of coffee when Hope finally poked her tousled head out of the tent.

''Good morning, sunshine.'' He smiled and hefted his mug. ''Coffee?''

His cheery greeting drove a stake through Hope's heart. It was how he'd hailed her every daybreak of their affair. Nor had she forgotten he'd always followed it up with the most slow, delicious morning lovemaking.

''Coffee,'' she croaked. ''Strong and black.''

''I know.''

From the solemn way he said it, Hope intuitively understood Ryder was remembering those long-ago mornings, too. The air crackled with memories. But if she acknowledged they existed, she'd open herself up to the admission that he still resided in her heart. She wasn't that stupid. Hope didn't trust him not to hurt her again. Steeling her resolve, she accepted the mug but didn't stick around to drink it. She walked to the rim of the plateau, instead.

Feeling her tension, Ryder drained his cup, then set about breaking down the tent. "I had a package of raisin-cinnamon oatmeal earlier. The water's still hot, if you'd like to eat before we get under way," he said gruffly.

She glanced sharply over her shoulder. "They're out there watching us, aren't they?" she asked suddenly.

"I suspect so, but I haven't seen a soul. Last I checked, workers had begun arriving for the first shift at the museum. With the sun breaking through, I can't afford to let any reflection bounce off a lens. You'll be safe taking a trip into the trees, though, if that's what you're asking."

"It wasn't," she said wryly, "but since you've brought up such an indelicate subject, McGrath, it's a good plan."

"Jones," he muttered. "Or call me Professor. You're Teri Harris, remember?"

"Yeah, yeah." She made a yakkity-yakkity motion with her hand as she set her cup on a rock and sauntered off.

He expended restless energy packing the Yukon. The minute Ryder saw her headed back, he mixed her oatmeal. While she ate, he carefully covered the fire with several shovelfuls of sand. They both used their morning ration of water to brush their teeth. For some reason they found that funny. A good laugh returned the balance to normal.

All day they slowly worked their way toward the strip of land where the birders claimed they'd been accosted.

Tagging jars and recording the unpronounceable Latin names had become second nature to Hope by sundown. Also monotonous.

"Did you use sunblock?" Ryder asked as they pitched the tent.

Her hand flew to her nose. "Why? Do I look like Rudolph?"

"Some. I should have noticed earlier. I forgot your skin is so fair."

There it was, Hope thought, that awkward tension again. "I'll take care of it with aloe if you start the fire. Tomorrow I'll wear long sleeves and a hat."

Ryder had just lit the fire when he noticed a vehicle kicking up dust as it angled toward them across the desert. "Uh-oh. Company." He took Hope her hat. "Wear this and stay behind me, near the tent." He put on the glasses Ted Evans had given him and tugged the brim of his Aussie hat.

In her nervousness, Hope forgot her own edict. She reached up and ran a hand over Ryder's dark stubble. "Good disguise. Your mother wouldn't even recognize you."

As they waited, a dust bubble rolled from beneath the tires of a black jeep that skidded to a stop behind the Yukon. Four muscled toughs piled out in the midst of a billowing mushroom, each man a clone of the other. Their hair was short, their eyes cold and their boots polished to a mirror shine.

Hope peeked from beneath her floppy hat. These weren't the men she'd seen at the museum. Carbon copies, definitely. The way they circled Ryder, blocking his avenues of escape, sent a chill up her spine.

CHAPTER EIGHT

HOPE HEARD RYDER introduce himself with his phony name and title. She decided to bide her time and let Ryder do the talking for now.

"You fellows been four-wheeling on the desert?" Ryder sounded friendly.

"We're with the civil defense patrol," growled the oldest of the intruders.

Ryder tugged an ear. "Civil defense? It's been a while since I took a history class, but I thought they disbanded after World War II."

"That's the trouble with you college nerds, you're out of touch with what's happening in the real world. It's a jungle out here, and our government's going to hell. Selling out. Somebody's gotta police our borders." The speaker looped his thumbs over his belt and puffed out his chest. "Me'n the boys are doing our part."

One of the clones noticed Hope. He sidled over to look her up and down.

She scowled and yanked her hat lower.

The first speaker, obviously the leader of the rat pack, tried to peek in the windows of the Yukon. They were too darkly smoked for him to see anything in the back well or on the floor.

"We're helping out border patrol tonight," he announced. "Looking for illegals. How about popping the hatch on your rig so I can take a look inside."

Ryder pulled his phony papers from the university out
f his shirt pocket. "My assistant, Miss Harris, and I
ave a right to be here, as you'll see from these permits.
he back of my Yukon is filled with the laboratory spec-
nens we've collected over the past two days. I doubt
ou gents will find them interesting." Ryder aimed his
omments at the leader, but he never took his eyes off
ie man inspecting Hope.

"What kind of specimens?" a third man asked bel-
gerently.

Hope shoved past the goon who was breathing down
er neck. "Let's just show them your collection, Pro-
essor," she said. "I still have to catalog today's sam-
les. At this rate it'll be midnight before we get dinner."
he jerked open the Yukon's hatch, forcing the men
ho'd crowded close to step back. Muttering a silent
rayer, Hope grabbed the jar with Ryder's prize taran-
ila. She swung around and waved it in the leader's face.
t the same time, she switched on a flashlight, allowing
veryone a full, illuminated view of the spider. He
ooked even bigger, thanks to the optical illusion of the
ir.

Hope's stomach heaved, yet she wanted to laugh at
ie way the four strapping fellows bellowed and scram-
led back. Hope frowned to hide the glee she dare not
xpress. "Dr. Jones, I don't think they appreciate our
nd."

"Ahem." Ryder cleared his throat. He took the jar
efore her hands started to shake. He also reached into
ie vehicle and selected the nastiest of the two scorpions.
'Isn't that a shame, Miss Harris? Take this *Centruroides
culptumtus*, for instance. I've known entomology teams
> search weeks for this poisonous variety." The light

drove the scorpion a little mad, as Ryder knew it woul
The creature lashed at the glow, tail curled high.

Sight of the grotesque bugs in such proximity sent t
four men hightailing it to their jeep. The leader fired
the engine before he spoke again. "You two are ev
dently here legitimately. However, this area is bei
heavily patrolled for illegals. It's my duty to warn y
that sometimes border patrol shoots first and asks que
tions afterward. For your own safety, I'd advise chan
ing locations. Try Phoenix."

Neither Hope nor Ryder said a word until the jeep ar
its occupants were completely out of sight.

"Phew," Hope whispered, slumping against the Y
kon's door when the taillights disappeared. Her kne
continued to knock. "Were they ex-military or what?"

"Awfully young to be ex-military," Ryder mutter
"I didn't detect accents, did you?"

"I wasn't listening, but now that you mention it, n
Were any of them working at the museum the day y
took the tour?"

"Not that I recall. They look so much alike it's as
they were photocopied."

"They train together, I'll bet."

"That's the second reference to a civil defense patr
You said a guide mentioned he belonged, too. First thi
tomorrow we'll hunt up their office and pay them a vis
If they're on the up-and-up, they must have a headqua
ters. Most volunteer organizations keep a list of mem
bers."

"Public domain?"

"Bet you a beer they'll claim it's not."

Hope shook her head. "I'm no dummy. No bet.
know several pilots who fly for the border patrol. I'

sure they're not connected to those thugs." She shivered in spite of the warm evening.

Ryder replaced the jars in the Yukon. In a reflexive action he hugged Hope. "You did some fast thinking there, lady. I thought for a minute they intended to search the Yukon. It wouldn't have been pretty if they'd discovered our surveillance gear."

Hope tried to shrug off his praise. His hands on her flesh made thinking difficult. From their first meeting, she'd felt…well, *safe,* in Ryder's arms. And she hadn't fully recovered from the unnerving strain of dealing with those punks—or the spider. It didn't take any urging for her head to find its way to Ryder's strong shoulder.

He accepted her weight with a sigh. Over and over he stroked her silky hair. God, but he loved the never-forgotten feel of holding her. Their bodies had always fit together perfectly. Still did. With a precision that left Ryder battling a rock-solid erection.

His conscience warned him to step away before she felt it, but he couldn't seem to move. He ought to stop touching her. But, oh, how he'd missed this. Missed holding and being held by her.

Hope came to her senses first. Clearly flustered by her lapse, she tried to fluff it off. "Here we stand, wasting time like two idiots. Shouldn't we follow those guys or something?" The breathless catch in her voice exposed her question for what it was, an attempt to deny what had happened between them.

But it had happened, dammit. If he sounded particularly edgy, Ryder didn't care. "Why? Thanks to you, they bought our story."

"Who are they really?" Hope persisted, careful to keep her distance.

"Hard to tell." He gave in to her tenacity. "Too many

gaps, as yet. But it's plain they don't want anyone snooping around this part of the desert. They definitely had us under surveillance. So we'll let them think they ran us off. Help me break apart the tent,'' he said, striding purposefully in that direction.

"Okay. Should I call Dad and tell him we're coming in?''

"No. That bunch may be monitoring the airwaves. I've no idea how sophisticated they are. The lengths to which they'll go to protect their operation depends on how bold, how secret or how foolhardy their master plan is.''

"They made my skin crawl.''

Ryder laughed at last. "Them or our spider?''

"Them. And he's *your* spider.''

"Not for long. As soon as we get packed, I'll backtrack a mile or so and let the critters go.''

"Oh, happy day. What are we waiting for?''

Ryder couldn't resist baiting her. "Too bad the punks showed up so soon. I was really starting to have fun.''

"Fun? No electricity. No shower. Sand in our food. Poisonous bed partners. You and I have different ideas about what constitutes fun.''

Ryder jerked out a tent stake. "We used to agree completely...on some levels anyway.''

Hope's stomach tightened. How was it that with so few words Ryder could evoke instant vivid recall of the wonderful weeks they'd spent together? They *had* had fun. In bed, as he'd insinuated, and out. For a too-brief period in both their lives, they'd been completely compatible. Some married couples couldn't even claim that.

Then again, how compatible were they, really, given the secrets Ryder had kept from her?

He ripped up the last stake, and the tent crashed to

the ground in a clatter of metal poles and a suffocating cloud of dust.

"Yuck!" Hope batted through the fog of grit. "Let's just roll it up instead of trying to brush the sand off here. I'll unfold it in the driveway tomorrow and sweep it."

"Deal. Open the side door of the truck. The tent should fit between the seats." He loaded it while Hope checked to make sure they weren't leaving any incriminating evidence behind. That accomplished, Ryder drove a zigzag course across the desert, using only the light of the moon to navigate. The clouds of the previous night had completely blown out of the area.

"This looks like a good spot to release the lot. Stay put. I'll be right back."

Did he expect her to argue?

"Are you positive you turned every last one loose?" Hope asked when Ryder switched on the Yukon's lights and again headed for the highway.

"Did you want me to save one?"

"No. Heavenly days." Hope shuddered.

"I shouldn't tease you. When it counted, you had what it took."

"Did you think I wouldn't? I've *never* let you down, Ryder." An eyeblink after her words shattered the truce they'd drifted into, Hope sucked in a noisy breath. Now she'd done it—opened a festered wound. And she'd promised herself she wouldn't.

"That sounded hateful, Ryder. Blank what I said."

Ryder still smarted from the venom lacing her first statement. When he finally trusted himself to speak, he said quietly, "Keeping all that anger bottled up isn't good, Hope. I know. I stockpiled plenty…starting with the loss of my son, and then April."

Hope grabbed the door handle. "Stop. Let me out. I

don't want to get into any of this,'' she shouted, tears leaking from her eyes.

Ryder eased up on the gas. He had only just pulled out on the main highway. He hated to add new tears to the long list of mistakes he had yet to atone for. ''Hope, if you'd listen a minute,'' he pleaded. ''My mom ragged on me for weeks to clean out April's things and get on with my life. You and I met the very night after I'd spent all day sorting and giving her stuff away. I never meant to take advantage. I was desperate to believe in something. In someone. You were everything I needed and more.''

Hope clapped her hands over her ears.

She wasn't ready to hear. To continue would drive a wedge deeper between them. Ryder couldn't stand to watch her suffer. If there was anything he understood, it was internal hell. ''Shh,'' he soothed her, sliding an arm across the seat, trying to bring her into the curve of his shoulder. Her seat belt wouldn't stretch, and he didn't see anyplace to pull off. Ryder had to let her control her emotions as best she could.

Which Hope did. Though not easily. And not until he'd withdrawn to his corner of the vehicle. Even then she couldn't look at him as she scrubbed the heels of her hands over her cheeks. ''I can't go home looking like this,'' she said as he came to the cross street that led to her parents' home.

Ryder glanced guiltily at her ravaged face. ''We passed a burger joint a few blocks back. We did miss dinner,'' he said quietly.

''I'm not hungry. You can order, and I'll use the rest room.''

''Hope, you haven't eaten enough in the past three

days to keep a hummingbird alive.'' He geared up to lecture her, but an unexpected giggle stopped him cold.

"Visit Tucson's Desert Museum,'' she said. "They have this great hummingbird aviary. Did you know those little guys eat half their weight in sugar every day because they expend so much energy flying? To produce the same momentum, a man would have to eat twice his weight in potatoes.''

She was talking too fast, but Ryder played along. "So I know bugs and don't know squat about birds. I stand corrected. You still ought to eat something.''

"Then order me a taco at the next stop. I don't know what got into me. I never cry. Never!''

Ryder came close to stepping in and accepting full blame. He was within one sentence of promising never to mention their past again. Which would be another lie. He intended to hash everything out—soon. In the end, he acknowledged her with a curt nod and pulled into a fast-food place off the highway.

Unable to think of anything else to say, Ryder simply kept out of her way as she hurried to the ladies' room. He'd nearly finished his burger by the time she returned.

She snatched the taco and wrapped it in a layer of napkins. "I'll eat this on the way home.'' Leaving him to pay the bill, Hope went out to the Yukon.

Ryder watched, but she didn't take a single bite. Pretending interest in the taco only meant she didn't have to talk on the drive home.

The minute they entered the Evans house, Ted commandeered Ryder. Hope's dad would have hustled them both off to a corner for debriefing, but Hope headed in the opposite direction.

"You tell the story,'' Hope instructed Ryder. "I'm going to soak off an acre of desert. Then I plan to crash in a real bed. You two figure out where the civil defense office is. I'll see you in the morning." She didn't wait for permission from her superior.

THE SO-CALLED civil defense headquarters was housed in a mobile home that sat on a vacant lot a mile outside of town.

The front door squeaked as Ryder and Hope entered a room that contained file cabinets, bookshelves and one desk, behind which sat another copy of the men from the jeep, although he was a few years their senior. The desk jockey also wore crisp khaki pants and a shirt with flat gold buttons and nonmilitary epaulets. Pseudomilitary, Hope thought.

"I'm Dr. Rhys Jones. I teach entomology at the university," Ryder lied smoothly. "I have a permit to collect desert-dwelling insects for my lab. Last evening my assistant, Teri Harris, and I were harassed by four men claiming to be part of a civil defense patrol looking for illegal aliens, or so they said."

"If you're local taxpayers, I should think you'd be grateful. Most residents are happy to have us watch-birding."

"These men came on a little strong. They wanted to search my vehicle. I had only their word on who they were. No credentials." Ryder paid lip service to a smile.

The man at the desk did not. "Our group is young and eager to do a good job. They're all volunteers."

"Are they screened? Who authorizes them to carry weapons?"

"They're carefully selected." The man deliberately ignored the second part of Ryder's question. "I'll have our senior trainer talk to them," he promised, his eyes a shade colder than his voice.

"It would help if your volunteers wore name tags. I assume you keep a roster of members. I'd like one in case we ever run up against them again."

"Impossible," the man snapped. "Our work demands confidentiality. Tell me where you'll be next, and when. I'll get word to the men on patrol to let you be."

Ryder rubbed his still-unshaven jaw. "Miss Harris and I are returning to my laboratory at the university with this batch of specimens. I'll have her phone you before our next expedition."

The man looked past Ryder to Hope, drilling her with cold blue eyes. "Catching bugs seems an odd profession for a woman," he said.

"We don't all like to bake cookies and powder babies' bottoms," Hope returned sweetly. She opened the door and willed Ryder to follow her out. She felt the man's reptilian gaze on her back even after stepping into the hot midday sun.

Ryder unlocked the Yukon. They both climbed in. Neither spoke until they were three blocks down the street.

"I'll stake my life on the fact that they're not locals," Hope said angrily. "Verde Vista is largely retired."

"Yes, but every last one is apple pie, mom, WASP American. *Not* the terrorists who dropped out of sight. I just don't get what this bunch is up to."

"No good."

Hope's savage denouncement surprised Ryder. "Did you see something back there that I missed?"

She shook her head. "A feeling is all. About this whole thing. Like evil at work. Maybe we shouldn't be so hasty in abandoning observation. The Smithsonian Astrophysical Observatory would offer a bird's-eye view of the missile site. It sits well above their radar towers."

"Um," he mumbled, thinking what he should be doing was ejecting her from this mess fast.

Hope noticed that Ryder kept glancing in the rearview mirror. She started to turn to see what he found so interesting.

"Don't look back," he warned, clamping a hand on her knee. "We're being followed."

"Since when?"

"A blue Ford pickup pulled in behind us right after we left the civil defense office. They shot out from behind the trailer. Someone must have been listening from the back room."

"Two someones," Hope said, catching a glimpse of the vehicle in her side mirror. "I don't see anyone in the back seat."

"We'll go straight to the university. I want to run this new development by my D.C. contact. Since he set up the office on campus, the phone should be a safe line."

"It's a cinch we've rattled a cage or two. I think we've stumbled onto something big, Ryder."

He watched the pickup drop back as he braked for a corner. "I'd be a whole lot more comfortable knowing what and how big."

Leaning close to Ryder, Hope muttered, "You don't suppose one of the guys we met last night attached some kind of a bug to the Yukon, do you?"

"Scared as they were of bugs?" Ryder winked at her.

"Be serious."

He sobered. "It's possible. Anything is possible when we're shooting in the dark. Base security can do a sweep for us, but we'll have to shake our bird dogs first."

"So shake them."

"I want them to see us go to the U. If we expect to

continue spying, it's better to lull them into complacency.''

"You're right. I'm not as good as I thought at all this cloak-and-dagger stuff.''

"Oh, I'd say you're coming right along.'' Ryder made an admiring survey of her features. "You've set them back on their butts a few times.''

Hope didn't know why she found it so hard to accept praise from Ryder. Time was that she'd basked in his adulation. Because she thought love was at the foundation. Now she wasn't quite so quick to trust his pats on the back.

Ryder sensed an uneasy shift in her manner. It provided the opening he needed. "Hope, I've been thinking. This investigation has taken on a new slant. I'm going to ask for someone to replace you.''

"Why? You just said I did good. Spying from the observatory was my idea. At least let me help with that.''

Ryder mulled over her request while he navigated the city streets leading to the university. There was no question that he wanted more time with her. His gut instinct, however, told him not to let her stay on.

"Well,'' she huffed after he'd parked near the science building. "Please.'' Her eyes softened to match her plea.

He'd never been able to refuse that steel-melting look. It cut right through him and wrapped warm sticky fingers around his heart. Against his better judgment, Ryder agreed to leave things as they were for now. "But at the first sign of trouble, you're out,'' he warned as she slid from the vehicle.

"No argument.'' Without appearing to check for the pickup, she walked to the rear of the Yukon and waited for Ryder to bring the key to the hatch.

"Our snoops parked across the street, about five spaces down," she murmured when he joined her.

"Here, take the notebook. There's a key in the binder that'll open the door to room 105. Act like we do this all the time. I'll make a show of loading the jars."

"What if they come over and see they're empty?"

"You think they will? I believe word has traveled about our choice of pets."

Hope's smile widened. "You know, I almost like that tarantula. I wish him a long and happy life."

What affected Ryder more than her grin was the sway of her hips as she entered the building. A swift ache pressed solidly against his jeans zipper. If he had half a brain, he'd replace her ASAP. That ache was also the reason he held back.

Inside room 105, Ryder asked Hope to stash the jars in a lower cabinet in the small laboratory. "Prop the outer door open in case our nosy friends decide to scope us out. I'm going to use the phone in the inner office."

"Your name's stenciled on the etched glass and everything. I'm impressed. However did you manage that?"

"Don't ask." He chuckled. "Be thankful my contacts are on our team. Any one of that tribe could heist the silverware from a state dinner without getting caught."

Hope considered that as she obeyed Ryder's loosely given order. Until this minute, she'd never given his duties with the air force much thought. Beyond the fact they were both officers, the bulk of their interaction had been confined to the minute and highly personal. Maybe she should have heard out his explanation. What if air force business had kept him from contacting her after she left Alabama?

There was a greater chance of polka-dot pigs flying.

She'd barely closed the laboratory cabinet door when the two men from the pickup hiked down the hall. Hope knew them at a glance. They were cut from the same mold as the others. Though her knees knocked, she didn't acknowledge the duo, nor they her. The minute they passed, Hope burst into Ryder's office.

He'd just hung up the phone. "What's wrong?"

She made walking motions with her fingers. "Our tag team."

"Ah. Open the door and pull up a chair. We'll act like we're hard at work in case they go by again. Then we'll give them time to take off."

"You think they will?"

"Why not? My guess is they were told to see if we're who we claimed to be." His hand panned the setting. "Voilà!"

She'd no sooner sat and opened the notebook than the men slowly ambled past again. Ryder vaulted out of his chair. "Are you students looking for my lab?" He stepped to the door. "My assistant and I just unloaded a rare and deadly scorpion. To say nothing of the biggest tarantula I've ever seen."

One of the men stumbled in his haste to leave. "We're…uh…on the football team. Me'n my friend got lost. This isn't the building we need."

Ryder and Hope exchanged grins as the two took off. She closed her notebook and set it aside as Ryder shut the door again. "What did your contact say? Any word on the terrorists?"

"None. But neither do they think these guys are anyone to worry about. Civil defense units are springing up all over. Apparently they're staffed by patriots so far to the right they're about to fall off the earth."

"Oh. Then what's next?"

"Another round of observation, as you suggested. We'll trade the Yukon for different wheels. A car in some neutral shade. Something an astronomer might drive."

"We're changing identity again? Shall I dye my hair?"

He cupped a handful of the glossy blond curls. "Never."

It was obvious to Hope from the lines creasing his forehead that Ryder was remembering when she'd worn it long. She pictured them curled together in the aftermath of love. Ryder had liked to separate the damp strands with his fingers.

Hope ducked under his arm. It wouldn't do for either of them to get caught up in that memory. "What are we waiting for?"

"Nothing." He stifled a groan as he locked up and trailed her out. "I'll drop you off to rent a car at a different agency. I have to swing by the base to check on a pot I left brewing. Meet me in two hours at the place we rented the Yukon."

She slid out of the Yukon at the new agency. Ryder had no more than driven off than Hope realized she didn't have enough cash to rent a car. He hadn't specifically said not to use a credit card or her real name this time. The men in the Ford were long gone. Hope weighed her options only a minute. She went in, selected a white compact and handed over her Visa. A young man filled the gas tank. Hope phonied up the contract and then drove off. What could be simpler?

Two hours sped by much faster than she'd anticipated. She met Ryder, and they were back on the road headed for Verde Vista exactly as he scheduled.

A side trip up to the observatory proved it to be too

far from the missile site to meet their surveillance needs. "I knew things were going too smoothly," Hope grumbled.

"How about if we hike to the top of one of those foothills?"

"Those aren't foothills. Remember I said they're mounds of mine tailings left from played-out copper mines? They've been here so long most are covered with vegetation and look like foothills."

"They're still mining the area," he said. "I passed a couple of big ore trucks the day I visited the museum."

"Could be. I'm not up on working mines."

"Looks like as good a prospect as any. Use the cell phone to call your folks. Tell them not to worry if we don't traipse in till dawn, but don't mention what we're up to."

Hope called. Ted understood the minute she hedged about that very question. Dory promised to have breakfast ready at the usual time the next day.

"Your parents are nice," Ryder said as they parked beneath some trees well off the gravel road. He shouldered the pack with the scopes and gave Hope a flashlight that had been taped to shine a concentrated beam of light.

"Mom and Dad enjoy life. They're nothing alike and yet they complement each other. Your folks do, too," she said as Ryder secreted the black duffel in a brushy area that jutted into a cleared promontory.

"My sis is planning a fifty-year-anniversary party for them next year. Shall I tell her to put your name on the guest list?"

Hope gazed down on his wind-ruffled hair as he assembled one of the scopes. "Oh, Ryder, that's unfair. You know what they'd think."

He glanced up, his eyes glittering. "They'd think it was nice of you to help them celebrate a very important event in their lives. They cared for you, Hope. Mom still asks about you."

A harsh rebuke was on the tip of Hope's tongue. She wanted to yell at Ryder that he wasn't being fair. She didn't know if she could visit Alabama again, pretending to be a mere acquaintance of the couple she'd once expected to call Mom and Dad McGrath.

Instead of saying that, Hope mumbled, "I'll give it some thought. Have Gail send me an invitation. Who knows where I'll be in a year. The air force could send me to outer Sloblovia."

The fact that she hadn't refused outright buoyed Ryder's spirits. For the first time since he'd seen Hope's name on his appointment calendar, he believed that they might mend their broken relationship. He would win her back with time and patience—and intervention from both their families if that's what it took. He was pretty sure Dory Evans sensed a connection between them and that she approved. Ted, like so many fathers, probably didn't see his daughter as a woman, let alone a desirable one.

"Are you going to look through that thing or sit there making cow eyes at the moon?" Hope demanded.

Ryder stirred. "I am. Why don't you assemble the transmitter-receiver. See if we intercept any radio messages."

"Won't they home in on us?"

"If they're not worried about detection, they may transmit without jamming."

Hope had been trained on high-level electronic devices, but this fancy setup proved to be beyond her. "Maybe you'd better assemble this yourself. I'll glue my eye to the scope for a while. Can you see inside the fence surrounding the compound?''

''All except behind the building itself. No cars. No activity at all. I wonder if we're wasting time. Those yoyos could just be gung-ho patriots looking for cheap thrills.''

''They didn't strike me as the rah-rah-and-glory types. But you're right about the museum being dead.'' She yawned.

''I brought a couple of blankets.'' Ryder handed her one. ''The smart way to do this is in shifts. I'll wake you at 2400. Then I'll catnap until you see the first glimmer of light in the east.''

An hour into his shift, Ryder divided his time between watching Hope sleep and peering through the glass. He woke her at the appointed time. ''Gonna be boring as hell,'' he warned. ''There's nothing moving in this corner of the world except an occasional owl. If you'd like, we can bag it and go home.''

''No. You pulled your stint, now I'll pull mine.''

More than once during the long, dreary hours until the moon faded into a gray outline, Hope lamented not having jumped on Ryder's offer to leave. On the other hand, she took pleasure in seeing his face softened by sleep. She hated to shake him awake. Yet shake him she did, allowing barely enough time to stow their gear and steal down the hill before sunrise.

''If your job isn't any more exciting than this, McGrath—'' Hope paused to cover a yawn ''—I may put in to train for Special Forces.''

He gave her an assessing look from the corner of one eye. After determining she was teasing, he cautioned in all seriousness, ''Don't spread around that I'm anything but an air staffer, okay?''

"As if I would."

BOTH DORY AND TED bustled around them as the two dragged in. The coffee had perked and Dory had apple muffins baking. "Guess what?" she said, her eyes sparkling as she poured tall, frothy glasses of milk and literally shoved Hope and Ryder into chairs.

"What?" Alert in spite of missing half a night's sleep, Hope knew something was up. Even her dad appeared more animated than usual.

"Chris phoned last night after we talked to you. He *has* met someone. A female someone," Dory explained in response to Hope's blank expression. "He's given her a ring and they're planning a Christmas wedding. Isn't that wonderful news?"

"Chris? Married?" The announcement stunned Hope. Then, as they all sat and the others chattered, the truth sank in. *Chris, married before her.* She was happy for him, yes. And envious. She said little, picturing handsome, slightly arrogant, cocksure Chris with a houseful of kids, while life passed her by.

Dory hummed the wedding march as she brought the steaming tins of muffins from the kitchen. Hope slipped into a contemplative mood. She'd enter the dating circuit again. Maybe join a hiking group or flying club on base. Still, she couldn't imagine marrying a military man other than Ryder. And he wasn't looking for wife number two.

Faced with Chris's newfound love, Hope felt angry at Ryder all over again. And angry at herself for letting so many years slip away. It was past time that she washed the cobwebs out of her brain and embraced a change in her life. Past time to come out of the deep freeze.

CHAPTER NINE

RYDER SEEMED to be the only one who noticed Hope's withdrawal from the conversation. He couldn't tell if the way she acted directly related to Dory's rambling speculations about Chris's fiancée and the couple's impending wedding or if Hope was brooding about the lack of progress they'd made with the investigation.

Amazingly, he'd become attuned to her mood swings in the past few days. If she was happy, so was he. If not, he took it personally. Like now, when she rose abruptly from the table and said, "I don't want breakfast. I'm going to sleep until noon."

The expression on Dory's face ran the gauntlet from surprise, to irritation, to concern.

"Night stakeout is tiring," Ryder said in her defense.

Ted crossed his silverware on his plate, selected a toothpick and leaned back in his chair. "I figured when you visited their office, those yahoos would tip their hand."

"They're organized," Ryder mused aloud. "But their discipline's shaky. Between the birders and us, we've annoyed them. One or two are ticking bombs." He rubbed a knuckle over stubble that had begun to itch.

"You kids going to take another stab at surveillance tonight?" Ted asked.

"Yeah." Ryder nodded. "Since they checked us out

at the college, maybe they'll feel safe enough to procee
with whatever the hell they're doing at the museum."

Ted stood. "I'm going to be late for my golf matcl
Son, you'd better catch some shut-eye, too." He helpe
himself to another muffin.

"Shower, shave and sleep." Ryder chuckled. "In th
order."

"I'm headed out to the grocery store," announce
Dory. "Sleep as late as you like. I'll walk softly whe
I come home to restock the shelves."

Never one to sleep well during the day, Ryder a
sumed that he'd be up again before Hope awoke, but th
slam of a car door woke him at 1500 hours. Not believ
ing the bedside clock, he struggled up on one elbow an
grabbed for his watch. There wasn't ten seconds' diffe
ence in the two timepieces.

Dressing quickly, he made his way through a siler
house. He found Dory curled up in the den in a recline
reading a book. "Where is everyone?" he asked, u
successfully covering a yawn.

"Ted's napping. Hope went to the club for a swim.
Dory closed her book and uncurled. "Did you and Hop
have an argument?"

"No. I don't know. Maybe. Why?"

"She seems, I don't know...out of sorts."

"I noticed that at breakfast," he said slowly, leer
about getting involved in a conversation about Hope
emotions.

"Ryder." Dory hesitated. "It's none of my busines
but...are you and Hope...?"

As the sentence hung unfinished in air gone suddenl
thick, Ryder propped a shoulder against the door casin
and faked interest in a group of athletic photos hangir
on the wall. "Is that Chris?" he asked, pointing to on

"Yes." Hope's mother set her book aside and rose to her feet. "Hope's a grown woman," she said, her lips pursed. "I'm probably the only one in the world who thinks she has a vulnerable side hidden under that tough veneer. Mothers sense when their children are hurting."

Ryder's eyelids shuttered. He wrestled with guilt as he met Dory's open gaze. "It's not my aim to hurt Hope," he muttered, unable to stop telltale sweat from beading his forehead. The sudden hammering of his heart and the pain in his voice revealed the truth. He had hurt Hope. Hurt her bad.

Ryder expected a tongue-lashing, or at least a stern lecture. But Dory patted his arm sympathetically as she squeezed past him, headed toward the kitchen.

"I'll bet you're hungry," she said. "Come. I made a chicken-pasta salad and a fresh pitcher of blackberry iced tea. It'll tide you over till dinner."

"Dory…" Ryder loped after her. "I want you to know that I…care about Hope." He couldn't bring himself to utter the word *love*. Caring seemed safer. More solid and lasting. Love got snatched away too easily.

Dory turned at the counter, her eyes calm and warm. "I know, Ryder. Ted would tell you I'm a silly, sentimental fool. But I've prayed a man would come along who sees our daughter as a woman first and an officer second." She began to rummage in the refrigerator.

If Ryder hadn't been self-conscious, he might have prevailed on Dory Evans to offer insights as to how to undo the mess he'd made of things with Hope. But a man thought twice about admitting to a woman's mother that he'd had a raging affair with her cherished offspring.

Hope's arrival precluded his asking, anyway. So it was lucky he hadn't risked making a damn fool of himself.

"Oh, you're eating," she exclaimed, focusing on the salad her mother slid in front of Ryder. "I intended to make sandwiches to take with us. That way we can get situated on the ridge before dark. We'll have more time to choose a better vantage point than we had last night."

"Sounds good." Ryder picked up his fork. "I'll consider this a snack. Didn't you work up an appetite swimming?"

"Not really," she said listlessly.

Ryder didn't like the dullness in her eyes. "Do you feel all right?" He paused with the fork halfway to his mouth. "I'll drive you back to the base clinic if you think you're coming down with flu or something."

"I'm fine. I just need to shower off the chlorine and wash my hair. I'll be ready to go at 1700. Wasn't that our initial plan?"

"Yes. If you have dark clothes, wear them. After I eat, I intend to change."

THEY DROVE OFF LATER under a sky piled high with fluffy white cumulus clouds. "Ice-cream-cone thunderheads," Hope called them. "This type are capable of building into a storm. Or, if a wind comes up, they're equally apt to blow over."

Ryder spared a glance. Behind the clouds a cherry red sun shot claret streamers along sawtooth tips of murky purple mountains. The evening kaleidoscope of colors was ever changing. Ever beautiful. And quick to disappear.

When dusk fell, he and Hope were still trying to decide between two sites. Ultimately they chose one offering automobile access. A road of sorts, possibly worn into the pile of mine tailings by weekend A-V'ers, ended in a stand of paloverde. The way it worked out, they hiked only half the distance they'd climbed the previous night. And once on top of the manmade hill, they were better hidden and had a clearer view of the missile site.

Ryder stashed the bag of scopes between two flat-topped boulders. "These trees will screen us from anyone looking up from below. Spread the quilt and I'll bring the picnic basket. What did you pack in it?" he teased Hope. "It weighs a ton."

"A boom box and a regular telescope either Chris or Rolf left when they moved. If any of our night riders pay us a visit, we can always pretend to be stargazers."

"Um. Point that lens at the moon. If anyone's keeping tabs on these hills, I'd rather we didn't have anything refracting back."

"Can't see the moon for the cloud cover. Without a moon it sure gets dark fast."

Ryder flopped down on the blanket next to Hope. She shifted and briskly rubbed her arms.

Stretching out his legs, Ryder leaned back on both elbows. "I'll let it get pitch-black before I set up the night scope. Have you always been afraid of the dark?"

Her head swiveled. "I'm not afraid of the dark. Only of the bogeymen." She fussed with the radio dials and finally settled on a country ballad.

Ryder's broad smile reached across the gap between them. "So what's to eat?" He sat forward and lifted the lid of the hamper.

Hope smacked his hand. "You just ate a huge salad. How can you be hungry?"

He drew back, looking boyishly contrite. "I'm always hungry, remember?"

She did. It was one of the things about him that'd always amazed her. How he could pork out and never gain an ounce. She'd put on fifteen pounds during their

affair. Of course, she'd lost the weight and more after i
ended.

"Don't frown like that. Six years is a long time t
remember the quirks of someone you barely knew."

"Barely knew?" Hope's head came up. She sat cross
legged facing Ryder. Her hands gripped her knees t
keep them steady. "The only things I didn't know abou
you, Ryder McGrath, were details you went out of you
way to hide. A little matter like a marriage, for in
stance." Wishing she'd held her tongue, she blinked u
at the drifting gray clouds.

He thrust a hand into the basket while her attentio
wandered and pulled out two sandwiches. Slapping on
onto her lap, he accidentally skimmed the inner seam o
her jeans. The sudden contraction of flesh beneath th
denim took Ryder by surprise. Glancing up, he saw he
pupils dilate. She quickly looked away, but did she thin
he wouldn't notice how she mangled the sandwich insid
its plastic bag?

"Eat that thing," he growled. "It's already dead."

By rote, she tore open the bag and bit off a smal
chunk.

"Are you still whipping everyone in sight at darts?"

"I don't play anymore." She laid the sandwich aside

Ryder had devoured his. He returned to the basket an
helped himself to a shiny red apple. Locking eyes wit
Hope, he casually polished it on his shirt. "Me, nei
ther," he confessed. "But I've put together those puz
zles you left about a million times each, I guess. Woul
you like them back?"

"No. No. If they help you pass the time, keep them."

"I don't need them much now. At first they were goo
therapy."

"Therapy for...?" The green eyes that pinned him clouded.

Scooting closer, Ryder set aside his untouched apple. "Do you know much about grieving?"

Hope ducked her head. A friend had told her that breaking up with someone you loved triggered the same steps as grief. She'd never tell Ryder, though.

He didn't appear to notice she hadn't answered. "People make a lot of wild promises to someone they love when the loved one is dying. Promises a person fully intends to keep."

"Like what?" she wondered aloud.

Ryder brushed crumbs off the quilt square that lay under Hope's knee. "The ultimate promise is to swear you'll love them forever. That you'll never love another. And you mean it...then."

Hope had to lean closer to hear him. It didn't take a genius to add two and two and get what he was trying to say. He'd given April that promise. Then he'd met Hope and he'd broken his word. Her heart beat itself up and bled for this man she'd loved six years ago. Who was she kidding? She still loved him.

Seeing her eyes flood with compassion, Ryder lifted a hand to cradle her face. "I didn't mean to hurt you, Hope. You gave me more joy than I had any right to exp... Than I had any right to, *period.*" His arm shook. Likewise his voice.

Hope turned her face into his palm. Letting her tears fall unchecked, she placed a hot, wet kiss on the work-textured skin she loved. "I'm sorry, Ryder. So sorry. If only I'd known. How you must hate me for barging into April's house. You should have told me no one could ever take her place."

He sat up and pulled Hope into his lap. "That's just

it,'' he said, begging her to hear him out. ''You put your sweet brand on every nook and cranny so completely I couldn't recall what April looked like.'' Ryder buried his head in the soft juncture of Hope's neck. As the shadows deepened around them, he sighed raggedly.

Breathing became difficult for Hope until Ryder pulled back slightly. ''After…after you left, and the guilt of what I'd done hit me, I went a little crazy.''

''Hush.'' She shut her eyes tight and kissed him. ''Am I so shallow that you didn't think I'd understand?''

Ryder trailed his fingers along lemony-scented curls that brushed her ears. ''You did nothing wrong, Hope. It was me.'' Wrapping her close, he rocked her back and forth. ''Outside of haunting my days and nights for six long years, you, my sweet, are totally blameless. When I reached a point where I finally managed to face the truth, I volunteered for a mission at Elmendorf. A colonel, a friend, one of the few privy to all that'd gone on, said you'd pulled strings to transfer out. So I bailed out of the project and went to Italy instead.''

''Oh, Ryder. If only you'd called me.'' Hope felt so cold. She put her fingers beneath his dark polo and stroked his toasty skin. Touching him had always thrilled her. That hadn't changed.

She pressed tiny kisses along his chin until he shifted away.

''If I dialed your number once, I dialed it a million times. I never let it ring. There are no words to express how much I missed you. I've never stopped wanting you, Hope.''

''I…I missed you, too, Ryder.'' Turning, Hope let her slight weight carry him backward to sprawl across the quilt. Memories flooded back. Good memories of how many times they'd lain like this, against one another—

quickly igniting the passion that always resonated between them just below the surface. "I've always been yours," she whispered shakily.

He stroked her back, then slowly traced the line of her bra forward. Her nipples were peaked against the lacy cups long before his thumbs rasped gently across the tips. "It's been so long," he murmured. "And you feel so damn good."

Heat rose between them, setting fire to needs, blocking out the world. It had been that way from the very beginning. There were days and nights they barely made it inside the door to Ryder's house before ripping off their clothes, coming fast and hard on the heap of clothing strewn there. They'd laughed and joked and fully appreciated the fulfillment wrought by spontaneous combustion.

Tonight was no different. They couldn't seem to shed their clothing fast enough. Couldn't touch enough. Hope was panting and begging when suddenly, as if struck by lightning, Ryder realized what they were about to do. The muscles in his arms shook as he eased back. The separation was like tearing out his guts.

"Stop," he said through gritted teeth as she ran her fingers and teeth up his tightly clenched stomach. "We can't do this, Hope."

She sat up dazedly, gazing at his face through slumbrous eyes. "Ryder?" Her shaking fingers reached for the quilt to cover her nakedness. His weight held it in place. "Is someone coming?"

Calling on every last bit of his control, Ryder got up and draped the quilt around her to keep her from getting chilled in the night breeze. He automatically smoothed her still-quivering muscles.

As the minutes ticked away and her heart quit its frantic pounding, Hope realized he hadn't called a halt because of unexpected company. A fierce cold invaded her limbs as she sat stonily watching him yank on his clothes. He hadn't said a word and refused to meet her eyes. Ryder didn't want to take up where they'd left off. Of course. He'd been trying to explain his feelings for April and the guilt he'd felt six years ago for taking her, Hope, to bed. What had she been thinking? She gathered her clothing with unsteady hands, seeing only his tense back as she fumbled with closures.

Ryder had turned away to zip his jeans. He knew by the rustle of fabric that she, too, was getting dressed. The silence stretching between them clawed at him.

"You understand, don't you, Hope? I...you...we've all been briefed repeatedly regarding the new climate. Right now you report to me. I'm your superior officer, for God's sake." Ryder angrily stuffed his shirt into his jeans. He shouldn't have let it get as far out of hand as he had. Even beyond reasons of ethics, he hadn't come prepared. *What if Hope got pregnant? She...she might die.*

Hope clamped her teeth on her bottom lip. *Excuses. Rules. She wasn't superhuman.* She *loved* him! He looked so bleak she didn't believe it was about air force rules at all. "I understand perfectly, Ryder. The sex was always powerful between us," she said coolly.

The frost clinging to her words reached out of the darkness. *Sex,* she'd said. Not that they'd made love. Semantics. Either way, he'd never risk her getting pregnant.

Ryder wriggled his feet into his boots, then turned to look at her, but the night was too black. He couldn't see her eyes, dammit. Only her outline was visible, an ebony shadow calmly assembling one of the scopes. And silence. Crushing, except for the distant call of a night bird and the stealthy rasp as she fit metal scope pieces together.

Ryder plowed a shaking hand through his hair. He certainly felt raw. It stood to reason she would, too. He did know her body language didn't invite further discussion. They both needed time. *Time* he could give her. This mission wouldn't last long. When it ended, he wouldn't be her superior. Things were shaping up fast on his parts-theft investigation, too. Then he'd cut back. Slow down. *And he'd be prepared.*

Then he could offer her a lifetime. But not now.

For tonight, if she felt more comfortable placing distance between them, he'd go along. He pulled out his notebook, sat and updated it.

THE NIGHT DRAGGED ON interminably. Hope hated sitting there elbow to elbow with Ryder as they gazed for hours through scopes that revealed nothing. She noticed he hadn't corrected her when she'd referred to what they'd once shared as sex. How many times did a woman have to be hit over the head? Ryder McGrath had buried his one true love, and he wasn't looking for another. He'd said it himself—sort of—he was a one-woman man. Apparently he didn't even want a female body to warm his bed. Oddly enough, she'd been willing to accept him on those terms. On any terms.

Where was the Evans pride? Surely she wasn't so wretched that she'd throw herself at a man who'd dumped her? Looking back, reliving those oh-so-blissful days with Ryder, it became patently clear that she'd been the only one *in love.*

She gnawed on her lower lip to keep it from trembling. Foolish woman—yet if she thought he might someday learn to love her—but that was silly, too. His wife had been dead for over seven years. Hope had heard the catch in his voice when he'd explained it to her mother. And not two hours ago, he'd admitted that he'd gone a little crazy when she, Hope, had made him forget. Wasn't that what normal people did? Try to forget and get on with their lives?

Oh, she was a fine one to talk. As if she'd ever be able to forget Ryder.

RYDER PRACTICALLY self-destructed with relief when the gray of dawn lightened the tension-filled darkness. For the past hour he'd spent more time watching the play of light and shadow sweep across Hope's tense features. He, at least, made an effort to pan the compound below at regular intervals. She didn't even do that.

The constant shifting of her eyes suggested she was doing some heavy-duty thinking. Maybe he should release her from this project at once and send her back to flying. "Hope." Ryder clasped her shoulder, and she lunged out of reach. Surprisingly fleet considering she'd sat cross-legged in one spot long enough to make most people's legs fall asleep.

He dropped his notebook into the bag and began to disassemble the scope. "It's time to go. I'll carry the scopes and picnic basket if you collect the quilts."

"Another wasted night." She shook the quilts vigorously before folding them.

"Not a total waste. We cleared up a few misunderstandings."

"Then we got carried away."

Ryder dumped the equipment into the long duffel bag and zipped it shut. That was a fine uptight little speech.

"I'm glad you said *we*, Hope. I know I wasn't the only one."

"I admit it." She hefted the picnic basket before his fingers curved around the handle. "Good old nostalgia. It's why so many divorced couples continue to have sex even after they split," she said, swinging down the trail ahead of him.

Did she believe that claptrap? She must. Daylight or not, Ryder wasn't sure this was a safe avenue for discussion even yet. He opened the trunk of the rental car, tossed in the bag of scopes. He cleared a place for the picnic basket.

She tossed in the quilts last, slammed the lid and stalked to the passenger door.

Ryder unlocked it, wishing he could turn back the clock. But maybe he was reading her wrong. She might be concerned for her spotless military record. "No one but us knows we almost got caught up in the past, Hope," Ryder said to the top of her head as she busily fastened her seat belt.

"Are you going to sit here all day yammering?"

"Okay. Have it your way. We won't even talk." He started the car.

She crossed her arms stiffly, looking neither right nor left.

Ten minutes down the road, Ryder was ready to pop. "Hope, what is it you want?"

"Nothing. I don't want anything more from you, Colonel." Which wasn't anywhere close to the truth. Hope wanted him to look her in the eye and say, *Hope Victoria Evans, I love you.* What would he do if she told him the truth?

He'd probably drive into a telephone pole.

Traffic had picked up considerably. Frustrated as he

was, Ryder didn't take his eyes from the road. After yet another night of nonactivity at the missile museum, he really couldn't justify spending much more time here on this wild-goose chase. Or was that an excuse to ship Hope back to someone else's command? What kind of officer let personal problems sway his judgment? Their relationship would have to be put on hold until he was satisfied no subversive activity centered around the missile site.

Such were Ryder's thoughts as he pulled into the Evans' driveway. To his surprise, the garage doors rose silently. Ted motioned him to drive on in.

"What do you suppose he's up to?" Hope muttered. "His car is parked at the curb."

Ryder shrugged but pulled into the garage. He climbed from the car, his questions ready. Ted had ducked out again. Ryder and Hope were left in darkness, staring stupidly at each other.

There wasn't much room to maneuver. They wove between Dory's sedan and Ted's golf cart. Suddenly Hope's father flung open the kitchen door and impatiently called for them to get inside.

"Dad, for pity's sake. What has you in such a snit?"

"One of those men called. For, you, Hope," he said in a hushed tone, as if the walls of the garage might have ears.

"One of what men?" Hope sidled past him into the kitchen, where, as usual, her mother bustled at the stove.

"I assume it was one of the civil defenders that you ticked off."

Hope blanched. "How…how would he get my name?"

"I dunno," Ted said. "He called last evening right after you and Ryder left. Said he was an old school chum from California. All slick-like, he asked where you worked now. Claimed he'd seen you in Tucson. 'Course, I didn't answer any of his questions. He wasn't so nice toward the end of our conversation. He insisted that you and he were once romantically involved. He described Ryder and wanted his name. Asked if the two of you were dating.''

Ryder and Hope gaped at each other. ''How in the name of heaven would he uncover your name?'' Ryder exclaimed. ''The department rented the office space at the university under my alias. I did the same with the Yukon.''

Hope flinched and looked guilty. Gripping the back of a kitchen chair, she said in a weak voice, ''May-maybe they fol-followed us to where you dropped me to rent the car.'' Her eyes offered an apology. ''After you left, I discovered I didn't have enough cash to rent the Toyota. I used my credit card. Did you see anyone following us? The Ford was gone when we left the U. Ryder, what'll we do now?''

He paced in a square, rubbing the back of his neck while the others stood by saying nothing. ''How would they know to call you here? Why not at your condo?''

At first Hope shrugged. Then she snapped her fingers. ''I didn't move in with Lissa right away. I used the folks' address for my forwarded mail. My bank statements and Visa bills still come here. I'm here enough that I never saw a need to change it.''

''That may prove to be very fortunate. And it tells me we've made these turkeys real nervous.''

''My assessment exactly,'' Ted broke in, smiling grimly. ''The minute the bastard asked where Hope *worked,* I knew he wasn't any old friend. Everybody knew she went to the academy.''

"Did you give the guy any information?" Ryder asked.

"Told him Hope was a graduate science student at the U. The minute I asked if I could relay a message, he hung up."

"It's not much, but at last we have something to report," Ryder said. "Let me grab my cell phone out of the car and I'll call Beemis and say I'd like to keep an eye on the museum for another few days. I thought about sending Hope back to her regular duties, but maybe she'd better lie low for the time being."

Hope and Ted nodded.

Dory held up a spatula. "Will the call wait until after breakfast? I have two plates of pancakes ready."

"You go ahead and eat," Ryder said. "It won't take me long to make this call. With the time difference between here and D.C., if I wait, they'll be out to lunch."

"Most of that bunch is always out to lunch." Ted snickered. "But go on, m'boy, make your call."

Ryder crossed the room to dial. Even though he spoke softly and paced the floor, Hope sensed his conversation wasn't going well.

"What's up?" she asked when he closed the phone with a snap and punctuated it with a disgusted snort.

"Beemis believes what we have is benign. Says we've probably locked horns with civilian flag-wavers. We've been ordered back to base. He's going to write a letter to the civil defense unit here suggesting they be less aggressive in the future."

"I have leave coming." Hope caught Ryder's arm. "I'll take thirty days and continue our stakeout for at least a week. If anything concrete turns up, I'll phone you."

"Not on your life. I might be able to swing some

ave, though. I don't want you poking around alone.
Understand?'' Ryder was considerably more concerned
or Hope's safety than he thought it wise to let her know,
given the emotional environment between them now.

"I have plenty of leave built up. It's no sweat to take
ome.'' She disarmed him with a smile. "After breakfast
ou can take me to pick up my car. Then we'll return
he rental and I'll drop you off at your place. We'll each
le leave papers.'' She turned to her dad. "Ryder can
hone me at my condo. I'll give you a jingle, okay,
Dad?''

Hope didn't bother reminding either of the men she
was quite capable of taking care of herself. If Ryder had
sked her not to poke around by herself, rather than or-
er in that imperious tone, she'd be more inclined to
ooperate. The way things stood, it'd be better if they
vent separate ways. Hope doubted she could handle an-
ther night of surveillance like last night's. Her emotions
ad gone through a wringer. She needed distance from
yder.

"That sounds like a good plan to me,'' Ryder agreed
fter careful consideration. "How about you, Ted? Are
ou willing to keep your hands off until Hope and I get
ack?''

Dory spoke for her husband. "He's getting too old to
aipse over mine tailings. Besides, we have tickets to
he opera in Phoenix tomorrow night.''

Ted looked sour. Ryder commiserated with the older
man's reluctance to listen to an evening of caterwauling.

Hope and Ryder pushed back from the table at almost
he same moment. Neither tarried in showering and
hanging. The ride to Tucson seemed inordinately short.
They managed to chat civilly about inconsequential
hings.

"What time shall I call you?" Ryder leaned in th
car window after she dropped him off. To keep compl
cations at a minimum, he dumped the scopes and h
notebook in the trunk of Hope's red convertible.

"Suit yourself. I have no plans."

"Then how about dinner?"

"No. I…ah…have a date with a pile of laundry."

"Okay," he said, rapping his knuckles on the fram
below the window. "I'll call one way or the other t
night. If I can't wangle leave, we'll come up with a
alternate plan."

"Sure," she agreed smoothly. "Well, gotta run."

He stood on the steps and watched her drive off. H
didn't understand the uneasiness that prickled along h
skin. Ryder frowned at the crimson car, wishing he coul
snatch her back. Berating himself for being foolish, h
got into his Hum-V and drove to the base. If he di
patched a week's worth of IFF code changes this afte
noon, then connected with the captain he'd set up t
infiltrate the equipment heists, maybe the powers-that-t
would agree to give him the time off.

His superior refused. It was Wednesday. The best de
Ryder could get was the promise of Friday, Saturday ar
Sunday off. And only then if he wrote a full report c
the burglary probe. He plunged right into the task. As
result, he didn't find time to call Hope until 2100. H
phone rang and rang. Thinking he'd dialed wrong, h
reentered the number. Still no answer. Giving up, Ryd
clicked off.

She'd said she had laundry to do. Probably laund
facilities were downstairs. He finished a rough draft
the report. Satisfied with his progress, Ryder picked u
the phone and tried Hope again. Counting through te
rings, he smashed the receiver back into its cradl
Where the hell *was* that woman?

CHAPTER TEN

HOPE FULLY INTENDED to wait for Ryder. Her request for leave went smoothly. It was a matter of waiting for his call. As she left her squadron command building, she had the misfortune of running into Lance Denton. He changed course and trapped her between his body and the door.

"The secret life of the Arctic Fox gets curiouser and curiouser," he drawled, casually sliding an arm over her shoulder, bracketing the door frame near her ear.

"Buzz off, Denton." Hope tried pushing him aside, but he only tensed his arm and became more sarcastic.

"According to the roster, you were at Holloman. I have a buddy there who swears not."

Hope leaned away from him. "Why all the interest in my boring life?"

"Is it boring? John Weaver, one of our tech supports, claims he saw you at the U. Said you climbed out of a dusty black Yukon and helped some guy in specs off-load a stack of boxes near the science building."

Hope rolled her eyes. She tried stilling the rapid beat of her heart. "Nonsense."

"Is it?" His fingers bit into her arm. "Johnny was so intrigued he followed you—or your twin—until a couple of tough paramilitary types stopped him and asked questions about you. Spooked Weaver. He split. Could sweet little Hope be trafficking on the side, I wonder?"

Hope didn't have to feign shock. She barely managed to hide her jumpy nerves. "You and Weaver watched the same late-night rerun." This time she broke free. *The plane parts. Ryder's investigation.* Denton must be hunting for leads. He was the type to try to strong-arm his way into a promotion.

She ran headlong down the steps and out to her car. Her hand shook as she started the engine. Of all the bad luck. Ryder needed to know she'd been spotted. Hope decided to swing by his office.

Airman Jackson recognized her. "You're not down for an appointment with Colonel McGrath." He flipped pages on a calendar.

"I know. But if he's in, I'm sure the colonel will see me."

The young man's face fell. "He's not."

She drummed her fingers on her thigh. "Is he with the base commander?"

"No. He's already seen him," the man said brightly. "If you'd like to wait, I'll fix you a cup of coffee."

Remembering her last experience, Hope declined.

"I could pencil you in with him tomorrow afternoon."

She glanced up sharply. "Isn't the colonel going on leave tomorrow?"

"N...no." The clerk frowned. "He's booked two IFF briefings in the morning."

"I see." Hope didn't, but she could only assume that Ryder had been denied the time off. "What I need to discuss will wait," she said. "Don't worry about squeezing me in. I'm sure the colonel's very busy. I'll catch him later."

She supposed she could have left a message. At least told him what Denton said. What niggled at Hope on the way out was John Weaver's description of the men from the blue Ford. *Paramilitary types.* If the possibility of them being militia had entered Ryder's mind, he'd never mentioned it to her. Their dress, their attitude— suddenly it made sense to Hope. Given the survivalists' extremist views, all the more reason to keep close watch on that group's activities.

She wouldn't put it past Ryder to have kept information of that nature to himself. Bossy as he was, he might decide to interfere with her leave if he discovered what she'd turned up. No sense getting Ryder's dander up. Or her father's, either. A few nights camped out on the side hill alone wouldn't hurt her. If she uncovered anything concrete, she'd notify Ryder.

Hope made a brief stop at her condo. She watered plants, packed her last pair of clean jeans and gathered all her dirty laundry to do at her parents' place. Her return to Verde Vista late that afternoon was both short and pleasant.

Ted and Dory were dressing for the opera when Hope walked in.

"Where's the colonel?" Ted eyed the bulky laundry bag his daughter hugged to her chest. He held the door open even after she ducked beneath his arm.

"He's still at the base. You look debonair." She flicked a finger across Ted's bow tie.

"Harumph." He cleared his throat and adjusted it beneath his chin. "Your mother makes me wear this penguin suit."

"Well, it's nice. What time will you guys be home?"

"Late," the general growled. "The Beckers always ask us in for coffee and dessert after one of these wingdings." A fan of tiny frown lines webbed between his eyes. "The colonel will be here soon?"

Hope breezed into the laundry room. She'd never been able to fib to her father. "That's the plan," she said as she dumped her underwear into the washer. "Laundry facilities at my complex are overcrowded. I thought I'd get a head start here. That's okay, isn't it?"

"Need you ask, dear?" Dory whisked out of the bedroom in a cloud of perfume. She wore a long silvery gown.

Hope leaned out to admire it. "You look elegant."

"Get on with you." Dory laughed. "For flattery like that, we'll let you and Ryder eat the quiche I prebaked for tomorrow's breakfast. Help yourselves to anything else you'd like." Dory transferred a few things from her leather purse into a beaded handbag. "You aren't planning to sit on top of mine tailings tonight, are you?"

"Um. Probably," Hope called, her head again bent over the machine.

"Oh dear. You two be careful. For some reason, I've been bothered by a jittery feeling all day." Dory slipped her arm through Ted's. "We have to run or we'll be late, but I'm happy to know you'll be with Ryder tonight."

Guilt left a bad taste in Hope's mouth. "Uh…sure," she told her mom with a sigh. Trailing them to the door she waved as they drove away.

Restless, she flipped through television channels. Nothing on but terrible reruns. Why had she let her parents think she'd be with Ryder when she knew he wasn't coming? Still, in all the time they'd sat in those desolate hills, their most aggressive companions had been a few curious rabbits. And she was, after all, a U.S. Air Force major. Her training had been thorough. Not as intense as Ryder's, but she could probably dispatch any vagrant who wandered into her camp.

After ten more minutes of vacillating, Hope made up her mind. She tossed her clothes into the dryer and filled a knapsack with fruit and cheese. In afterthought, she jotted a note to her parents. "Stakeout as usual, see you at breakfast." Tuning out a guilty conscience, she left.

RYDER FINALLY CALLED a halt to his hectic day. Off and on he'd tried phoning Hope at her condo to no avail. A call to her squadron commander late in the day netted him the information that she'd signed out on leave. No surprise there. But what did her continued absence from home mean?

While debating whether or not to work late, Ryder decided to phone Ted. Maybe Hope had contacted her parents. Their line rang until it connected to the answering machine. "Well, damn!" The way he felt now, he'd wring her neck when he did find her.

Airman Jackson stuck his head in Ryder's office right before he left for the day. "I almost forgot, Colonel. Major Evans came by to see you. At 1500. She thought you were going on leave tomorrow. I set her straight. She said she'd catch you later."

"Thanks, Jackson. Have a good evening." So Hope knew he'd be delayed. Hmm. Maybe she'd gone out with friends. He wouldn't put it past her to go on to Verde Vista to avoid riding down with him on the weekend.

If the three Evanses were out together, he'd reach them sooner or later. Ryder couldn't help wishing that it were sooner. The news, however, sparked his decision to go home.

Once there, he unloaded a briefcase full of paperwork and slapped it on the dining-room table. He pictured Hope acting smug over the repeated hang-ups on her parents' answering machine. Damn, he hated being predictable.

He could take a quick run down there, but considering the shaky way they'd left things between them, that'd probably annoy her to no end. Instead, he sat and plowed through a pile of memos on the IFF changes. Wearing two hats got to be tricky at times. He really couldn't spare the time to play hide-and-seek with Hope. *Dammit!* He wouldn't relax until he saw her.

Just as he made up his mind to go, the operative he had working undercover on the missing-parts case paid him a visit.

''There's no question but that these are the men involved?'' he asked. His infiltrator replied emphatically that he had photos to prove it.

Accepting the packet of film, Ryder phoned his boss in D.C., who ordered him to have security pick up the suspects. ''You interrogate them personally, Colonel McGrath.''

So much for his quick trip to Verde Vista.

After three hours of grilling, Ryder had two solid confessions and one holdout. In the wee hours, he stumbled home again to compose and fax his report. He fell asleep at his computer and awakened later with a jolt. It was 0330. Scrubbing a hand over gritty eyes, he realized it was too late to call the Evans house again. Fate had decided for him, he thought as he ripped back the covers on his bed and fell in fully clothed.

HOPE REACHED the stakeout site before museum volunteers left for the day. She munched a banana and reread the notes in Ryder's notebook. In print the whole thing sounded bizarre. It felt a little as if they'd stumbled into Oz. Tossing the book aside, Hope bagged the banana peel to avoid an invasion of ants. She sipped water and watched a smattering of clouds drift over the sun.

Activity around the museum ceased before daylight faded to dusk. For a dime she'd go home. This was going to be another tedious night. Made more tedious for lack of Ryder's company. For a while she sat on the quilt and counted stars, which made her remember what it had been like to observe them with Ryder. Lethargy stole over her. She wished they *had* made love, rules or no rules. Was that really why he'd called a halt? Rules and everything else flew out of her head when it came to Ryder McGrath.

Excuse me? Did your mother raise a total dummy?

Determined to forget him, Hope crawled back over to the night scope and fitted her eye to the viewfinder. Hours later, an involuntary yawn knocked the scope askew and threw objects out of focus.

A silver moon bobbing in and out of wispy clouds saved the night from being horribly black. Still not enough light to fix the lens. Hope snapped on the small flashlight to accomplish the task and to check her watch. She wanted to log a report in Ryder's notebook every hour on the hour as he had. It wasn't quite 0200. Dousing the light, she eased an eye to the viewfinder again. She panned the compound haphazardly, already dreaming of the next break.

Movement? Burrowing flat on her stomach, Hope squinted at the shrubs and trees planted inside the fence. It could be nothing more than wind shadows. Except, up here, the air seemed perfectly calm.

Hardly daring to blink, Hope found the range again. Her heart began to skip erratically. Sweat slicked her palms. Oh, God! Unless she was hallucinating, people in camouflage gear were moving around inside the grounds of the missile museum. Three. At least three. Maybe more. It was so far away. Too far.

She rubbed her eyes and reached for the long-range binoculars, which in the end proved less satisfactory.

Her conscience decreed that she should run, not walk, to notify Ryder. The trained officer in her said to stay and get more detailed information. Both distance and the proficiency of the disguises worn by the figures below continued to hinder her from forming an accurate picture of exactly what they were doing.

Unwilling to admit defeat, she scouted the area and found a knoll that afforded a clearer view. There were no trees or shrubs to use for cover, but the scope was black and Hope had dressed in dark clothing. From the new vantage point, she was able to identify two husky men using some kind of high-speed saw. Her heart drained of blood and plunged to her toes. They were sawing through the concrete barriers that cemented open the silo doors.

Two additional stalwarts swept up debris as it flew from the saw. After each cut the sawyers completed, two men filled the crevice with something out of a can. Paste—no, putty. Hope scrambled upright, then plopped back hard on the rocky cliff when her quaking knees gave way.

For a moment she was too frightened to let her brain assimilate the significance of what she'd just seen. Little by little, fright blossomed into stark terror.

Someone did intend to launch the missile.

Where? At what? She recalled having asked Ryder those same questions.

Once she'd calmed herself enough to be rational, Hope concluded that those facts were unimportant. If launch was imminent, the men wouldn't be taking such care to mask the cuts. And they were painstakingly making certain everything appeared normal. Business as usual to the public.

Hope rubbed between her eyes, smoothing worry lines lodged there. "Darn," she whispered. "Ryder, I need you."

He'd taken the cell phone, or she could call him from here. *A pay phone.* The closest one was probably two miles away at a convenience store.

No. Not yet. First and foremost it was crucial that she record everything she'd seen, step by step, in Ryder's notebook. She sneaked another peek to be certain she hadn't dreamed the whole messy incident. But no, the men were still working like a colony of ants.

Lugging the scope, Hope scurried back to the quilt. At first her nerves were too jumpy and her hand too slick to grip the pen tightly enough to write legibly. Ordering herself to stop it—to calm down—she began again. Date. Time. Observation. Eventually she'd logged every last detail to her satisfaction. Her fingers were cramped by the time she set the book aside.

The pages ruffled in a sudden gust of wind. Hope swiveled in surprise. A stiff breeze had sprung up and she hadn't even noticed. The snap of a twig spooked her. She wedged the book between two rocks that sat near the blanket. Scolding herself for being so skittish, Hope decided to verify the activity one more time before reporting to Ryder. Thinking a new angle might show more detail, she shouldered the scope and headed for a higher ridge.

Without warning, two shadowy figures sprang out of the night. One knocked Hope's feet out from under her. The other clamped a hand over her mouth.

She kicked and bit instinctively, lashing out first with

one elbow, then the other. Trained she might be, yet she got in only one good lick to an iron jaw before the men subdued her.

"This is public property," she panted, trying to ram her head into the closest fellow's solar plexis. When she only succeeded in hurting herself, fright jellied in her stomach. As quickly, anger spun her back to reality. What could she do to trick them into revealing who they were?

It was a cinch they weren't wearing night-camouflage gear as a practice run for Halloween. These slimeballs meant business. One taped Hope's mouth, the other her wrists and ankles. Their precision and their total silence gave her the creeps.

Why, oh, why hadn't she listened to Ryder?

As the initial surge of adrenaline receded, bile rose in Hope's throat. Soundlessly her captors collected her belongings. The quilt, the knapsack, the bag with the equipment. She didn't see them pick up the notebook. For an instant her spirits lifted. Then they began to sweep the area, systematically destroying all tracks. These men weren't amateurs. When they'd restored the landscape to their liking, the ugliest of the two patted her down. Luckily, he seemed immune to the fact she was a woman as he dug her car keys out of her pocket.

Panic licked through her veins. Her convertible had a decal permit to enter the airbase, and her purse held her military ID. Gagging against the tape, Hope fought not to retch as fear for her life threatened to choke her.

RYDER LEFT for work early, circling past Hope's condominium. Her car wasn't in its assigned space. Late now for his scheduled IFF briefing, he was plenty ticked that she'd skipped out without a peep.

At 0900 he left the briefing. He'd no sooner stepped inside squadron command than Airman Jackson jumped up and handed him a message. "This guy, a Ted Evans—claims to be a retired general—said to tell you his call is urgent."

The word *urgent* struck him like a right-cross to the jaw. "No message? Just urgent?"

Jackson nodded. "That's all he said, sir."

Ryder couldn't get to the phone fast enough. His fingers beat an impatient tattoo on his desk as he waited for someone in the Evans household to answer.

Ted himself snatched up the phone. "Hello."

"This is Ryder."

"Have you seen or heard from the major today?"

Ryder's mouth and tongue went numb. "Isn't she with you and Dory?"

"She came in yesterday afternoon. Put laundry to wash and said you'd be along. Or that's what her mother and I understood. We got home late from the opera and found a note. It said, 'Stakeout as usual, see you at breakfast.' She hasn't rolled in. I suddenly realized there's not an extra car in the driveway. Don't mind telling you I'm some worried to find you at the base."

Ryder was more than some worried. He smoothed a damp hand over a close-shaven jaw. "Maybe she had car trouble." *But her car was nearly new.* Ryder attempted to tamp down the fear squeezing his lungs. "It'd be hard to give you directions to the site we used. I'll meet you in twenty minutes at the convenience store on Duval Mine Road. If you're not there, I'll assume you found her and I'll go on to the house."

"Got it. Hurry, Colonel, but don't break your neck."

Ryder didn't care if he got reprimanded for leaving. He swiped his desk clean, shucked his flight suit, turned out the lights and locked the door. "Field my calls, Jackson. I have an emergency off base. If anyone asks, I'm on official business."

The surprised clerk bobbed his head.

Ryder tore out of the building like a madman, refusing to listen to the negative possibilities hammering in his brain. He kept to the speed limit—barely—but his hands were tense and white-knuckled as they gripped the wheel. His heart plummeted when he reached the rendezvous point and saw Ted pacing impatiently outside the store. Ryder vaulted from the cab of his Hum-V almost before the engine shut down. "No word?" he panted.

"No. I wish somebody would explain what's going on."

"I don't know, Ted. You heard our plan. Then I couldn't get off today. Hope found that out from my clerk. I tried calling her all last evening. First at her place, then at yours. I forgot you and Dory had an engagement. Damn, I'd have run down here last night no matter how late if I'd remembered."

"Why would she disobey orders?"

Ryder sighed. "We had words. Technically, she's no longer under my command."

"So what now?"

"I suggest we go have a look around. Hell, I can't say for sure she'd go back to the same spot, but I don't know where else to start."

"Let's take my car," Ted growled. "Your rig stands out."

"I know, but it's all I had available. We'll still need to hike a ways."

Fifteen minutes later they puffed to the top of the rise and stared at a rocky clearing that looked undisturbed.

Ryder broke off a long stem of deer grass and stuck it in his mouth to keep from swearing. Which was okay, because Ted did it for him.

"No sign of her. Nor did we see her car stalled along the road. Got to admit, son, I'm getting damn rattled."

Dropping to his haunches, Ryder sifted a handful of gravel through his fingers. He closed his eyes to block the vision of how he'd nearly made love with Hope at this very spot.

"Are you thinking what I'm thinking?" Ted knelt. "This area looks as if it was swept with a broom. Or a tree branch."

Ryder looked closer. Ted was right. Mooning about Hope almost let him miss a valuable piece of information. "Let's split up. Check for signs of a struggle. Hope thinks fast on her feet. If she met with foul play, maybe she managed to leave a clue."

They worked the area. Ted found the branch used to sweep away tracks. Ryder discovered broken fronds on a paloverde. At one point, while crawling around on his hands and knees, quite by chance he dislodged a rock and out fell his black notebook. His exultant cry brought Ted running.

It was Ryder's breakthrough, so he flipped through the book. Thumbing fast, he found the cramped notes Hope had added. If he had an ounce of color left when he read Hope's last entry, it drained.

"This is crazy!" he exclaimed. "Insane!" He glanced up and into Ted's eyes. They mirrored his pain.

Ted ran a hand through his shock of gray hair. "Those bastards. I knew it," he ranted, slapping his forehead with the butt of his hand. "They're going to try to launch that Titan. Well, I hope it blows them all straight to hell."

"Don't even make jokes like that," Ryder said harshly. "We have to assume they have Hope. One misstep and they'll take her out, and possibly this whole valley."

Sick to his stomach, Ryder gazed out over the facility that stretched placidly below them in the brilliant sunlight. With the naked eye he could just make out the Stars and Stripes waving atop the main building.

Ted's hands balled. "I want to rip them to shreds. Damn, I feel helpless."

Ryder pulled out his cell phone. "Past time for heroics. Time we call in the big guns." He punched in a string of numbers, then wore tracks in the soil while he waited for the call to go through. Throughout the conversation that ensued, his voice rose to a shout at times. Instead of hanging up when he clicked off, he flung the plastic case against a rock, looking grimly satisfied when it flew apart. "Damn those pigheaded morons. They're pulling the plug on us. The CIA found the lost terrorists in Lebanon. Beemis insists all we have is a flaky hoax and a few crackpots. He told me to turn it over to local authorities."

Ted's jaw flexed as he scooped up the pieces of Ryder's mangled phone. "I heard you tell him what the major verified. Didn't that cut any ice?"

"Beemis and his sidekicks are convinced there's no way this rocket could be fitted with engines, a warhead and fueled. Said he'd reread the report on the missile's deactivation. End of discussion. I'm tempted to go over his head."

"And get yourself court-martialed? We'll solve this problem ourselves."

Ryder gave the older man a tired smile. "We have no other choice, as I see it. Let's collect my wheels, go back o your house and draft a plan. Oh, but will we upset Dory?''

''She's a military wife.''

Taking the general at his word, Ryder tucked the evidence into his pocket and led the way at a dead run to Ted's car.

A strange car sat in the Evans' driveway. Ryder flew out of his rig, praying that Hope had hitched a ride home. But from the way Ted, who entered the house two bounds ahead of Ryder, gripped the stranger's hand and pounded him on the back, Ryder's expectations were dashed.

''Chris!'' Ted exclaimed gruffly. ''You're a sight for sore eyes, son.''

''You, too, General.'' The blond man spared less than a curious glance at Ryder, tugging his father toward the kitchen. ''I brought someone I want you to meet. Jennifer, hon,'' he yelled over the louvered café doors.

A striking brunette appeared at once. She let Chris draw her into the curve of his arm.

''Jennifer, this is my father. Dad, Jennifer Richards, soon to be my wife.'' Bending, he nibbled at the pretty woman's cherry-red lips.

''Nicetomeetyou.'' Ted's polite sentence ran together as he deftly separated Chris from his intended bride. ''Son, your timing couldn't be better. I want you to meet Colonel Ryder McGrath.'' Ted dragged Ryder forward. ''The colonel and your sister were on a mission involving surveillance. Near as we can tell, someone snatched your sister. We're about to devise a plan to get her back.''

Chris Evans studied Ryder with cool green eyes so like Hope's that Ryder's heart kicked over. He let the hand he'd extended fall away.

The younger Evans doubled his fist and belted Ryder in the mouth. Ignoring his fiancée's alarmed cry and Ted's shock, he rubbed his knuckles and sneered at the man who now held his jaw. "McGrath, I've wanted to meet you out of uniform. What's my sister doing messing with you again? And since when do pilots work surveillance?"

Ryder rocked his jaw from side to side and glared back. He didn't owe this upstart any explanations. Spinning on a heel, he started to walk out.

Ted blocked his way. "I don't even want to know what that's all about," he thundered at both men. "There's bigger trouble afoot than a couple of young bucks' egos. Whatever your beef with Ryder is, Chris, put it aside until we find your sister. That's an order."

Dory sneaked out of the kitchen and tenderly slipped an arm around the pasty-faced Jennifer. Neither Chris nor Ryder questioned the older man's right to issue orders. Keeping their distance from each other, both trekked after Ted into the dining room.

BLINDFOLDED, Hope huddled against the floorboards of some hot, smelly vehicle where her captors had tossed her. Her mouth felt like cotton, and the tape on her wrists was too tight to budge. All in all, she was damn uncomfortable.

But she was alive. And though shaky, she still had her wits. At first she had assumed they'd take her to the missile museum. After all, what better place to bury a witness than somewhere in a silo one hundred and forty-six feet underground? Hope almost wished she didn't know so much. For instance, that people who played deadly games couldn't afford to leave behind witnesses.

But the absence of smooth road beneath the tires of

the vehicle in which she rode made the first prospect less likely. And a lot less likely that anyone looking for her might find her. It felt as if they were bumping across the desert. Hope was sure people died on the desert, never to be found again. By the time anyone figured out she was missing, these jokers could fuel the rocket. Funny how she remembered the finite details of her dad's spiel. The Titan II took a minimum of forty-five minutes to gravity-load the propellants—and precisely one minute to launch. The worst part, once launched, the missile could not be redirected or called back.

Her heart jackhammered. Why, oh, why hadn't she waited for Ryder? All the things she wished she'd told him tumbled crazily through her brain. That even if he loved April till eternity, Hope still loved him. *Still and always.*

The vehicle stopped suddenly. Straining, she heard low, abrasive voices. Apparently her captors had reached their destination. Her gravesite? Renewed panic surged through her.

Rough hands yanked her out, cut the tape that bound her legs and stood her on unsteady feet. She felt the presence of a large body in front of her and one behind. She stumbled when a hand shoved against her back. Suddenly furious, Hope straightened. She limped forward as best she could in the conduct befitting an officer of the U.S. Air Force. Whoever these men were, they were scum compared to the protective legions that stood shoulder to shoulder with her.

Still, when a calloused male hand jerked her to a stop and ripped off her blindfold, Hope cringed. She shut her eyes against a bright light and opened them again slowly.

Rock walls surrounded her. It was dank and much

cooler here. Her sleeveless blouse was no protection, and she shivered. Once her mind clicked forward, however, it didn't take Hope long to judge the cave to be part of a defunct mine. Who knew which one? She'd heard the area was honeycombed with them.

Though she was left alone for the moment, the cavern bustled with muscular young men. Crates lined the walls. *Crates of munitions.* The place was a veritable arsenal. And the men wore precision khaki uniforms. Their pant legs were bloused military-style over spit-polished black boots.

Army? Maybe a group on maneuvers. Hope's heart lightened a bit until she realized they wore no tags or insignia. *Not military.* And she was the only sane person who knew what evil they were up to. She had to stop them.

But how? One person. Hope was only one person. *With one life to give for her country.* Ryder's teasing words from the other night didn't seem so laughable now.

Amazingly, everyone seemed to ignore her and went on about their business. When she grew tired of standing in the middle of the uneven floor, she edged over and sat on a crate that said it held government-issue rifles. Apart from one bathroom break, she sat there for hours.

Finally a short man who reminded Hope of a bantam rooster confronted her. He ripped the tape off her mouth and smiled when she sucked in a ragged breath to offset the pain.

"Major Evans, suppose you start by telling us who sent you to spy."

Hope shied from his hate-filled black eyes. In the absence of rank, she didn't imagine the Geneva rules for the humane treatment of prisoners applied. But as she'd been schooled, Hope supplied her name, rank and serial number.

His upper lip curled. ''I already have that information.'' He proceeded to pull her ID card from his breast pocket and tapped it menacingly on his fisted left hand.

She shrugged, and as a result, missed seeing the back-handed slap he dealt her until her head spun around. The signet ring he wore bit into the soft flesh of her lip. Hope gingerly pried her teeth away with her tongue and tasted blood.

She still didn't look at him. Instead, her eyes checked out his ring. She'd seen one like it before. In the picture she'd taken of the guide at the missile site. A furtive glance revealed that all the men wore similar rings. Like a fraternity, she thought hysterically. A deadly fraternity. If she'd ever doubted that her captors were tied to the group at the museum, she doubted no more.

Two men stepped out of the shadows. Hope recognized them as two of the four who'd accosted her and Ryder in the desert.

''We're interested in the whereabouts of your bug-loving friend, Major.''

Smiling out of the side of her mouth that didn't feel numb, Hope said, ''He left before your goons grabbed me. I'd keep an eye over my shoulder if I were you. Are you familiar with the term Special Forces?''

The leader swore and hit her again. This time Hope's cheek puffed, and she refrained from lifting her taped hands to see if there was blood.

Swinging away abruptly, her attacker hauled out a field phone. After making a string of calls, he charged back, wrapped a hand in the front of her blouse and dangled her off the ground. ''So, you go by the code name Arctic Fox.'' It was a statement, not a question.

Even so, she felt a chill raise the tiny hairs on the back of her neck.

"Are you CIA?"

Hope only glared at him. He pushed his face so close to hers she knew the pupils of her eyes dilated in fear.

"Tell me," he demanded. "I want the name of your contact. You're not in any position to protect his butt."

Seeing the loathsome face twisted in crazed fanaticism, Hope made a snap decision. Maybe, just maybe, she'd survive if she fed them a crumb. "I...I was roped into this scheme because I knew a little about the museum layout. My dad used to volunteer there. I swear I don't know their plans or what they're after. The Strategist, he's the leader."

The man released her. "Well, that's better. What's his real name?"

"I don't know." Hope did her best to look dumb.

He rubbed his hands together, his eyes glittering wildly. "His code name may be enough. Get her out of here," he ordered the two who'd brought her in. "Take her next door and feed her. I'll decide by morning what to do with her."

Grateful for the reprieve, however minimal, Hope didn't mind the oafs' silence this time as they led her to a rocky cavern where the smell of soup filled the air. She wouldn't eat a bite these devils cooked, but she said how starved she was so they'd untape her wrists. She rubbed them as she glanced at her watch and realized she'd been shackled for thirteen hours.

She played with the food, letting her mind drift. She had to make her move before a new day bloomed. Otherwise she wouldn't give a plugged nickel for her chances of seeing another sunrise.

Keeping her head down and her ears open, she heard

enough talk to know they planned to launch the missile within the week. *At Camp David.* The presidential retreat. The president and his wife were due to spend a week vacationing there. She wanted to vomit.

It was almost too unreal to believe something like this could happen. As near as she could make out, these men were protesting the lack of presidential intervention after an attack on a U.S. military barracks in the Middle East a few years ago.

Clinging to the bowl of soup more for warmth than for nourishment, Hope fretted so long over all she'd pieced together, she almost missed the advent of thunder. Then a bolt of lightning cracked right outside the entrance to the mine shaft and set a bush on fire, which provoked a flurry of activity. Even the man guarding her ran outside.

Crossing the desert on foot in the middle of an electric storm held little appeal to Hope. However, she'd never have a better opportunity to slip away. Depositing her bowl on a crate, she sidled along the cave wall, sneaked around the knots of men involved in the ruckus and melted into the blessedly stormy night.

CHAPTER ELEVEN

RYDER HAMMERED OUT a plan with Ted and Chris. He put everyone in the family to work. Dory and Chris's fiancée were dispatched on a tour of the museum. As Chris had flown a twin-engine plane in from Maryland, he and Ryder paid lip service to a truce, agreeing to conduct a thorough flyover of the surrounding terrain.

"I'm going to round up as many guys from my air force association chapter as I can and bring them up to date," Ted said. "If the big guns on the hill won't take our complaints seriously, we'll nab those no-goods ourselves."

"Hold everything," Chris warned. "Ryder and I don't want to lose time and grade over this. We just want to get Hope home safely."

Ryder shifted in his seat. He folded his hands together and rapped his knuckles against his forehead. "If I hadn't read Hope's notes, Chris, I'd agree one hundred percent. I still agree that her safety comes first. But I've seen these characters. The prospect of them being paramilitary is a whole lot scarier than when we thought they were overeager flag-wavers."

Chris stood. "It's 1200 now. Shall we meet here and debrief at, say, 1530?"

Ted agreed. Ryder and Chris left in Chris's rented car and went to collect the plane. On the drive to the airport, Hope's brother relentlessly grilled Ryder. After evading his questions for ten minutes or so, Ryder finally turned in his seat and caught the belligerent major's eye. "Look, I've no intention of airing Hope's or my dirty linen so you can feel vindicated for chewing out my butt. All you need to know is that there hasn't been anyone since her and that I love your sister. If those creeps hurt her, this may well be the end of my career. If I have to, I'll take them out one by one."

A smile spread slowly over Chris's face. He lifted a hand from the wheel and stuck it out for Ryder to shake. "You won't be alone, Colonel. I'm not much on hand-to-hand combat, but I'll be there covering your back."

"Fair enough," Ryder growled.

Their first flyover revealed no sign of Hope's car. Ryder had had such high expectations. His gut churned as he noted the miles of rugged terrain.

"The area is spotty with old mines," Chris complained. "They're even working one a few miles from where you say you found the notebook. Messy, the way they pump tons of water over the ore. I wonder how deep that sludge lake is. It's so murky someone could shove Hope in, car and all, and we'd never find her."

"Stop it." Ryder shot him a dark look. "They've seen us together. I can't help thinking they'll be anxious to know what's happened to me."

The waning sun reflected off Chris's mirrored sunglasses. "Will they abort their mission if they discover the two of you are military?"

Ryder gazed at the pilot. "They know. She had the scopes, and her car had a base sticker."

"Damn!" Chris exclaimed. "We're coming up empty here. Would it do any good to visit that phony civil defense office and threaten to shave a few ears off?"

"I'd like nothing better. However, instinct tells me

she'll be safer if they don't discover we're onto them. What I know about survivalists, and that's damn little, they consider themselves true patriots. God only knows where they've programmed that missile for. Moscow, Baghdad, Sarajevo.'' Ryder slumped in his seat. "It'll never occur to them that none of these Titans were ever tested. That they could toast half of Arizona and themselves if anything goes wrong."

Chris made a smooth landing. "I never thought beyond Hope's disappearance. Special Forces is your field, McGrath. Make the brass listen. I'm just a simple pilot, dammit."

"I tried to make them listen. My contact hung up on me. He believes reports that say this Titan isn't flyable and that the warheads have all been destroyed. I've tracked down too many terrorists and smugglers to be that sure."

"So what now?"

"Now we rendezvous with your dad. We find out if the women saw anything out of the ordinary at the museum. Then we put everything together and regroup."

Dory and Jennifer were climbing out of Dory's car as Ryder and Chris pulled in.

"See anything?" Ryder asked them.

"The tour was the same," Dory said. "The only difference was that the guides seemed nervous and made everyone sign the guest book—which used to be optional. I made up a first name and borrowed Jennifer's last name. I put ditto marks for my address so they'd think we were both from Maryland."

The four continued into the house, where Ted entertained approximately twenty-five men, all of them about his age.

"Ted," Dory said worriedly once they'd all reported in, "shouldn't we notify local police?"

"And let them blunder in and get Hope killed? No way. I'm for snatching one of those young punks and intimidating information out of him."

Ryder held up a hand. "That's kidnapping, Ted. Until we get Hope back, we need to work within the law. You know, I noticed something out near one of those abandoned mines. It ate at me, and now I know why. There were tire tracks worn in since the last rain. In the middle of rusted equipment, I saw a newer piece...an old military cherry picker. Now it strikes me that anybody who planned to refit the engines on that missile would need a crane of that type."

"What are we waiting for?" Chris asked. "Let's go."

Jennifer glided to Chris's side. "Isn't that dangerous, babe?"

"Yeah," Ryder answered for him, then turned to Ted. "I see you fellows have assembled some pretty fair camouflage gear. I propose we wait until dark and that I go in on foot. Alone."

Jennifer appealed to her fiancé. "Chris, all of this is crazy. I know she's your sister and you love her, but shouldn't you be working through channels?"

Chris gathered her close and swayed with her a moment but otherwise ignored her outburst.

Dory wrung her hands. "On the way home from the museum, Jennifer and I heard on the radio that another storm is moving in fast from the Baja. Forecasters predict more thunder, lightning and rain than we had the other night, Ryder."

"I won't melt, Dory. These guys live off the land. If they have dug in some kind of base out there, one man has a better chance of getting in and out undetected. If it turns out a dead end, we've only wasted a few hours.''

''Take a weapon and our cellular phone,'' urged Ted.

Ryder shook his head. ''No electronics that'll give any signal they can track. And no weapon. This is strictly unofficial and unauthorized. If we bust up this group, we'll have to do it unarmed if at all possible.''

The others showed concern.

''I used to be fair with the martial arts,'' said a bald man who still looked fit. ''While you're gone, Colonel, maybe the old gang'll brush up on moves and counter-moves.''

''Good. So it's settled?'' Ryder glanced around the room for confirmation. The minute he got consent, he began assembling gear. Night goggles for himself and a pair for Hope should he find her. Two clip-on canteens, four energy bars and a tube of black grease to take the shine off his face and hands. Though he wore boots and camouflage shirt and pants, he removed his dog tags and all other ID.

That brought home to everyone in the room what a serious game they were playing.

Chris, who'd been standing at the window watching the gathering dusk and the approaching storm, turned suddenly and slapped Ryder on the back. ''I'm driving you to the drop point. Dad and I will keep a running patrol of the perimeter road leading up to the operational mine. Between us we can come up with a variety of cars in case they're monitoring traffic. You find Hope. Haul her out to the road. One of us will pick you up.''

Tears glittered in Chris's eyes. Ryder couldn't have asked for clearer acceptance from Hope's protective sibling. They clasped hands briefly. Ryder tugged a cap low over his eyes. ''Let's do it,'' he growled.

Chris kissed Jennifer solidly. He hugged his mother. The two youngest of the assembly left in the wake of loud thunder and bolts of lightning. The storm from the Baja had begun to pound hell out of southern Arizona.

HOPE KNEW the minute the men put out the fire they'd discover her escape. She didn't have much time to pick a route and throw them off the track. Especially as she paused in a thicket of mesquite to get her bearings and felt the beginning patter of rain. It'd help put out the fire faster. *Darn and blast.*

A jagged bolt of lightning that followed a particularly long roll of thunder lit a swath across the desert, including her hiding place. If the lightning kept up, it would slow her down. She could only make progress between flashes. Hope wished she had something to cover her hair. In this darkness, it would act as a beacon for her trackers.

Hope hadn't so much as a handkerchief. Her captors had picked her pockets clean. This was probably an idiotic move. Desert storms weren't to be messed with. They could produce flash floods in a matter of seconds. But if she died out here, she'd at least know she'd died trying.

Hunching, she took a deep breath and charged into the wind. A faint cry went up from the direction of the caves, and Hope knew someone had discovered her disappearance.

She panicked a moment, positive they'd expect her to head for the mine road and follow it into town. Indeed, she had very little choice. To try to climb the mountain of tailings in the dark would be suicide. Her dad once told her there were abandoned sludge pits throughout the area. He'd taken a helicopter ride over this section once.

Huddled up against a paloverde, she racked her brain trying to recall what else he'd said. Between corkscrew flashes of light, she dashed to the next clump of trees. Rain soaked her sleeveless blouse, and cactus thorns grabbed at her jeans. She stumbled and cracked her knee on something hard. *A rock.* No—an iron bar.

Hope knelt and ran her hand along the metal. Her first thought was that maybe she could use it to defend herself if they caught her. Further exploration revealed it as part of a railroad track. A spur leading into a mine? Would it intersect the road at some point? Seemed logical to Hope. And offered the best news she'd had in some time. Crouching low, she trailed one finger along the wet metal and scurried as fast as she could. At least now she had direction and purpose.

She'd begun to breathe easier, when in the pitch black that followed an extra brilliant flash of light, she smacked face first into a brick wall of a man.

Swallowing a scream, Hope tried to knee him in the groin. Her efforts failed, but the attempt sent them crashing to the ground. Terrified of what would happen if this man, who was obviously a perimeter guard, took her back to the leader who'd already bloodied her face, Hope kicked and gouged for all she was worth.

Her assailant swore. She ducked as he tried to grab her around the throat and succeeded in tripping him. As he fell, she ran, no longer caring if she followed the train tracks. She'd barely gone three steps when she slammed into another broad chest. Beyond panic, she aimed her fingernails at the man's eyes. No matter how she tried to remain silent, tiny whimpers of fear worked their way out.

She feared she was done for when the new foe wrapped her in a viselike grip and held her defenseless as the one she'd shaken off crashed through the underbrush.

"Hope? Hope? Calm down," a voice murmured as she struggled harder. Her ears rang. Adrenaline spurted furiously. It was hard to say exactly the moment she realized this invader meant her no harm. But it was before he thrust her behind him and dropped her first adversary with a karate chop to the neck.

Suddenly joy crushed her already overtaxed lungs. "Ryder," she whispered. Scrambling up, she launched herself into his arms and spoke his name more loudly.

He clamped a hand over her mouth, though he stumbled awkwardly as he accepted the kisses she rained over his face. "Stop," he ordered in a hushed tone next to her ear. "Someone's coming. We have to get out of here fast."

She knew he was right, of course, but as so often happened after an ordeal when a person knew that danger had passed, Hope started to shake. Pluck that served her well throughout her capture and subsequent escape fizzled and her knees began to knock.

During a forked bolt of lightning, Ryder evaluated the situation. He didn't like what he saw. Rather than head for the road and face the probability of running into more of the men who were chasing Hope, he decided to take his chances by holing up.

Because he could see she was almost played out, he picked her up and slung her over his shoulder. He was in good shape, and she hardly weighed more than a full backpack. The problem, as Ryder judged it, was that the subversives knew the lay of the land far better than he. Still, he thought he had surprise and advantage on his side. Only one man knew he was out here. The others would undoubtedly expect Hope to make for the high-way.

So what if they worked their way over top of that next ridge of old tailings and angled toward the working mine? The more he chewed on the idea, the better Ryder liked it. Mines likely had shifts working twenty-four hours a day. And phones. They surely had a telephone. Decision made, Ryder took off at a run. He only paused to take cover each time lightning struck.

He couldn't say how long he'd been carrying Hope when suddenly he felt her pounding on his back pockets. Dropping to one knee, he gulped a tortured breath and set her on her feet. "What's wrong?" he whispered. "Are you sick to your stomach?"

Though she ran an unsteady hand through her soaking hair, she shook her head. "I can walk, Ryder. I don't know what came over me. I was so afraid they'd found me and would take me back." She shivered, wiping at the rain pelting her face.

"Shh." Ryder massaged the back of her neck. They didn't have time to waste, but he hated to push her.

All at once several wicked forks of lightning illuminated the sky and the hill where they stood. He got a clear look at Hope for the first time. The puffed, cut lip. The ugly bruise on her cheek.

"They hit you," he snarled, reaching out to touch her injury, then drawing back. "Tell me which one. What'd he look like? I'll teach him to put his filthy hands on you." His voice shook.

"Ryder," Hope murmured, clutching at his sleeve. "We have to get away from here. You have no idea what they plan to do."

"Launch the missile." He sighed. "I know. We found the notebook. All right. But when we round them up, you're going to show me which one hit you. I'll settle the score.''

"You found the notebook?" Her relief was overwhelming. "I thought *they* had. Oh, Ryder, I have to tell you that I called myself forty kinds of fool for not listening to you. All I could think was that no one would have the vaguest idea where I was."

He hugged her fiercely, then set her away and clamped a tight hold on her left hand. "Running into you was a lucky shot in the dark, Hope. Your brother and I crisscrossed this section a hundred times by air."

"My brother? Which one?"

"Chris. He brought his fiancée to meet the family." Ryder allowed a small chuckle. "The poor woman stepped into a hornet's nest, what with all of us running around looking for you."

Just then he heard the sound of a vehicle churning up muddy sand somewhere below and off to the left. He tugged Hope flat behind a granite boulder a second from being trapped by a bank of powerful searchlights.

So, the hunters hadn't bought the most logical theory—that Hope had headed for town. Either that or the man Ryder had stopped cold came to and made his way into camp. Now Ryder regretted not taking the time to gag and shackle the jerk. Had he and Hope left tracks? In this weather, probably footprints the size of Sasquatch.

If they were lucky, the rain would soon wash the prints away. If not... Ryder didn't finish the thought. Paramilitary were well trained in tracking. If they were like the zealots at a camp in Texas he'd helped dig out, they had the latest military equipment, too. But maybe not. The minute the idling truck doused its lights and plowed into the desert behind them, Ryder unclipped the two pair of night goggles from his belt. He slipped one set over Hope's head, hesitating a moment to stroke a thumb along her cheek before donning the second set himself. Once Hope adjusted the goggles to her satisfaction, he snugged his wet hat over her bright curls. She started to thank him, but he tapped his forefinger against her lips to indicate that from now on they'd run silent.

He hated not being able to follow the truck. Nor did he like stumbling around hostile land with hostile forces nipping at his heels when he had Hope in tow.

Keeping a firm grip on her hand, he led out, taking care to avoid brushing any of the shrubs. No telling what kind of night-observation equipment the men in the truck carried. Some devices detected body heat or bent twigs at fifty yards.

They hadn't gone far when Hope pulled frantically on his arm. It was in a fairly open area. Ryder slogged toward a thicket, barely made out through rain-drenched goggles. Hope's signal grew more insistent. Winded from the exertion of jogging in a half crouch, Ryder hauled her close and let go of her hand. "Wh...a...at?" he wheezed.

She forcibly turned his head toward a clearing.

Ryder expected to see the truck bearing down. What he saw was almost more chilling. Four sets of slanted amber eyes blinked at them through the rain.

"Coyotes?" he muttered, breaking his own vow of silence.

Her teeth chattered as she stretched close to his ear. "Wolves, I think."

"God," he breathed. "Just what we don't need."

"I saw one a while back. I thought we'd go our separate ways. Then the second one appeared. Oh, Ryder, I hate to say this, but they appear to be stalking us."

The creatures looked lean and mangy. Where had they come from? Ryder figured food was probably slim pickings on these old mine tailings. Unless maybe the militiamen fed them scraps. He wouldn't put it past them.

"So far they're keeping their distance. Only thing I know that scares them off is fire. Too bad that lightning storm has moved farther north."

Hope shivered. "You are armed, aren't you?"

"A knife is all."

"How far is the mine from here?"

"To be honest, I haven't a clue. You stay to the left of me. I want to be between you and the wolves."

"Great," she said. "So I'll have to watch you get eaten."

"Nobody's going to be eaten. See how they're hanging back. Let's move."

She did, but felt clumsy and awkward as she tried to keep one eye on the scavenging beasts.

"I know we shouldn't be talking, Ryder, but how did you get out here? If you left a car, wouldn't we be better off heading for it?"

His voice, off to her right, grated roughly. "Chris dumped me on the road about two miles from where we'd seen some old mining equipment and what looked like a military-issue portable hoist. It fit in with the other stuff until I started thinking it's what they'd need to lift the missile out of the silo for refueling. Anyway, to make a long story short, that's where I was headed. To take a closer look. Finding you was pure unadulterated luck."

"Ryder, I know the piece of machinery you mean. It was right outside the series of caves where these nuts have set up camp. A cherry picker isn't all they've got. They have enough munitions to put a crater the size of Lake Michigan in this area."

Without warning, Ryder gave her a massive shove that sent Hope flying behind an outcrop of rocks. He dived right behind her, curling his body over top of her.

Nerves on edge, Hope started to sputter indignantly at the uncalled-for treatment, but even as she opened her mouth, the blinding searchlight they'd seen before cut through the shroud of darkness and lit up the countryside on both sides of the mound.

"Come on, bitch, we know you're out there." A gravelly menacing voice bounced off the outcrop and rolled over them.

Hope tried to disappear into the soaked earth but shook so hard from fear she was afraid her trembling would give away their hiding place.

The voice spoke again, saying something that touched off a series of swearing. "Lookit there! I'll be a monkey's uncle if it ain't a pair of wolves. Pass me the gun, Weasel. Come on, man. The light's stunned 'em. I got me a clear shot."

Ryder willed the wolves to hightail it away, and fast. If the men shot one and came after the carcass, he and Hope would certainly be discovered. Yet he didn't dare throw anything to scare them off. Or did he? The men with the searchlight appeared to be arguing among themselves.

Chancing it, Ryder picked up a small stone and tossed it between the ears of the big lobo. It glanced off another rock with a tiny ping, but it was enough to startle the animals. They bolted and scattered. One tore off into the underbrush, and the other scrambled up the hill.

"Dammit!" shouted an angry voice. "I could have had me a nice fat wolf tail to hang on my truck antenna. Why didn't you gimme the damned M16?"

"For one," a deeper voice growled, "we're not hunt-in' wolves, we're lookin' for the broad. Second, automatic gunfire is just gonna bring the dude helpin' her down on us.''

"Really? Well, Weasel, we wouldn't have lost her if you'd done your job. Catch me lettin' some skirt deck me with a rock.''

"I'm tired of saying it wasn't the broad that hit me. It was a guy. This big dude stepped outta the storm and laid me out with a chop to my neck.''

"Oh, yeah," jeered another, higher-pitched voice. "Like he knew lightning was gonna strike that bush and give her a chance to run. You're strong as an ox, man, but don't try and lie. You're about as bright as Alaska in January."

This was followed by some guffawing and backslapping. Hope and Ryder heard doors slam. Suddenly the light was snuffed and an engine coughed once, turned over and purred. The sound grew softer as the truck lumbered away.

In spite of the rain that continued beating down, neither Ryder nor Hope moved for ten minutes. Not until total silence engulfed the desert once more.

When Ryder finally did venture out, he indicated by a signal of his hand that he wanted Hope to stay put.

She, of course, popped up, sticking to him like glue. With the wolves going in one direction and the men who'd held her captive in the other, she wasn't about to get separated from the only person she trusted to keep her safe.

Trusted. The thought froze her for a second. She trusted Ryder to get her to shelter. Trusted him with her life. But not with her love, or so she'd thought. How foolish. Why had she let herself get embroiled in a useless tug-of-war? The minute they landed somewhere

where they could talk, she'd do her best to convince him that life was too short to spend alone pining for a lost love. April was dead. He needed someone alive to care about him. Hope knew he did.

Her heart hammered so loudly it almost deafened her as she swallowed her fear and stumbled along at Ryder's heels. As one step followed another, Hope blotted out the bone-numbing discomfort and blanked all worry from her mind. What if they never made it to safety? Those men out there were armed. There'd been at least three in the truck, maybe more. She and Ryder were a long way from town, and they were walking in the opposite direction. What would happen if the two of them failed to get back? If they didn't stop the extremists' plan to kill the president, who would?

Yet, after a time, though her heart was willing, Hope's physical strength waned.

Ryder sensed when the wet sand that sucked at their each and every step began to sap her stamina. Furthermore, he'd kept an ear tuned for the truck. And unless his radar was off, the distant growl of the engine was circling toward them again.

At a point when Ryder half led, half carried Hope, luck smiled on them for the second time. They ran into a cluster of abandoned mining outbuildings. The entire area was fenced. Regular chain link and not electrified, Ryder noted happily.

"Here." Breaking silence, he hauled Hope close to the wire. "I'm going to boost you over. Then I'll follow. Try not to touch any part of the fence."

"Why? Is it electric?"

He shook his head. "No, but this time they've brought dogs. It's to be expected. Underground militia brag about their hunting skills. All are trained trackers."

Several levels of fear made Hope pinch her lips into a thin line. "Then we're done for. At least I am. Leave me, Ryder. You've got to stop them. I eavesdropped enough to know their target is Camp David. They've scheduled a hit while the president and his wife are vacationing there."

Ryder swore, then said, "I'm not leaving you, Hope. I didn't figure they were mad at a simple grocery store. Whatever their target, it was bound to have political repercussions. That's how they operate. Please, honey, just do as I ask. Get over the damn fence."

The endearment helped her to make up her mind. She used the last bit of her energy to clear the top links as Ryder tossed her high. She didn't, however, see that being corralled, so to speak, would help them one iota. They'd merely be like rats caught in a trap.

But Ryder vaulted the fence as if he hadn't a care in the world. He landed in a spray of water and mud. He hurriedly checked the buildings, seeking one he'd deem least likely to be a hiding place were he the tracker. Most were falling down. A storage shed, a bunkhouse with broken windows. A general store. An assay office—the sign still intact. This must have been one of the gold mines Ted mentioned, as opposed to the pit copper mines.

Ryder's eyes lit on a rickety ladder leading up to an old water tower. From the size of several holes in the bottom of the rotting tank, the thing didn't hold water.

"No," Hope protested feebly as he tried the ladder. "Ryder," she protested. "There's no telling what's taken up residence in there."

"It may not even hold our weight," he muttered. "But as I see it, it's our only chance. We don't have much time—the baying's closing in.'' He reached down a hand.

In an act of blind faith, Hope lifted her hand and clasped his wrist. She stifled a scream when one of the rungs broke and they slid back two steps. If anything, Ryder only climbed faster.

At the top, he shone the flashlight he hadn't dared use before inside the structure. The far side seemed to be solid. At least it wasn't broken, and he didn't see any squirrels' nests or rats.

Turning off the light, he fit his hands around Hope's narrow waist, lifted her over the edge and deposited her inside. ''Welcome home, sweetheart,'' he whispered. ''Step lightly. Go all the way to the west wall and sit.''

''Where are you going?'' She couldn't prevent the note of terror in her voice.

''Nowhere. I'm going to dismantle this ladder and bring it inside.''

She heard his labored breathing and little else as she crept to the corner he'd indicated. Actually, it wasn't such a bad hiding place. The roof of the water shed still covered this section, leaving it fairly dry and providing a respite from the pounding rain.

Piece by piece, Ryder tore off the rungs of the rotting ladder until he had a fair stack of wood inside. The last thing he did was use one stick and rub it repeatedly around the rim. Then he dropped silently to his feet and moved to Hope's side.

''Why did you do that?'' she asked. Hope really wanted to ask how they were going to get out when the time came but was afraid of jinxing their chances if they should be fortunate enough to escape their present danger.

''I didn't want to leave any sign of fresh wood.'' Ryder froze for a fraction of a minute, then flattened his fingers over her lips. "Company," he said softly. "And we aren't going to invite them up for supper." He ripped off his goggles and indicated she should do the same. Stripping off his jacket, he snugged it around her shoulders.

Shivering in spite of the coat's warmth, Hope listened to the rumble of a truck engine and the deep-throated baying of hounds. When light from the spotlight danced through the many holes in the body of the structure, she hid her face in Ryder's warm coat and held her breath, awaiting the discovery that would surely come.

CHAPTER TWELVE

FOR WHAT SEEMED like endless seconds, the dogs lunged at the chain-link fence, yapping and howling. A crash and the horrendous tearing of metal alerted Hope and Ryder that the men in the truck must have driven through the fence, rather than scaling it as he and Hope had done.

Dread trickled into Hope's heart. She fought claustrophobia. She couldn't breathe.

Sensing her unrest, Ryder sought her face in the velvety blackness. Cradling her chin with his palms, he sheltered her with his body and stole a soul-sustaining kiss from her lips.

As she was drawn into the kiss, Hope's panic subsided.

Below them, men shouted as they sloshed through the muddy mine yard. Gutter language mingled with the frantic yip of the hounds. Every sound echoed in the chamber that hid Hope and Ryder's reunion from prying eyes, and though he could have drowned in Hope's kisses, a disciplined part of Ryder's brain followed the progress of the angry trackers. Their erratic actions, he judged, were fast growing out of control.

The most vocal of the trackers kicked in a door to an outbuilding. Soon his buddies followed suit, demolishing the empty shacks along the crumbling boardwalk.

Ryder imagined he could smell the wet fur of the dogs

snuffling back and forth beneath them. He tensed and drew back from Hope. The hounds' masters swarmed around the rickety tower, obviously convinced the dogs had picked up a scent.

Hope clung to Ryder, afraid to breathe. Someone bumped one of the tower supports. The old tower swayed. Hope cringed, fearing it would tumble.

Ryder identified the release of a rifle safety a heartbeat before a stutter of bullets bit holes in the weathered wood opposite them. Reflexively he curled around Hope's body, all the while cursing himself for having set them in this death trap. He hadn't dreamed that in their frustration the hunters would riddle the tower just for kicks.

A second volley sprayed over their heads. Ryder felt a searing heat high on his left shoulder. His only thought was that if anything happened to Hope, he'd dive out of here and kill the one responsible with his bare hands.

Burrowed tight against him, her slight body shook like the ground below a passing freight train. All Ryder could do to reassure her was hug her tighter and press soundless kisses in the wet hair above her left ear. Any sudden movement on their part would surely invite further wrath by their would-be executioners.

"Dammit, Weasel." A rough voice from directly below them rose through the broken boards and the new bullet holes. "What in hell are you doing? You wanna bring the law down on us, you stupid son of a bitch?"

"Old Blue acted like he'd treed a coon."

Ryder heard a slap of wet material and a scuffle of sorts.

"Hold it, brothers," a sterner voice ordered. "Old Blue probably got wind of a rabbit or skunk. Weasel, take a good look at that old tower. The dame'd have to have sprouted wings to be hiding up there. I scouted this whole site. I say we're wasting time. Eventually she's gotta try and reach the road if she hasn't already slipped past us. I tell you we'd be smarter to patrol the mine road.''

''Yeah, Weasel. I don't know about you, but I'm mighty sick of tramping around in this rain,'' someone with a sulky voice put in. ''I'd a whole lot rather drive up and down the road in a dry truck, and maybe play some tunes to pass the time.''

''Okay, dudes, but if we don't find her skinny butt, the boss is gonna kick yours.''

''We'll find her.'' The voices receded slowly. Following a shrill whistle, the dogs also pattered away.

Hope stirred. Ryder tightened his hold on her to warn her not to be too hasty. They had yet to hear the sound of the truck's engine.

Even after the roar, the grinding of gears and the skid of tires over wet sand, Ryder wasn't in any hurry to abandon their dry nest.

When he tested his shoulder with his free hand, he found that his arm was bleeding profusely. And what if they'd left a guard behind? Ryder had a sick feeling that the man called Weasel was blessed more with the mentality of his hounds than his pals gave him credit for. A man who worried about repercussions from his boss might strike out on his own.

Ryder wished he knew the name of that sickest of all the sick minds involved in this scheme. To rally men and convince them he could pull off a missile launch under the very nose of the air force required a powerful, charismatic leader. Most of those types were listed on a database at the Pentagon. A hint that one of them had his fingers in this pie, and help would come running. Provided he got to make the call.

Apart from the residual runoff dripping into the structure through missing sections of the roof, Hope didn't hear a sound. "Ryder? What are we waiting for?" she murmured.

"I need time to think our options through." He rolled her off his lap. The pain in his shoulder almost caused him to black out.

"You sound funny." Hope peered through the darkness. "How many options do we have? Shouldn't we work our way to the mine or back to my folks' house?"

"I've been hit, Hope. Help me rip the tail off my shirt so I can bind my arm."

"Hit? Hit how?" She scooted closer.

"Weasel's target practise came a little too close for comfort."

Hope sucked in a breath. She touched the hand he had clamped over his arm and hers came away sticky with the blood that oozed between his fingers.

"Why didn't you say something sooner?" Yanking her blouse out of her jeans, she tore off a strip of fabric around the bottom. "Can you slip your shirt off? Dare we turn on a light? Oh, Ryder, the bullet isn't still in there, is it?"

In spite of the wave of nausea that washed over him when he tried to shrug off his shirt, Ryder laughed tightly. "My shirt is off. No light. And the bullet passed through. Could we dispense with the questions? They're making my head swim."

Hope had climbed to her knees and now crawled close to Ryder's left side. Since her eyes had finally adjusted to the darkness, she had a fair idea as to the length of the ragged hole in the fleshy part of Ryder's upper arm.

"We should clean it," she muttered, more to herself than to him.

"I have two canteens of water, but that's all, I'm afraid."

"You have water and haven't offered me a drink?"

"We were in the pouring rain. I figured if you wanted a drink, you'd stick out your tongue."

She huffed a little but made him bend over so she could pour the contents from one canteen over his wound. "Sorry," she said as he gasped and flinched.

"Forget it," he said. "Just bind it tight enough to stop the flow of blood."

She did, ever mindful of his pain.

Once she'd tied the final knot and helped him thread the shirtsleeve over his arm again, he leaned over and kissed her hard.

Her fingers faltered and stopped doing up buttons. "What was that for?"

"Between you and me, I always thought if I took a bullet, I'd slough it off like the men in those old war movies. I hate to tell you how queasy I am. We should take off, but I don't think I can just yet."

She laid her head on his good shoulder and slid her arms around his waist. "You're allowed, Ryder. And you were very cool. I didn't even know you'd been hit. My mom cut her hand once while she was washing a glass. She hollered for my dad to get her a towel. He came in, saw all the blood and fainted. Real blood is a lot different than those fake packets they use in Hollywood."

"Um. I suppose. Speaking of your dad, he and your brother are probably going out of their minds with worry. They intended to take turns patrolling the mine road. I'd hate for them to run afoul of our good buddy Weasel.''

''I'm sure they'll be careful, Ryder. And our surly pals with their macho truck, spotlights and dogs are pretty obvious.''

''All the same, instead of hiking up to the mine, maybe we'd better try to cut straight to the road. Your dad and Chris planned to switch cars every so often and run the perimeter road. They shouldn't be too hard to spot. There's not a lot of traffic.'' He levered himself up with his good arm. ''Ready?'' he asked her quietly.

''Let's not rush, Ryder. You need to rest. I could go alone and direct Chris and Dad back here to pick you up.''

He rolled his eyes. ''Not only no, but hell no! We'll blow this place together or we'll rot here. Come on. I'm feeling better already.'' He climbed to his feet, then almost toppled.

''Liar. You're white as a ghost. Why don't you catch a nap? Another half hour or so won't make a difference to the ultimate outcome of this mission.''

Ryder slipped back down the wall. He fumbled in his shirt pocket and brought out two flattened energy bars. Passing one to Hope, he said, ''I wish we knew the ultimate outcome. These boys play hardball. Unless we can convince the brass in Washington they mean business, there's you, me, your brother and some thirty over-the-hill-gang members in this backwater posse. We've no authority to invade their camp. Nor will I risk going in with weapons.'' He closed his eyes and leaned back against a board that had cracked as a result of one of the bullets. ''It'd help if we had an estimate of how close they are to launching.''

She chewed and swallowed a bite of her honey-and-raisin bar. "They won't launch until next week or the week after. That's when the president is slated to go on vacation. At least according to the news report I heard."

"You have to know they'll rush the shot now that we're onto them."

"Still, it won't do them any good to fire before the prez gets to Camp David."

"What's to keep them from reprogramming and, say, aiming it at the White House? They're single-minded fanatics, Hope. Not a conscience in the lot."

Hope touched a tongue to her still-swollen lip. "Believe me, I know."

Ryder hooked the back of her neck with his good hand. "I forgot about that bastard hitting you." His thumb traced circles around the soft flesh underneath her chin. "Did I hurt you when I kissed you a while ago?"

"No. You couldn't." Her lashes fluttered down over her bright eyes. "When we kiss, you make me forget everything."

A warmth blanketed all that remained of Ryder's fury at her captors. He coiled one of Hope's drying curls around his forefinger, let it loose, then touched another. "Doesn't seem right to get personal with so much at stake."

Her eyes swept the craggy lines of his face. *Get personal!* she wanted to shout. But of course she didn't. She only allowed herself to stroke Ryder's wrist. It was a strong wrist attached to a gentle hand.

"There's so much I want to tell you, Ryder. Being held captive makes a lot of things crystal clear. The past crashes in. The here and now stretches into infinity. The future means nothing. I discovered a person shouldn't hold anything back. There are no guarantees we'll have tomorrow."

His eyes looked tawny in the shifting light. "Duty knows no calendar, Hope. But before we leave our safe little cocoon, I'll let you in on a secret. I had exactly the same experience when your dad phoned the office to ask if I knew where you were. I can't explain the emptiness I felt after finding the notebook. Then, when Chris and I flew over every inch of this countryside without unearthing a trace of you or your car..." Ryder's gravelly voice broke. He swallowed repeatedly.

"I wonder what they did with my car? It'll be next to impossible to explain to my insurance company if it never turns up."

"Will you stay put right here?" Ryder cut in. "I hate the thought of them getting their filthy hands on you again. I have a better chance of evading patrols if I hike out of here alone."

"Don't insult me, Ryder. Can you honestly say I've slowed you down?"

She had. She'd tired and lagged, which was why he'd taken cover in the first place, but she probably would have stuck with him all the way to the mine even if she'd been dead on her feet.

Ryder glanced away from her hurt yet faintly accusing eyes, and ran an inquisitive hand over the bandage she'd applied to his arm. It seemed to be solid. "Then if you're ready, I suggest we go. Before the moon decides to show her face."

"All right." She straightened and attempted to stuff the uneaten portion of her energy bar into her jeans pocket. They were still damp and stiff and resisted her efforts.

"Eat that thing. No need to save it. I have two more. We'll need every ounce of energy this sugar has to offer." Taking his own advice, Ryder ate the remainder of his own bar. He washed it down with a swallow of water and passed her the canteen.

"Okay." She made a face as she folded their discarded paper wrappers and tucked them in his shirt pocket. "I'm ready to jump over tall buildings in a single bound if you are."

Her attempt at humor made Ryder smile. "That statement may be more truth than fiction, Hope. The closest and best way out of this tower is to bust out more of these floorboards and drop straight down."

If he thought the threat of dropping blind would deter her, he soon found he was wrong. She crept to the largest gap and began prying up boards with her bare hands.

Since Ryder only had the use of one hand, she did most of the work. Nevertheless, they were both sweating by the time they had uncovered a space large enough to allow Ryder's shoulders to fit through. Even then, he scraped his arm and broke the bullet wound open. He said nothing even though he felt blood trickle over his elbow and drip down his arm.

Remembering what Hope had said earlier about the uncertainty of the future, Ryder stayed her with a hand, pulling her back into a quick, unexpected embrace. "If...when we get out of this mess, Hope, I want you to know that I'm never letting you out of my sight. Lord knows I'm no prize. I foolishly let you go once. Consider this fair warning, lady. This time, well, you're not getting rid of me."

Her feet tangled in the trampled fence. She blinked up at him. "Not getting rid of you? What exactly does that mean, Ryder?" Her heart, still pounding from the long drop into the muddy black void, tripped even faster as she waited on tenterhooks to hear the long-awaited declaration of love.

"I guess I mean mar...marriage," he stammered, unable to marshal all his scrambled thoughts. She looked so vulnerable, mussed and muddied. "Yes," he said tenderly. "That's what I mean." He thought he sounded supremely confident, considering how he'd lost faith in the vows and the promises that went with the ritual—especially the part about in sickness and in health.

Hope picked right up on the absence of the L-word. Six years ago she'd assumed he loved her. She had never heard from him again. Why was she so terribly afraid Ryder's current proposal was due to the insanity of their situation? Hadn't she said that a person got pretty maudlin when forced to face their mortality?

The bald truth in her case was that Hope doubted very much she could survive another six years if Ryder McGrath faded into the sunset again. Was she selfish not to want to open herself up to that kind of pain? She didn't think so.

"Whose career gets set aside?" she asked brutally. "Mine would be the logical one, seeing as how you have the higher rank. Except I happen to like flying, and I have a lot of time invested, too."

Careers? Ryder hadn't thought that far. "I...ah...well, never mind. We'll talk about this later."

Hope shut her eyes. "According to my mom, everyone in the military needs a wife to keep the home fires burning when Uncle Sam sends us into the wild blue yonder for months at a time. Who will tend our kids if we're both off and gone?"

From the shaken look on Ryder's face, Hope knew her question had not been well received. As he sprinted off, fading into the shadows, she fought a deep desire to retract her careless words. The truth. The bottom-line truth: she'd take him on any terms. A person could survive in a one-sided marriage. He said she'd made him forget April once. If that were so, perhaps in time he'd store memories of his wife and child in their rightful place. Why hadn't she had the courage to live her life according to her newfound convictions?

Her heart had so many fractures in it now, it seemed silly to be so protective of it. Especially as it now sat like a lump of coal in her chest. And from the set of Ryder's shoulders, she'd venture to say he was having second thoughts. A sigh, the biggest yet, almost turned her inside out.

The mere mention of Hope having kids had sent Ryder into a tailspin. April's doctor—hell, everyone—said her death wasn't a result of her pregnancy. Intellectually, he knew that. Emotionally, the two were tied inextricably. And losing a child—well, Hope didn't know—the pain never completely went away.

He deliberately blanked his mind to everything but setting one foot in front of the other. Ryder couldn't bear the thought of Hope suffering as April had. He'd almost rescinded his offer of marriage. Would have if he hadn't caught the lights of a vehicle off to the right. Did they belong to the men he and Hope were doing their best to avoid or to those with whom they wanted to connect?

His wound throbbed incessantly. If he could put on an extra burst of speed, he might be able to flag the car down. Motioning for Hope to hurry, yet cautioning her with a finger to his lips, Ryder set off at a bone-jarring run.

Hope shied at shadows caused by dark clouds sailing by overhead. Deep pockets in the loamy soil still held water from the recent rain. Slop sucked at her shoes, and more than once she landed in puddles that squished over the top of her sneakers.

Twice she slowed and nearly lost sight of Ryder.

"What's gotten into him?" she wondered, dodging a tree branch he'd let fly back. She could only imagine that the two of them must sound like a couple of buffalo charging through the underbrush.

Finally, when a stitch in her side demanded she ask for a break, Hope saw him lying flat behind a row of fat spiny yuccas. *Had he passed out?* She started forward at a lope. He gestured frantically for her to be cautious. Sinking to her knees, Hope crawled forward on her belly. She swallowed a yelp when her elbow connected with a broken cactus pad. When she stopped to pluck out a row of spines, she realized an arc of light illuminated the thicket that should have concealed Ryder. Beyond the flimsy covering, within spitting distance, ran the gravel road that led to town. The light came from two parked vehicles. Fear lanced through her. One of the vehicles was the black pickup.

Ryder was wearing his night goggles. Hope tugged hers on with shaking fingers. Burned into her mind was a memory of Weasel brandishing an M16. What was Ryder thinking, sneaking this close to the enemy?

Her heart almost stopped beating when the goggles brought into focus a clear picture of her brother Chris, spreadeagled across the hood of a light tan car she didn't recognize. Two men in camouflage gear similar to what Ryder wore, appeared to be arguing with Chris, though she couldn't hear what they were saying. If the dogs were still in the back of the truck, they were being remarkably quiet.

Now where was Ryder headed? Slithering forward like one of the desert snakes, Ryder used his good arm to propel himself closer to the parked cars. *Had he gone nuts?*

Not wanting to be left behind alone, Hope made sure her hair was all tucked beneath Ryder's cap, then she followed.

He stopped before he'd gone more than a few yards and shoved a metal tube of camouflage grease into Hope's hands. He'd already smeared his face and hands.

Taking it gingerly, she opened the tube with a grimace and did the same. She wanted to laugh, and wondered if the danger and lack of sleep had finally triggered hysteria. But with the grease, mud and goggles, Ryder looked like some space alien. Hope supposed she did, too. Ah, well, she thought, capping the tube, now the man she loved had truly seen her at her worst.

When they drew as near to the group as they dared, Hope saw this was a different black truck. *What did those jokers do, buy at fleet prices?*

She hadn't seen Chris in almost three years and allowed herself a moment to drink in the sight of him. Though she and he had gone through life as fierce competitors in academics and sports, they'd also been best buddies. Hope loved him without reservation, and she regretted that it'd been so long between visits.

The two men hassling her brother were young and fresh-faced. Like the others in their outfit, they had buzz cuts and looked as if they worked out with weights. And Chris wasn't much of a fighter, Hope knew. Unless he'd changed, and she doubted it, he preferred to call himself a lover.

She tensed when the two punks started to shove him around. So did Ryder. It showed in the way he gathered his lean frame into a crouch, as mountain lions did right before springing on their prey.

He wouldn't—would he? He was already wounded, and they didn't even know if these yokels owned guns.

But he did lunge out of the bushes. Right before her very eyes. Though it took Hope a minute to collect her wits, she probably wasn't so far behind after all. Fortunately they had the advantage of surprise. Also the advantage of three against two once Chris discovered the idiots who flew out of the cactus patch screaming like banshees were in his corner.

The men—boys, really—were subdued in due course. Chris's belt served as handcuffs for the one who struggled the hardest. Hope ripped a second strip off her blouse to bind the second one's wrists. "Crop tops are in," she joked.

"You're a sight for sore eyes." Chris hugged her, then held her away and grinned. "A sight, anyway."

She slugged him even though she felt like weeping for joy.

Chris gripped Ryder's right hand. "Clipped your wing, I see, old man. If you got that freeing Hope from the clutches of these sons of bitches, the family's much obliged."

"Save your thanks till the work is done. We tangled with clones of these two about an hour back. I'd hate to let them have another go at me tonight. If you roll these clowns into the car, I'll drive the truck and we'll go someplace and interrogate them."

Chris smiled. "I have just the place. Dad's ragtag army commandeered the air force association office at the armory. It's handy to the museum. Some interesting activity there tonight. We delayed a strike until you rescued Hope. You sure took your sweet time doing it, McGrath."

Ryder's grin was more cocksure than his condition warranted. "And I was just beginning to like you, too, flyboy." Helping himself to the pickup's keys and getting spit on in the process wiped the smile from Ryder's face.

"I hate to take any more of that blouse, Hope, but we really need to gag them. And don't take your eyes off this one for a minute. It's going to be my pleasure to extract information from Big Mouth here."

Shackling the men's feet proved to be wise. Both, though silent, butted at their captors and attempted to make a run for it. Ryder ended up karate-chopping one into snoozeville. The other took the hint and entered the car peaceably.

"You know," Ryder told Chris, "it'd be better if we ditch their truck fast. Follow me to that strip mall. The one that's well off the highway. We'll park it behind one of the buildings and let the police have it after we round up the rest of these characters."

"Unless they sold my car across the border," Hope said. "It's really not a fair trade for my convertible, but if it's the best they can do…"

Ryder gave her a thumbs-up as he climbed into the fancy black Chevy.

"You bought a convertible?" Chris demanded after the two of them entered his rental car. "Man, how can you afford the insurance on that?"

"I don't spend everything I make trying to impress a battalion of men from my little black book, little brother." She winked.

A sappy look changed the contours of his face. "I guess the folks didn't tell you, huh? My black-book days are done."

"They told me." She shifted her gaze, still not sure how she felt about the news.

"You'll love Jennifer. She isn't just another pretty face. She's funny and smart, too."

"Not so smart," Hope said cheekily. "Or else why'd she choose you?" He was so far gone on Jennifer he didn't even rebut her insult. *Sickening*. On the other hand, it was good to see how hard the mighty had fallen. Smiling to herself, Hope thought she might like Jennifer after all.

Chitchat dissipated after they met up with Ryder. He spent the next few minutes attempting to interrogate the peepless chicks.

"Real talkative, ain't they?" Chris drawled.

"Yeah," Ryder muttered. "In case our presence at the armory isn't all that secret from the honchos at the museum, I suggest muzzling the Bobbsey twins here. Can we smuggle them in through a back door?"

"Sure. We'll swing by the house and pick up a roll of duct tape. Mom'll sleep easier knowing Hope's been found, too."

"I wasn't lost," she said sourly.

"Oh, no?" Ryder said. "What do you call it then?"

"Misplaced," she shot back. "And don't forget I'd already escaped before you showed up, hotshot."

His eyebrow arched. "Well, excuse me all to hell for interfering in the wrestling match between you and Weasel."

At hearing the name of their compatriot, the smallest of the prisoners jabbed his elbow in the other's ribs. Only he was still out like a light. Hope picked up on the move. "Know Weasel, do you? You ought to choose your friends more carefully, kid. Weasel is going down for assault with a deadly weapon, for carrying a banned automatic rifle and for anything else we can nail him for. I predict Weasel's going to be doing hard time till he's old and gray. Might go easier on you if you sing a bit."

"You cops?" the kid snarled. "The creampuff's ID said he's a prostitute for Uncle Sam."

Chris glared in the rearview mirror. "Who're you calling a creampuff? This one's mine, Ryder."

"You'll get your turn. The way I see it, since we're working unofficially, the Geneva rules don't apply."

Chris's high-beam smile could have been classed as feral. The wattage was still turned up as he swung into the driveway at his parents' home.

"Don't tarry with your lady," Ryder warned. "And grab a change of clothes for your sister while we're here. Who has the Hum-V? My duffel is in it."

"Dad borrowed it to collect the spare gear his cronies had squirreled away. He's assembled quite an arsenal. Wait until you see all the pilfered USAF junk. I think he expects you to forget that you saw it, though," he added with a chuckle.

Ryder didn't remind him that he'd said no weapons. He hadn't figured on having to go up against such a well-organized group. Weapons didn't have to be loaded to make an impact.

He continued to mull over the strategy of attack after Chris returned and they'd gotten under way again. His mind assembled and rearranged details when Chris doused the car's lights and eased quietly down a shadowy path.

"Why don't you and Hope take the lively lad in first. I'll stay here with Sleeping Beauty. You can send someone back to help with him."

"Okay." Ryder already had an armlock around the neck of the troublemaker in case he had any ideas about making a break.

What Chris hadn't said, or maybe didn't know, Ryder

thought wildly when all at once he and Hope were hit from two sides, was that Ted Evans had posted lookouts.

A hard head rammed his bad shoulder. Ryder grunted in pain and lost his grip on the prisoner. From behind, someone bashed his skull. Ryder crumpled in a flash of stars, a tuneless song rattling around inside his brain. He slumped to the ground, not quite understanding what Hope cried out. Had he failed her again? Ryder struggled to keep his eyes open, but darkness overtook him.

"Mr. Fletcher!" Hope howled, grabbing the raised arm of her dad's oldest friend. "Stop! You're killing Ryder. He's already injured. Help him inside. Right now!" Hope didn't realize her woman's voice was the only thing that kept her from getting bonked, too.

At least not until her dad poked his head out the door to see what the noise was about. He immediately hefted Ryder over his shoulder in a fireman's carry.

"I'm sorry, Major," he said over and over as Hope knelt beside the prostrate Ryder applying cold packs to the goose egg on his head. "We've had such comings and goings here that I posted guards and gave everyone passwords."

"Oops," said Chris as he staggered in under the weight of the unconscious prisoner. "I plumb forgot about the password. Frankly, sis, if you'd take a look in the mirror, you'd see why Fletch made the mistake."

"If you've caused serious injury to the man I love, Chris Evans, you'll soon be laughing an octave higher."

Hope flung herself down at Ryder's side again, sponging his face tenderly. Her worry was such that she didn't fully register the shock on her brother's face.

CHAPTER THIRTEEN

GROANING, Ryder blinked several times. Hope's anxious face came slowly into focus. He rubbed his head and felt a good-size lump. "Did we get ambushed?"

"Yeah, in a manner of speaking." Hope cast a humorless glance at the men who milled around the room. "By our own side."

"Ooh. Ah." Ryder didn't object when Hope guided him into a sitting position. He finally managed to zero in on the other anxious faces hovering above him. "Where are our prisoners?" he asked testily.

"We've got 'em. Never fear." A man stepped forward and handed Ryder a cup of coffee. "I'm damn sorry, Colonel. It was dead black out, and, well, we weren't expecting you to drop in unannounced."

"It's okay…Fletcher, isn't it?"

Ted's friend looked abashed. "Yep. I sorta hoped you'd forget who I am. Hafta say I feel like a fool."

Ted Evans slapped his friend on the back. "It's good you didn't hit him any harder, Fletch." Hunkering down beside Ryder, the elder Evans stuck out his hand. "Mighty glad you're back, my boy. Mighty glad. The major already briefed us on the particulars. I took the liberty of separating your prisoners and interrogating them. You've caught yourself some bad-ass boys."

"Who?" Ryder asked, halting with the cup partway to his lips.

"Well, one told us to go to hell, so we only have the younger fella's word. He boasted that they're a branch of the Lightkeepers."

"Damn." Ryder's coffee slopped over the cup's rim. A cold bead of sweat trickled down his spine when he thought of Hope's having been in their clutches. "Guess I was wrong about their discipline being shaky." Setting his cup aside, he raked a hand through his hair. "They're one of the most organized of the fanatical groups, Ted. Suspects in several political kidnappings. Antigovernment from the get-go. Slippery as eels. So far the CIA hasn't been able to pin anything on them, but if they're bold enough to steal a missile and target the president, they will."

"I know decisions aren't up to me, but I figure we've only got three hours until daylight. If we don't round 'em up fast, those bastards will scatter."

"You're absolutely right," Ryder said. "We've got three targets to hit simultaneously. The museum is yours, General. I'll take the hideout. Chris can hit the civil defense office in town. So pick your men carefully. Does anyone have a phone? It's time I let Beemis know exactly how things stand. We'll still have to do the dirty work, but he'd damn well better send in a mop-up crew to cart the trash out of here." Ryder climbed to his feet with less alacrity than he'd have liked.

"Pick your *men?*" Hope, who'd been silent throughout, elbowed her way between Ryder and her father.

"You're not going, Major," Ted stated flatly.

Ryder tried to be more diplomatic. "We need someone to stay here and keep an eye on the prisoners, Hope. An active-duty person to brief whatever crew D.C. decides to dispatch. It's hard telling who's available or where they'll fly in from."

"A chimpanzee could brief them. If anyone stays, it should be you. That shoulder wound is in danger of infection. Besides, who'll pinpoint the hideout? You and I connected quite a ways from the actual caves where they've set up operation."

Ryder delivered his most persuasive smile. "Mark the spot on the map your dad spread out on that table." He turned to Hope and gave her a friendly push in the right direction. "I have to go make that call."

"So you're saying I can't see this through to the end?"

Ryder let his eyes slide away from her searing gaze. She knew as well as he that since Beemis pulled the rug out from under this investigation, he was no longer in a position to give her orders.

"You've been in the field two nights and a day without sleep. You're half-dead on your feet. Please…wait here?" He wanted to kiss her, but settled instead for filtering his fingers through her hair as he fell short of begging for her cooperation.

"Okay. Sure, Ryder." She pulled away, walked over to the table, bent over the map and picked up a felt-tipped red pen with shaking fingers.

Ryder swiveled, locating Ted and Chris. Did they think it odd she'd capitulated so fast? Both men shrugged. Ryder figured they knew her best. Relaxing, he continued into the room Ted indicated, shut the door and dialed General Beemis—who seemed truly rattled when Ryder reported all that had transpired in the past forty-eight hours.

Still the man in charge made no concessions.

Ryder's forehead puckered. "I agree my proposal is highly unusual, sir. I know these men are civilians. They're also here and ready, General. We don't know if the missile has already been fueled and armed. Major Evans eavesdropped enough to know their intended target is the president's vacation retreat. Since the devils know we're onto their scheme, what's to stop them from beefing up their launch date and targeting Capitol Hill?''

Ryder listened intently as he paced the length of the phone cord. "Not being privy to their fuel source, I can't recommend bringing it down with antiballistics, sir. Can we afford to gamble that they haven't stolen nuclear fuel?''

The general's voice squeaked back urgently. Ryder gingerly touched his bandaged shoulder. "I understand. You'll do everything you can. But, General, waiting for authorization takes time—and we don't have any to spare." He scowled. "So be it. If anything goes wrong, I'm acting on my own. Yes, I'll take that risk."

Ryder replaced the receiver slowly. For a moment he did nothing but stare at the large framed air force insignia that hung on the wall behind the desk. And at the photographs of men in flight suits and bomber jackets, some dating back to early Vietnam. There was a good possibility the men he'd committed to battle were some of the same ones whose pictures graced these walls. Retired men with rusty skills. Civilians in every sense of the word, as Beemis had pointed out so caustically.

No sense telling himself they were embarking on a joyride. There was a distinct possibility he was about to flush his entire career down the toilet. Involved in a battle with his conscience, Ryder wasn't aware that Hope had opened the door quietly and stood watching him.

"D.C. still doesn't believe you, Ryder?" Crossing the room, she clutched his arm.

He rested a hip against the desk. "There's no mistaking those SOBs' target, is there, Hope?"

"No. Why?"

"Beemis has to go through channels. He's worried about sticking his neck out. So mine is on the chopping block." He gave a self-conscious laugh. "He'll send backup, but if we're wrong..."

"Oh, Ryder. No. What are you going to do?"

He kissed the tip of her nose and for the first time tumbled to the fact that she'd changed clothes and washed her face. He felt all the grungier. "It's called making a field decision. Promise me, Hope, if anything goes wrong, you and Chris will clear out. You two have never heard of me, understand?"

She smiled into his wonderful, beautiful face and nodded, daring no more. "I came to tell you Dad is ready to finalize strike details." She casually linked their hands. "The bathroom is two doors down, Ryder. I left you a towel and a change of clothes in there. A team leader should look the part."

He grinned at that. "Pilots do hate to get their flight suits dirty." Ryder scrubbed at a grease stain on his shirt. "At least it's honest dirt, Hope. A couple of pilots in your squadron got real dirty. Remember my telling you my real mission at Monahan was to corral a ring of airplane-equipment thieves?"

"Yes. Are you saying it's someone I fly with?"

"Beemis confirmed. The last of the pilots we arrested confessed. A Major Denton. Denton and two others, Major Todd Phillips and Airman Second Class John Weaver, along with three flyers from Luke, smuggled plane parts into Mexico, then sold them abroad to the highest bidder. Not to our allies, either."

Hope's mouth gaped. "Lance Denton? A thief?" She broke into a grin. "Prison couldn't happen to a more deserving guy. Here I thought his biggest crime was harassing defenseless women. Well, well, you've made my day.''

"If you have something concrete on Denton's treatment of female personnel, I'll gladly listen. I can't imagine he'll get off, but I've seen some slippery legal eagles get some real scum buckets off with no more than a slapped wrist. I want these guys nailed."

"It'd do my heart good to see Denton taken out of circulation. I'll tell you everything I know when we're finished here."

"Did that jerk hit on you, Hope?"

"He tried. He was more obnoxious than threatening. The other day he had the nerve to suggest I might be up to something shady. John Weaver saw us carting boxes into the lab at the U. I never got a chance to tell you. What causes men like that to go bad, do you suppose?"

"If I knew, Hope, I'd market the formula and make life a whole lot easier for all the poor devils who have to do my job. Speaking of jobs," he said, grimacing, "I'd better get on with the one that fell into my lap."

"Right. What's next after you tie this up, Ryder? Will you zap off to parts unknown to solve another crisis?"

He fingered the points of her collar, urging her to within kissing distance. "I'm not going anywhere," he said huskily. "When I negotiated leave, I requested to stay put until you and I hammer out our future."

Their future? Hope's heart did handsprings one minute and bottomed out the next. Ryder sounded sincere. She wanted, with all her heart, to believe him. Hope might have questioned him further, but Chris stuck his head around the corner and told Ryder to step on it.

"In a minute," he said, brushing a kiss across Hope's lips before he moved away. "Give me five minutes to wash up."

Chris withdrew.

Rattled, Hope lingered in the hall. Not wanting to appear obvious, she drifted into the outer room and wandered from group to group, absorbing the various plans. She'd come so far with this mission, and now she felt a bit left out.

"Dad." Hope touched his arm. "You have the toughest task. Your enemies will be protected in the silo. Even if you get lucky and sneak past their radar, they'll overtake you when you break the seal on the door."

Ted dangled a set of keys under her nose and chuckled when she crossed her eyes to see what he held. "They're either awfully arrogant or awfully dumb. No one bothered to change the locks, and no one asked me to turn in my set of keys."

"You old fox. Be careful, though, please. Ryder and I can attest to how mean they are. I'm worried. What if they panic and push the button?"

"My theory is, if they were ready to launch they'd do it instead of chasing after you and Ryder. Maybe I'm all wet, but I'm betting they figured to silence you two then get on with arming the missile."

"They did seem to be playing for keeps."

Chris joined them, flinging an arm around Hope's shoulders. "You want us to leave Fletch here instead, sis? Your eyes look like you're coming off a ten-day drunk. Why don't you go home and sleep it off?"

"Thanks a heap. Although—" she yawned hugely "—I am ready to crash. Would you lend me your rental car for the drive home?"

"Sure. I'll catch a ride with Dad." Chris dug into his pocket and handed her a car key. "But I guess you'll stick around long enough to see Ryder off." He sounded as if it was a foregone conclusion.

"I would if I thought he'd give in and let me go. He won't, I know."

"Izzatso? Don't you have him wrapped around your pinkie?"

"Chris, if the sun were shining, I'd think you had heatstroke."

"Come on. I saw that kiss. And not twenty minutes ago you announced that you loved him. It's *your* brain that's scrambled. Don't gape at me like I'm losing it. I heard…we all heard you. What's the matter?"

She stared at him in horror. *Her record. Ryder's. What if Chris blabbed to the wrong person?*

"I…was…upset by Colonel McGrath's injuries," she explained feebly.

"He…ll…o! This is your brother you're trying to snow. A few years back I heard that you two had a fizzled fling. I planned to punch his lights out if we ever met. I did try. Now…well, I like him. Hell, sis, I guess I'm doing a bad job of saying this, but if you two want, I'll ask Jennifer to make it a double wedding."

"I…I had no idea news of our…fizzled fling, as you so bluntly called it, circled the globe. You never asked me about it, Chris."

"Didn't have to. I told you I planned to punch McGrath's lights out in due course."

She threw up her hands. "Why would I expect you to understand my feelings? You, who cut a swath a mile wide through the female population. Men don't concern themselves with broken hearts."

"Not true any more than you lumping all men under the heading of insensitive brutes. Jennifer is the only woman I've ever promised to love. All the others knew up front I wasn't offering anything permanent. Our splits were mutual."

"That's your perspective. Partings are rarely mutual. Oh, it happened years ago, Chris. Why flog a dead camel? Shouldn't we focus our energy on capturing those creeps."

"Our energy? Aren't you going home to catch some shut-eye?"

"Shows how tired I am. The *we* slipped right out. Maybe I won't wait for Ryder."

Chris cracked a smile. "Come on. I'll walk you to the car. It'd never do for our sentry to bonk you on the head. Your poor brain is already stretched beyond its limits." He yanked on a curl, and she jabbed him in the ribs. A ritual they'd observed since childhood.

RYDER BUNDLED HIS dirty clothes as he came out of the bathroom. He'd have preferred a shower, but scrubbing his face and putting on clean things made a big difference. He was glad Hope had badgered him into taking the time.

He glanced around the room, wanting to thank her, and was disappointed when she wasn't there.

Ted rapped his knuckles on the table before Ryder had a chance to check any of the back rooms.

"Quiet, everyone. Here's our strategist. Colonel McGrath is attached to Special Forces, for those of you who haven't met him. It's been a while since most of us participated in this type of briefing, so it's imperative we listen closely and commit each step to memory."

"I have CRS," shouted a jolly bald man in Chris's group.

Chris eyed the man with concern. "Is that some sort of palsy?"

"Nope." The fellow laughed until his belly shook.

"Has to do with aging, boy. Those initials stand for 'can't remember shit.'"

Ryder didn't mind the men releasing tension by telling bad jokes. He'd toss a few out himself if Beemis's words weren't still ringing in his ears. Especially the part about him standing alone if it came to sucking up a failed mission.

Ryder favored his injured arm as he repacked his duffel.

"Timing is the most important issue," he said to the men. "I want everyone to synchronize his watch with mine." He read the time and told them to mark it. "I'm giving you a specific hour, minute and second for our individual strikes."

"Why does it matter if we all hit at exactly the same instant?" a man wearing horn-rimmed glasses asked.

"Because," Ryder answered sharply, "we don't want point A contacting point B or C and giving the enemy time to prepare for our arrival."

"Gotcha. But won't it take less time to round up the group at the civil defense office, supposing anyone's even there at this hour, than it will for your team to drive out to the caves?"

"Right. Which is why my outfit will leave first. Mine, then Ted's. Chris's group leaves last. Speaking of the caves, maybe Hope has a more accurate guess at how long it'll take for us to get there." Ryder scanned the room again, this time looking more than puzzled when he didn't see her.

"She left," Chris told him. "Fletcher's staying to guard the prisoners and meet the men you have flying in." When Ryder didn't resume speaking, Chris added, "Hope looked beat, Ryder. Sorry. I had no idea you'd want her.'' He checked his watch. ''She ought to have reached the folks' place by now. You could call her.''

Ryder puckered his lips with his fingers. For a moment his mind remained on Hope. He'd expected her to stick it out to the end if for no other reason than the satisfaction of seeing the gang rounded up.

Though reluctant to admit it, Ryder was disappointed that she wouldn't be here to finger the son of a bitch who'd dared strike her. Ryder looked forward to some private interrogation time with that particular militiaman.

''I'll phone if you'd like,'' Chris offered.

''No,'' Ryder said, slowly emerging from a fog. ''Let her rest. I know the type of terrain out there, and she marked the caves on the map. Give me a minute to do the calculations.''

He did them and double-checked figures. ''Okay, men. Here's the plan.'' Counting the recruits off by twos, Ryder again cautioned everyone to make certain their weapons weren't loaded. ''You may all be ex-military, but your status now is civilian, as my D.C. contact so kindly stressed. You all know those Washington cats have hard heads, so here's the deal. Zero authority, and I have one hundred percent of the liability if this mission goes sour. Anybody who wants to walk, I'll understand. No hard feelings.''

No one even glanced toward the door.

''All ri...ght!'' He closed a fist in the air. ''Then let's get down to it. You men set to raid their office—don't tear through town looking like a bunch of commandos. For you, easy does it.''

''Yo.'' Chris agreed for everyone on his team.

Ryder's eyes met Ted's. ''I trust your crew knows more about the museum and the silo than I do.''

''We all worked there,'' Ted told him. ''Our goal is

to take them by surprise. We don't want the devils escaping into the blast-lock area. The doors weigh six thousand pounds each. If they engage the hydraulics, depending on how far they are in the load-launch process, we might not be able to stop them.''

"We have to stop them," Ryder said through gritted teeth.

Ted nodded. "Don't expect you'll walk in and secure those caves without a few rough minutes. The major said they were dug in tight. They're sitting on a munitions keg of dynamite. They could decide to torch it.''

"Anything's possible." Ryder searched through a pile of gear. He handed out tubes of grease, hats and all the night goggles he'd been able to lay his hands on. Each man took a roll of duct tape to bind the feet and wrists of prisoners. "Okay. We know we're not headed to a birthday party. The main thing is to stay alert. Avoid their gunfire and cover each other's backsides." Ryder again marked the time, then led his eleven men out to a volunteer's van. He planned to ditch the van and hike over the top of the mine tailings where he and Hope had set up surveillance, then sneak down the other side to the caves. He counted on the fact that sentries would only be posted in the vicinity of the camp.

The men inside the van said little as they left the armory.

"I forgot to mention that they have at least four hounds," Ryder muttered. "Anyone know how far human scent carries?''

No one did. On reaching the appointed site, one man ventured timidly, "If we're going in above them like you say, Colonel, I doubt the dogs'll sniff us out.''

"Thanks." Ryder told him. "We need the element of surprise to get between the bozos and their stash of weapons. From here on, there'll be no talking. Securing that cache of arms is our first priority. Nothing else interferes. *Nothing.*"

IT WAS A RUGGED HIKE. They ran into a sludge pit that necessitated changing course in order to skirt it. It cost them time. Ryder worried that Ted's and Chris's teams would beat them, which meant that his target might get tipped off. Sweat trickled into his eyes and plastered his shirt to his chest.

He breathed easier after they'd wriggled on their bellies to a crest above the caves and overlooked a camp that appeared normal. Small groups of men sat around fires drinking coffee. Although, at 0330, Ryder would have expected more to be asleep.

The wind shifted suddenly, and so did Ryder's sense of well-being. Too many militiamen were up and about. A sixth sense he'd depended on more than once to save his hide punched Ryder hard in the gut. Then he saw what made him jumpy and why the enemy appeared calm.

"Hope." Her name scalded his tongue. The bastards had her lashed to a spindly tree. Tape covered her mouth. There was a cut over her left eye that'd leaked blood down her cheek. A black-and-tan hound dozed at her feet. Within arm's reach sat a bruiser, whittling. His six-inch blade gleamed evilly in the firelight.

Stomach heaving, Ryder crept back from the ledge lest he upchuck and give away their position.

He saw tension in the faces of his cohorts and knew they'd also identified the problem. For the first time since he'd joined Special Forces, Ryder felt the odds were too great to risk going in.

But his rationale was purely personal.

Even as he wanted to die inside, Ryder knew in his frozen heart he'd have to do what needed doing. Seconds ticked by as he played out all the angles. No matter how he looked at it, the odds stank. Sweat ran thicker and colder. His timing had to be perfect. If ever he earned the name Strategist, let it be now. Somehow he had to sneak silently into the viper's den and reach Hope at the exact moment his team created a disturbance by swarming down from above. And he had to pull it off within his original time frame so as not to jeopardize Hope's dad's and brother's campaigns.

Ryder made decisions fast. He whispered terse instructions and barely waited for confirmation before he belly-crawled down the slope. He had no other choice but to trust Ted's inductees to do their jobs.

It took him eight seconds longer than he'd allotted. Which turned out to be just as well. The noise of volunteers landing in camp with their rebel yells startled both the whittler and his dozing hound. Flying past Hope at a low run, Ryder hit her knife-wielding guard with a two-footed karate kick to the upper gut that dropped the creep like an imploded building.

The hound ran in confused circles. Then as if sensing Ryder held the upper hand, he slunk toward the colonel on his belly. "Good dog." McGrath spared him a pat before he ran to loosen Hope's bonds. As tenderly as possible, he peeled the tape from her mouth.

"Ryder, I'm sorry," she started to say. Midsentence she broke off, dived around him and rammed an elbow into the throat of a goon brandishing an automatic rifle. The blow stunned the man. Ryder ripped the weapon away and felled the man with the gun butt.

"Hope, get the hell out of here." Panting, Ryder dislodged the clip and tossed the weapon aside.

She gave him a withering look. Then she entered the fray shoulder to shoulder with Ryder.

If he landed a blow to an enemy's neck, Hope aimed for the guy's groin.

Twice Ryder ordered her to take cover. Both times she nodded, but when he met the next challenge, she stood glued to his side like his shadow. After a while he gave up and accepted her help. They feinted, ducked and kicked as if choreographed, deftly moving in and out among Ted's recruits, who gleefully punched out militiamen right and left.

The fracas didn't last long in clock time. Their luck ran high. The men seated around the campfires were the only ones holding this camp.

"Where are the others?" Ryder gasped after he and Hope together decked an Uzi-wielding oak of a man whose full beard failed to cover a scar that ran from his right cheek to his ear.

Hope shuddered. She didn't answer Ryder until they had the giant securely taped and dragged into the cave with his pals. "It's my fault," she said for Ryder's ears alone. "The bulk of their force went to the missile site. We have to hurry and help Dad."

Ryder never questioned the validity of her statement. He assigned three of his team to stay behind to guard the prisoners and the munitions. He asked another to hike back and collect the van.

"My vehicle...er...Chris's car is parked a ways off the mine road," Hope said. She patted her pockets and eventually produced a key.

"You drove yourself into this hotbed of thieves?" Ryder caught hold of her elbow and spun her around. Anger and disbelief erupted in a string of curses. "Is that what you meant by saying it was your fault?"

"What do you take me for? A fool?" She touched two fingers to the ugly bruise on her cheek. "They had men watching the armory. I'd driven less than a block. Four men forced me off the road. One held a gun to my head, another had a knife at my throat."

"It's okay, Hope." Ryder wanted to take her in his arms, but he didn't dare. The mission wasn't over. He allowed himself only a brief touch, a fingertip outlining the fragile curve of her jaw. "When I think they might have killed you rather than use you as a decoy…"

Hope clamped a hand on his wrist. "Don't. I wasn't afraid. I knew you'd come."

Ryder softened his expression. "Whoever hurt you is going to regret it."

"It could have been worse, as you said. I let them think you and I had a disagreement, which was why I left the armory. I said I wanted to try and talk them out of firing the missile." Her shoulders slumped. "Their leader is crazy, Ryder. He has Satan's eyes. He's the one who hit me. He uses that signet ring they all wear like brass knuckles. I believe he would have killed me this time, except a younger man, his second in command, I think, convinced him you'd try to take the caves. It was the assistant's idea to use me as bait."

"If we can connect with Chris's crew and meet his team at the museum soon, will we be in time to lend your dad a hand?"

She bobbed her head. "I'm sure they haven't loaded the fuel."

Setting her aside, Ryder barked orders at his volunteers. "Three of you stay and wait for Harry to bring the van so you can haul this garbage out." He nudged the toe of a bound dissident. "And round up the hounds. We can't leave them out here to starve. The rest of you come with me. We'll take Hope's car. I don't care if we have to sit three deep and get stopped by the police. About now I'll take all the help I can get.''

"Dad's cell phone is in the car," Hope told him as they hiked to the vehicle and began to squeeze in. I stuffed it between the seats before they forced me to open the doors."

"What good will a phone do? Chris doesn't have one."

"No, but we can call the armory. Maybe your recruits arrived."

Ryder smiled. "We do make a good team," he said.

Embarrassed by his praise, Hope busied herself digging out the phone, glad she'd committed the phone number there to memory. Fletcher answered on the fourth ring. She gave sketchy details. In return, he said Chris and his crew had returned. Also the men General Beemis had dispatched.

Greatly relieved, but still concerned for her dad, Hope passed the phone to Ryder.

"Fletcher. Get every available man over to the museum site on the double. Tell them to lie low and wait for us. Our ETA is five minutes. We're driving Chris's rental car. Yeah," he muttered after a pause. "That's a long story."

"I suppose you'll have to report my kidnappings," Hope said after Ryder closed the phone. She bit her lip. "If…if anything bad happens to Dad, they won't have to ask me, I'll resign."

"That's the last thing your dad would want, Hope. He's loving every minute of this. Ted knew the danger going in. I pulled and read his military file, as you suggested. He's a wily, tough old wolf. I predict he'll live to dance at our wedding."

His easy reassurance rekindled Hope's fading dreams. *Our wedding.* Suddenly she was impatient for their crusade to come to an end. If she had a future with Ryder, she wanted to know.

"Will you wait this out in the car, Hope?"

It pleased Hope that he asked rather than commanded. "I can't sit idle, Ryder. Not when the majority of the men I love have their lives on the line." *Men she loved.* It had a nice ring. Ryder, her father and Chris.

"You know I don't have authority to stop you. Don't take unnecessary risks. Please!" This time he did beg.

TED AND HIS MEN were in the middle of a heated skirmish when Ryder, Hope, Chris and their band of volunteers stormed the silo area of the museum. Luckily the militiamen weren't stupid enough to fire the weapons they carried. Zealots or not, it was obvious none of them wanted to fry if a nuclear propellant tank ruptured. The fight merely bloodied noses and bruised a few heads. Ryder's old bullet wound was the worst casualty.

He only needed one look at the pack of shackled toughs to know which man led the band. No one, Hope included, objected when Ryder indicated he had a score to settle with him. Ted clapped Ryder on the shoulder and discreetly hustled the others out. Chris stayed.

Ryder held back purposely. It would have been too easy to kill the SOB after what he'd done to Hope, but the slimeball didn't know he was dealing with an ethical man, and that served Ryder's purpose. He circled the bastard's neck with his hands and pressed until he had the pleasure of seeing fear blot out every last shred of cockiness. "I won't kill you," Ryder said, easing his grip. "I want the satisfaction of watching you hang for treason. Take him away." Ryder shoved him at Chris, who happily prodded the fellow up the narrow, winding flight of stairs. "Bind him so tight that if he moves it'll cut off his circulation to vital parts," Ryder growled when they reached the top.

"Roger that." Ted beamed, jerking the spitting, choking man toward one of the vehicles.

Back at the armory, the natural evolution of a successful mission progressed into noisy chatter, cigar smoking and back-slapping. Ted Evans strutted along the row of bound prisoners. "I know where these dirty dogs are headed. What are we going to do with the real bowsers?"

Ryder swung around to look at the sleepy-eyed hounds. "Damned if I know. I hate to take them to the pound. Any suggestions?"

"Do you think they're trained sniffers?" Hope asked. "If so, I can check with a couple of guys I know at border patrol. They have a big dog unit."

"Good idea, Hope." Ryder smiled. "We can vouch personally that these dogs can track. Go phone your friends, why don't you?"

During the time she made her call, Ryder compiled a list of the captives. They weren't forthcoming with names. Dawn was breaking by the time he had enough information to phone Beemis with a report.

Ryder had a hard time swallowing the gushing reception he received from the general. Fortunately Beemis wasn't the man to whom he usually reported. Ryder phoned him next. General Tolliver was out of pocket. Ryder left his number. Before all hell had broken loose, he'd filed paperwork asking for a duty change. Tolliver should have his request by now. It'd be nice to be able to tell Hope he was staying put.

His two duty calls completed, Ryder went out to relay Beemis's congratulations to the men involved in the raid.

Then he had things to settle with Hope. Ryder tried unsuccessfully to corner her. Someone always interrupted, although he kept her in sight. She should be falling-down exhausted, but she handed out endless cups of coffee, each with a smile.

At 0600, Dory and Jennifer, having been summoned by Chris, bustled in carrying dozens of doughnuts. That prompted another round of stories. All Ryder wanted was to escape with Hope to some quiet hamlet where they could talk. He was tired of rehashing a mission that might well have ended badly.

Dory clapped her hands and gained everyone's attention. "You all have reason to be proud. But now that security police have carted off your prisoners, shouldn't you grab a few hours' sleep before the media descends? What do you say to reconvening at a barbecue potluck in the park at 1600? While you men rest, I'll phone your wives and arrange it."

"A first-rate idea, Dory," Fletcher shouted. "Give the reporters one whack at us."

She held up a hand. "I hope you don't mind if we consider it Chris and Jennifer's engagement party, too. Poor Jennifer. I think she's beginning to wonder what kind of nutty family she's marrying into." The observation earned scattered laughs. She'd succeeded, however, in prompting them to tie up loose ends.

Ryder pulled Dory aside. "I need to talk privately with Hope. Do you have any idea where we can go to be alone?" He studied her gravely. "If things go as I'd like, you may have a second engagement to celebrate at the barbecue."

Her answer was to hug him gleefully. "Privacy,

huh?'' Dory thought hard. ''Atmosphere wouldn't hurt, either. There's a quaint Spanish-style motel at the edge of town.'' She supplied the name. ''You'd better call for reservations now, before the news networks book all the rooms. Your whereabouts will be our little secret.''

''Not too secret. I have a call in to my superior,'' he lamented. ''Who knows what he'll say about the way I stepped out on a limb. Would you do me a colossal favor, Dory? Run Hope over to that motel in about half an hour. I need time to arrange a couple of surprises for her.''

''I like the way you do things, Colonel. Ted proposed to me in front of his entire squadron. It was the last thing I expected. He swept me off my feet.''

''I'm not that showy,'' Ryder said uncertainly.

''I'm sure you'll make Hope feel special, anyway.'' Dory patted his arm. ''Signal me when you're ready to leave. Oh, this is so romantic.'' She scurried off.

Ryder wound down quickly. His head reeled as he left. Hope *was* special. The million-dollar question was how to convince her she was the most special woman in his life.

CHAPTER FOURTEEN

RYDER LEFT a second message on General Tolliver's voice mail. Ending assignments always left Ryder antsy. More restless this time because, depending on Hope, he entertained the idea of taking a new direction in his life. If Tolliver agreed, nothing more exciting than pushing papers from A to B.

Before last night's raid, he'd never suffered such bone-numbing fear during an operation. Finding Hope tied to that tree, odds stacked against rescuing her, he'd lost all objectivity. He'd lost the necessary ability to coldly block out all but the ultimate goal. Granted, none of his superiors would know, because it hadn't been an authorized mission and his would be the only report. It was enough that he now knew there were stakes so high he'd never be willing to pay the price. For a wild moment, Hope's welfare had taken precedence over the mission's outcome. And as long as he knew at a gut level that his capabilities had a cap, he'd always and forever face that niggling doubt. True, he'd faltered for only a second, but in this job, seconds often stood between success and failure. Between life and death. He had limits. He could never have sacrificed her. Never.

Besides, he thought ruefully, he was getting too old for scaling water towers in the dead of night. Too old for snaking down rocky sidehills on his belly. His body had protested a few rounds of kickboxing after that fast five-mile hike, too. There were plenty of young guys itching to take his place. So let them. Precisely what he'd tell Tolliver when he called.

Arguments in place, Ryder turned his thoughts to more pleasant matters. Namely, his date with Hope. Heady anticipation erased his sore joints and aching muscles as he pulled up outside the motel office.

Pale golden rays of sun backlit the distant mountain range. A perfect day, he thought as he filled out the room registration and instructed the desk clerk to give Hope a key.

Rushing out again, Ryder made up his mind to buy Hope a ring. A visual token of his intent. He'd also pick up a sexy nightgown. Silk, he thought. Green to match her eyes. Eyes that would go soft and dark when he slowly peeled her out of the cool material. This time there would be no barriers to stop him. None that were real or imagined. Except, he realized with a jolt as he entered the town, no stores were open yet. It was too early.

He had to settle for an all-night grocery store. At least he had no one else to fight for a choice parking place.

Once inside the nearly empty store, Ryder paused beside a cooler displaying champagne. He reached for a bottle, then remembered Hope didn't like the taste. As he shut the door he noticed cut flowers in the next case. He vacillated between a bouquet of yellow roses or one of pink carnations. His heart skipped a little as he realized he didn't know Hope's favorite flower. Pressed for time, Ryder chose the roses because he liked them best.

Next he picked up a box of chocolates. Afraid flowers and chocolates were too clichéd, he added an assortment of helium-filled balloons. All stated what Ryder hadn't as yet told her—*I love you.*

On his way to the cashier, he passed an aisle of stuffed toys. Sappy? Probably. Shrugging, he added a funny-looking, soft, floppy-eared dog to his stack of purchases.

The clerk, a wrinkled man with snowy-white hair took in Ryder's torn and dirty camouflage clothing, his face still streaked with traces of black grease. "A newlywed headed home after a week on desert maneuvers, huh?" the old man teased.

Ryder paused, a hand on his wallet. "Overkill?" he asked, checking out the array of gifts.

"Nothing of the sort, son. The trouble with couples today, they're too busy earning money to spend any of it on keeping romance alive in their marriage. Me, I've been married fifty years. Still try to take my wife a surprise present at least once a month. These flowers are nice. Believe I'll buy my wife some, too."

"We're not married yet," Ryder told the man as he paid the bill. Then he felt stupid for confiding in a complete stranger.

The clerk winked as he returned Ryder's change. "Asking is real painless. What you gotta know is, does it hurt to think about spending the next forty years without her, and does she hurt the same? Forty years go by fast if you spend them with someone you love. If you spend 'em alone, they'll trickle by one darned day at a time."

Ryder considered the clerk's advice as he gathered his purchases and carried them to his vehicle. For six years he'd avoided the issue of wanting Hope in his life. The years had dragged. Then one day he'd known it was time to see her. Time to square things. He'd wangled a project at Elmendorf. Hope had transferred out.

Had he wanted her so much he'd just assumed she'd toss six years of hurt aside and welcome him with open arms? How many times over the past weeks had he witnessed her pulling away?

A lot.

Perhaps holing up with her in a motel room wasn't a good idea. It was entirely possible he needed to rethink things. Give her more time.

But it was too late. As he turned into the motel, he saw Dory's car speeding off down the street. Which probably meant Hope had picked up her key and was even now wondering where he was and what she'd gotten herself into.

Well, he could still play it cool. Take things slower. No sense pouncing on her the minute he walked through the door. No sense going down on bended knee, declaring his undying love for her until she gave some sign that she wanted to hear it.

What might that sign be? He didn't even know what excuse Dory had used to get her here. Ryder fumbled his plastic key card in the lock, wishing he had a clue as to how to proceed.

Hope stood in the center of the room looking dazed. "Oh, there you are," she exclaimed inanely as Ryder stumbled inside, balloons twisting, bouncing and catching on the knob.

"Mom said you wanted me to stop here and that you'd run me home later. I suppose you need me to add to your report."

Ryder dumped the items he'd bought on the bed, except for the flowers, which he carefully set on a nightstand that stood next to a king-size bed. Stepping back, he nudged the door closed. In the artificial lamplight, the bruises on Hope's face stood out. Her eyes looked bruised, too, he thought.

"This has nothing to do with reports," he admitted in

a shaky voice. "We need to talk. People were always barging between us at the armory. Now I think talk can wait. You're hanging on by a thread. You need sleep. I have a clean shirt and sweatpants in the car. Why don't you shower while I get them?"

She picked up the stuffed dog, which had flopped on its face. She smiled in spite of her bewilderment. "Balloons, toys, chocolates and flowers. Are we celebrating someone's birthday at the barbecue? Or did you get these for Chris to give Jennifer? I know Mom said it'd be an engagement party, too."

He shook his head. "I…ah…wanted to give you a gift, Hope. The grocery store was all that was open." He crossed his arms and dropped his chin to his chest. "Pretty bad choices, huh? Who'd eat chocolate at this hour?" He rattled the balloons. "These are really tacky. And cut flowers wilt fast in this heat. The dog…" Ryder gave the plush toy a really hard look. "At the store, I never noticed his eyes were crossed."

Hope extended her arms and studied the droopy stuffed body. "He's priceless, Ryder. He looks like I feel. And the rest…" She waved offhandedly at the bed. "Are chocolates any worse at 0600 than the ten boxes of jelly-filled doughnuts my mom brought us for breakfast?"

Pleased by her attempt to be gentle with his feelings, Ryder released the balloons and let them float to the ceiling. "Say the word and we'll clean up and go find a restaurant. I…uh… Coming here was presumptuous of me."

She circled the balloon bouquet. Their inscriptions were all similar. All bore the word *love*. A word Ryder studiously avoided. Had he bought them for their cheery color? Surely he wouldn't buy balloons that sent a message he'd never let cross his lips.

No. She was so tired her thoughts were getting rummy. It was more likely that, in his haste, Ryder hadn't even realized there were words on the Mylar. And it'd only embarrass him if she pointed it out.

The excited thrum that had kicked over in Hope's abdomen began to fade. He wanted to tell her something, all right, but she was too tired to figure out what it was. Hope laid the toy on the bed and linked her hands in front of her as she stared at the muddy toes of her boots. "I guess, if anything, I deserve a reprimand for jeopardizing the mission. Is that why you asked me here?"

Ryder sounded cross as he stomped to the door and yanked it open. "Maybe we're both too tired to communicate effectively, Hope. Go shower. I'll bring you clean clothes."

She winced when he stepped outside and slammed the door hard enough to jiggle the pictures on the wall. Hope exhaled loudly. She and Ryder never used to have trouble communicating. Since that night they'd back-slid into the old routine and had almost made love on top of the mine tailings, it was as if they'd been walking on eggshells around each other. She looked for ulterior motives in every move he made.

The problem didn't lie with Ryder, but with her. She wanted with all her heart for him to say he loved her. Truth was, no amount of wanting on her part would put the words in his mouth. Why did she have such a difficult time getting that through her thick skull?

When he didn't come straight back, Hope elected to go ahead with her shower. If she didn't, he'd likely find her collapsed in a heap on the floor. Flying AC-130's was a cinch compared to what Ryder did for a living.

Every bone in her body ached. What had enticed him into this dangerous field? When they'd met, she had been so smitten he could have done anything or nothing and Hope wouldn't have cared.

Had April found it difficult to correlate the two sides of him? The tender lover as opposed to the stone-cold protector. Or maybe his wife never saw the Ryder McGrath Hope had encountered last night. The Ryder who would rescue a woman or die trying. How difficult it must have been on that Ryder to lose his unborn son and his wife to an enemy he couldn't fight.

Hope adjusted the temperature of the shower, then stripped out of her clothes. In Ryder's shoes, she'd have gone crazy with grief. Her heart ached for him as she stepped beneath the cool spray. If only he had shared that sad part of his past with her, the two of them might have built their love on a solid foundation. Instead, she'd erected sand castles on shaky daydreams. The future she'd prattled on about must have seemed unreal to Ryder, who on all levels had experienced quite the opposite.

Was that what he'd been trying to tell her over the past few weeks? That he hadn't meant to shut her out, but at the time he'd been incapable of believing in happiness? If so, Ryder hadn't deliberately hurt her.

For a moment, her cares sluiced off her shoulders and disappeared down the drain. Maybe it was possible for them to erase their tragic history and start over again.

RYDER HEARD the splash of water as he walked in. He frowned down at the T-shirts and two pair of sweatpants he'd dug out of his duffel along with his shaving kit. What was he supposed to do with her set? Did he barge in on her or wait for her to come out wrapped in a too-small towel? Neither prospect seemed judicious given his present mood. But of the two, slipping into the bath to drop them off while she was safely hidden behind a shower curtain was probably wisest.

Not so wise as it turned out. The shower curtain was clear plastic. And as Ryder opened the door, air whooshed in and molded the damn thing to Hope's naked body. His mouth went dry, and he was incapable of backing away.

Feeling the rush of cold air, Hope shrank from the spray. The bar of soap shot from her hand and bounced at her feet. She panicked as the plastic curtain wrapped her in a wet cocoon. As she scraped dripping hair from her eyes, fought off the cocoon and chased the soap, Hope sighted the hulking shape of a man. Her scream bounced off the tile walls even as her foot found the missing bar of soap. She wobbled and flailed, losing the fight to regain her balance.

Ryder, used to acting fast, dumped the items he was carrying, ripped the curtain aside and caught her in his arms before she toppled out into the room.

"Are you all right?" he asked, trying to breathe normally as he felt the slick soapy heat radiating from her wet, naked flesh. Hurled into old memories, he paid no attention to the fact that his dirty camouflage shirt was getting soaked by the spray. Urged on by the rapid drumming of his heart, Ryder let his mind take him back six years.

Showering together had been an extremely provocative aftermath to lovemaking. A ritual that had always left him wanting Hope again. But now he held himself in check, waiting, wanting, needing her permission.

Willingness smoldered in the sea-green depths of her eyes, all but begging him, or so he fancied as the water cascaded around them, pooling on the bathroom floor. His body strained toward her, clamoring for fulfillment. She ripped open his shirt and ran wet fingers through the hair on his chest. But it was the words Ryder needed. A simple *I want you, Ryder* would do.

Growing harder by the moment, he slid his hands down over her smooth buttocks and pulled her close to the pulsing, rigid shaft that only she could offer release. "Tell me," he finally growled when he saw her throat working and her lips moving in a silent plea. "What, Hope? What do you want?"

"You!" she cried, releasing the buckle of his belt. "Always you. Only you, Ryder. In me. I need you inside me. Fill me, please, before I die."

He needed no other invitation. Though he favored his injured arm, Ryder tore off his boots and shed his pants with the speed of light. He stepped into the shower still clad in socks and shirt. There'd be time for finesse later, he decided.

Crazy with need, Ryder took only long enough to see that she was ready for him. A touch revealed she was. The instant her legs tightened around his hips, he lost all thought of going slow. He backed her against a cool mosaic wall, and with a groan, buried himself inside her with one thrust. She convulsed around him. Ryder's legs quivered. He braced them clumsily against the wall with his good arm before they both tumbled. *Home. Together at last.* Nothing else mattered.

Tears filled Hope's eyes and her tiredness slipped away. Joy threatened to burst a heart that brimmed over with love. She had to tell him. She just had to. "I love you, Ryder. Love you," she panted, nipping his chin, kissing his lips.

Her words gave him strength to hold out a little

longer. His head felt so light, his heart so buoyant, Ryder barely managed a reciprocal "And I love you" before he climaxed into her, leaving them both shaking and drained.

As they clung together, spent, crying and laughing, Ryder realized he'd forgotten all about protection again. In Alabama he'd always remembered. Always! Alarm grew to overwhelming proportions.

Fighting an old terror, he gathered her tight to his chest, relishing the feel of her stomach flattened against his. *It would be all right.* April's doctors swore that his getting her pregnant had nothing to do with her cancer. Likewise, her miscarriage at six months had been happenstance, they said. A fluke. Only they'd never fully convinced Ryder. If he hadn't given in to April's plea to have a baby, she might still be alive.

"Ryder?" Hope's muffled voice emerging from somewhere in the vicinity of his breastbone, shook him from a fear that gripped him still.

As she laughingly drew away to reach around him and shut off the stream of cold water, he lifted her off her feet and kissed her hard.

"Everything is going to be all right, Hope," he whispered brokenly into the softness of her cheek. "We'll get you to the doctor right away."

She plucked two towels off the rack and pressed one into his hands. "Doctor? Ryder, I hate to be obtuse, but why do I need a doctor? Oh, or do you? Your arm. The bullet wound. Was I too rough? Did it break open again?" She eased the shirt off his injury and saw that the bandage had gotten soaked.

"My arm is fine." He tried awkwardly to wrap her in the towel. Their eyes met. Hers were dark with concern. God help him, but Ryder wanted her again. Knowing all the protection he had was in the small duffel still out in his vehicle, he clenched his teeth and stepped out of the stall and well away from her. "I was talking about the risk we took just now in getting you pregnant, Hope." He looped the towel around his waist and gave a vicious tug on the knot.

"Risk?" She seemed to be having a hard time taking all this in. Granted, she was tired, had been two days without sleep. However, for the life of her, if he meant what he said about loving her, well, none of it made sense. She heard his breath escape in a hiss as he turned his back on her.

"Ryder," she gasped, really missing his point. "I... do...ah...you have some disease?" Her heart galloped madly. She thought surely he must hear the fright in her voice.

"I don't have any disease," he snorted. "What if you get *pregnant?*"

"What if?" She moved in front of him and smiled. "Nothing says married officers can't have babies." Hope yawned, tried to stop, couldn't and yawned a second time. The last came out a purr. She knew she must sound warm and sleepy, like a woman sated. She kicked aside a pile of clothes and tugged Ryder into the outer room. Literally dragging him to the king-size bed, she curled one foot under her and sat. "I feel like a cat that slurped down an entire bowl of cream. I need to sleep, Ryder, so don't tell me if your long-term plans don't involve marriage." Her tone teased, but she needed to hear the truth.

"They do. Of course they do," he said, digging in his heels, afraid she didn't see that marriage and pregnancy didn't always add up to bliss.

She yawned wider, her eyelids drooping as she

flopped back on a pillow. "Come, hold me while I sleep, Ryder. And stop worrying. Last month I had a flight physical. I'm healthy as a horse." Smiling, she curled on her side and fell asleep.

He watched as her fingers went limp and her hand dropped away from his. Her easy assurance that she was completely well pole-vaulted the last fence that cordoned off his heart.

Hope was well. She loved him. He loved her. They'd be married soon. And maybe they'd even have a child together. Someday.

Ryder allowed himself to imagine her blossoming with his child. Their child. The ultimate gift. He lay down beside her, and curved his body protectively around hers. He stroked her arm and smiled when she didn't stir. She would get cold, he knew, so he moved the chocolates and the stuffed dog and pulled the spread up.

Ryder couldn't help himself; he combed his fingers through her wet hair. He sprinkled butterfly kisses from her ear to her chin. She continued to sleep like the dead. Eventually he put an arm beneath his head and just lay there, basking in the happiness of having her beside him in bed again.

During a pleasant lull that invaded his limbs, right before sleep overtook him, Ryder murmured in Hope's ear, "Few people ever get a second chance, sweetheart. Nothing will go wrong this time," he said fiercely. "Nothing."

NOTHING, Ryder discovered, moments after the telephone ejected him out of a sound sleep an hour later, *except his obligation to the U.S. Air Force.*

He sat next to Hope's tightly curled body, already

missing her warmth while he shook cobwebs from his brain and listened to General Tolliver's assistant lob orders.

Ryder limited his replies to monosyllables. There wasn't any sense trying to talk to Tolliver's aide about the request for a duty change he'd filed. He needed to talk directly to the general. Swearing, Ryder slammed the receiver into its cradle after the caller disconnected. Hope slept on. He placed a hand on her shoulder but she didn't move. He shook her lightly at first, then harder. All she did was flop over on her back like a rag doll. She was out like a light. "Damn."

Some jackass at the Pentagon had overridden his request for extended leave. He had forty minutes to get to the base and meet someone from Special Operations who'd brief him on a new assignment. He shook Hope again, but her eyelids didn't even flicker. If her covers weren't moving up and down rhythmically, he'd think she was dead. "Double, double damn."

Ryder pulled on sweats, ran a razor over his jaw and gathered his gear. Maybe he'd be able to drive to the base and straighten things out with General Tolliver before she woke up and realized he'd been gone.

Bending over, he kissed her nose, then her lips. It'd be better if he told her what was happening. Still she didn't stir.

He had time to leave her a note. He scrawled, "0900." Below, he wrote:

Something's come up at the base. Tried to wake you. Couldn't. Will square things away and pick you up here in time for the barbecue. If for any reason it takes longer, ask your mom for a lift and I'll meet you at the park.

The pencil hovered above the pad a moment. Smiling like a fool, he scribbled, "Love, Ryder."

His sleepy gaze rested briefly on the phone. Likely everyone in Hope's household was still zonked. It wouldn't be fair to wake them over a silly misunderstanding involving his paperwork. The worst-case scenario would be that he'd have to do one last mission. If it came to that, he'd just call her and explain.

Ryder was confident he had everything under control.

Wrong! He squealed through the gate thirty-nine minutes later, only to be halted by an M.P. with orders to drive Ryder to a plane that sat tuned up on the flight line.

Impossible, Ryder kept saying to himself.

Inside the plane, a terse Special Ops briefer explained that he understood Ryder had a request in for extended leave and a rotation assignment. "Too bad, Colonel. But General Tolliver needs two men with your expertise to go undercover ASAP. A plane. A brand-new prototype with highly sensitive equipment on board disappeared while on the ground for refueling in Panama."

Ryder's mission: find it before it fell into the wrong hands. The plane in question was so new and so secret that Ryder was warned to tell no one about the nature of his mission. *"No one,"* Tolliver's man stressed. "Overall, Colonel," he continued, "we haven't a minute to lose. Corbett Jordan will be your partner. He's already en route from South America, along with our liaison for Latin American affairs. We have reason to suspect local guerilla forces. Our task force doubts they know what they have…yet. That plane carries enough fire power to wipe several small nations off the map. It's imperative they don't discover its capabilities, Colonel McGrath.''

Ryder went on autopilot. ''When Corbett and I make contact, what are we authorized to ransom?'' He listened, committing everything to memory, then zipped into a flight suit while Tolliver's emissary drummed his fingers on his briefcase.

''I still need to make a phone call when we stop to refuel in Miami,'' Ryder said.

''Negative, McGrath. This is so sensitive you're not to even notify family.''

Ryder felt a sharp pang in his heart. ''I'm still responsible for a temporary assignment at Monahan.''

''Not anymore, Colonel.''

''I have friends in the area. What if they call the office and ask for me?''

''They'll be told you've been transferred.''

''Just that?''

''That's all, McGrath.''

Ryder buckled in for liftoff. He glanced out the window as the air base dropped away. To mention Hope to anyone up the ladder might invite a probe into their relationship. Strict enforcement of the nonfraternization rules had spawned senseless witch-hunts. When all was said and done, Hope would understand. She was, after all, military. Following orders was in her blood.

AN IRRITATING, insistent peal of bells pulled Hope from a comfortable black void. She opened her eyes slowly, and a few pleasant aches, mixed with some that were less pleasant, reminded Hope where she was and the reason behind the pleasurable pain.

Was that the telephone? It sat on Ryder's side of the bed. Why didn't he answer it?

Soon her outflung hand told her why not. His side of the bed was empty. Bright light filtered in around the blinds. What time was it? Her eyes felt as if they were filled with grit and her mouth with cotton. The phone had finally stopped ringing.

Hope found her watch on the nightstand. To get it, she knocked a notepad to the floor. *It's 1600?* "Oh, no," she muttered. "The barbecue started an hour ago."

She stood on legs that protested the move. "Ryder?" When she got no answer, Hope spoke his name louder. She'd just assumed he'd gone to the bathroom. Now she realized the place was devoid of sound. No water running. No shaver. Her heart accelerated. Hope forced her wobbly legs to move faster. She pushed open the door to the only other room. The towels still lay in a soggy heap on the floor. Ryder's clothes were missing, as was his shaving kit.

Hope caught sight of herself in the mirror. Eyes puffy. Hair spiked out around her head. A scabbed cut on her cheek and another on her lip. And were those Ryder's handprints on her upper arms, or were they the marks made by her last captor?

The phone bleated again. This time she had the wherewithal to dash over and pick it up.

"Hope? Is that you?" Her mother's voice sounded altogether too cheerful.

"Ye…ee…s." She covered a yawn with her free hand. "Ryder must have thought I needed the sleep.

Send him back to get me. I promise I'll be presentable by the time he arrives.''

"Isn't Ryder with you, dear?"

Hope licked her dry lips with the tip of her tongue. "Quit clowning, Mom. I'd expect as much of Chris, but not you.''

"The colonel really isn't here, darling.'' Dory's voice faded as if she pulled away from the phone to look for him.

"Wait.'' Hope's foot kicked the notepad. Her heart did a joyful dance the minute she saw the message. "It's okay. He left a note. They called him back to the base. Looks as if he expected to be back by now. He does say if he's detained, he'll go straight to the park. So can you come pick me up? And if it's not too much trouble, grab me some clothes? Don't forget underwear.''

"All right, dear. I'll put Betty Fletcher in charge of restocking salads. Expect me in about fifteen minutes.''

By the time she hung up, Hope had noticed how Ryder had signed the note. She tore off the page to save. This wasn't like last time. He'd just gone to the base for something simple. The capture, probably. Ryder loved her. He'd said so last night, and now he'd put it in writing.

Hope hummed as she showered. Running the washcloth over her stomach, she recalled Ryder's concerns. He'd really sounded upset at first. But having lost a son and a wife, he had good reason. Hope wanted children. She wanted Ryder's children. She was very glad they'd cleared the air.

She was seated on the bed, swaddled in a towel, combing her hair when her mother arrived. Hope waved Dory into the room's lone chair. She took the clothes and disappeared into the bathroom.

"I asked Chris and Jennifer to wait until we got there to do their engagement toast. Maybe Ryder will have arrived by then, too. He hinted earlier that you two might be making an announcement, as well," Dory said.

"Announcement as in a wedding date?" Hope shook her head as she reappeared, and stuffed her blouse into the waistband of plaid walking shorts.

"No?" Dory sounded extremely disappointed.

Hope paused in the midst of gathering the gifts strewn around the room. "Well, maybe that's why Ryder's late. He's so sweet, Mom. He bought all of this to say he loved me. It'd be like him to think he has to give me a ring in order for it to be a proper proposal."

Dory hugged Hope. "I've never seen you look so happy, honey."

They detoured by the house to leave the candy, flowers and other things. Hope was positive Ryder would beat them to the park. It was already two hours past the time he expected to return.

But he wasn't there. People asked Hope about him. And they asked. They continued to ask as she wandered aimlessly among the picnic tables.

Where was he? He was a hero for goodness' sake. He ought to be there to get his own pats on the back. The later it got, the less congenial Hope felt about listening to how he'd single-handedly saved the nation. "My father was the *first* to recognize something was wrong at the museum," she snapped at a television reporter who only wanted to meet Ryder. "The air force retirees played a huge part. No, I haven't seen the colonel. Maybe you should call Monahan and request an interview.''

In fact, why hadn't she thought of phoning him before this? Hope borrowed her mom's car keys and retrieved the cell phone. It wasn't until after the squadron office phone started to ring that Hope realized she was missing Chris and Jennifer's toast.

''Airman Jackson?'' Hope recognized his voice. ''This is Major Hope Evans. Do you remember me? You do? Good. I'm trying to reach Colonel McGrath. Has he left for Verde Vista yet?''

Hope listened. She put out a hand to steady herself. The laughter coming from the park faded in and out as she repeated Jackson's words in a thready whisper. ''He's been transferred? No, that's all right. I understand that they don't tell staff where a temporary duty officer's been reassigned.'' She clutched the phone to her lips long after she'd shut the flap.

But Hope *didn't* understand. Why hadn't he phoned her with the information?

CHAPTER FIFTEEN

NO MATTER HOW hard Hope worked to put on a happy face in order not to ruin the party for anyone else, everyone there knew something was troubling her.

The former military men chalked it up to the letdown that often followed a tense mission. Her family suspected it had to do with Ryder's continued absence. Ted Evans followed her to where she stood alone, gazing out at the highway.

"Why the long face, Major? You, of all people, ought to understand how much time it takes to fill out reports in order to process all those hoodlums."

Hope settled into an empty swing and pushed off gently with one foot. "I called the base. Ryder's clerk said he'd been transferred, Dad."

"The clerk is probably confused. I expect the colonel had to accompany the prisoners. The CIA will surely get into the act. Interviewing those clowns will take days. McGrath will call us with news when he can. He knows we have a vested interest."

Hope stopped the swing. Was Ryder's absence about paperwork? Then why did she feel so uneasy? So lost? Possibly because of something her father didn't know. History had taught Hope that with Ryder it was out of sight, out of mind.

Maybe he'll call tonight. And maybe not, nagged a little voice.

"Dad," she said abruptly. "I've got time left on my leave. Chris has a plane. Why don't we book a bungalow in Acapulco? Jennifer hasn't had any time to get to know the family. We all need a break. It'd be fun." Hope really needed to get away. They all did, she told herself.

For all his bluster, Ted Evans was pretty transparent. He was as hooked on deep-sea fishing as he was on golf. Hope knew the trip was a done deal.

"Great suggestion. A family vacation. I heard Jennifer tell your mother she planned to invest in a fake tan before the wedding. A week at the beach and she'll go home with genuine color." He snapped his fingers. "Say, it occurred to me that Colonel McGrath could use a getaway, too. Those bungalows sleep eight or more. I'll call Pug and get a number for the colonel right after I run this by your mother."

Hope stilled the fluttering in her heart. She'd pay for a day of deep-sea fishing for her dad if he managed to hog-tie Ryder for this trip.

Ted's efforts to track down Ryder that evening all hit snafus. Next day, while the women shopped for their minivacation, he contacted another old friend who worked for the FBI, again to no avail.

Hope got sick and tired of hearing her family's hourly updates on how thoroughly Ryder had disappeared. By day three, she figured if Ryder had wanted to get in touch, he'd have found a way to call.

Dory remained staunchly in Ryder's corner. "Quit fretting." She fluffed off his failure to communicate. "He'll show up when he's finished doing what he's doing."

"Mom." Chris sounded exasperated. "Give us one good reason why he'd duck out without so much as a message? How can you stand up for the guy? Look at the way he's treated Hope. And it's not the first time.''

Ted paused on his way to carry a load of suitcases to the car. ''Treated her how? She only met McGrath at my insistence. They've worked together for a few weeks. Now he's been reassigned. That's the way of the air force.''

Chris faced his father. ''Hellfire! Where have you been, Dad?''

Hope's stomach did double flips. She tried to get her brother's attention. It was bad enough that her mom and Chris knew she'd been stood up twice. She could do without announcing her shortcomings to the world. But typically, Chris plowed ahead with what he had to say.

''Hope and McGrath were having a flaming affair six years ago. This is the second time he dumped her.''

''Thanks a heap, brother.''

''Is that true, Major?'' Ted's complexion turned florid.

''Look,'' Hope said in her own defense, ''I'm not a child. My love life is no one else's business. The Acapulco sun is waning while we stand here talking about it.'' Her voice cracked a little. Unshed tears glossed her eyes. Swiping at them angrily, she turned away.

Ted Evans puffed up to say something. A warning glance from his wife, and he yanked the door open and walked out with the bags.

Dory sidled up to Hope. ''You've always loved Ryder, though, haven't you? Then, and now?''

Hope caved in under her mother's gentle probing. ''Yes,'' she said slowly. Then, tucking a lock of hair behind one ear, she squared her shoulders. ''Yes, yes and yes on all counts. But I'm going to get over him. I never want to see Ryder McGrath again. Nor do I want to hear about him the whole of our vacation. Promise me that if he ever calls here asking for me, you'll tell him the air force sent me to Timbuktu.''

"Are you positive, dear?'' Dory worried her lip with her teeth.

Chris, who stood across the room, scowled at his mother. After persistently tugging on Chris's arm, his fiancée finally succeeded in leading him away.

"I am sure," Hope said bleakly. "I have to cut him out of my head and my heart, Mother. Otherwise, I'll never survive.''

"So be it," Dory murmured, although she looked sad. "Ted has the car started," she said on a brighter note. "Unless we want him to go to Acapulco alone, we'd better hustle our bustles out there.''

THEY RETURNED a week later, the whole group fit and tanned. Hope's bruises had faded, as had the two cuts she'd sustained at the hands of her captors. If her eyes still lacked luster, and if at times they filled with a deep, abiding sorrow, the family was careful to let these moments pass.

Ted, who paused at the sideboard to leaf through a stack of mail their neighbor had collected during their absence, pulled a heavy cream-colored envelope from the center of the stack. "Lookee here!" he exclaimed, waving the item in front of the others' noses.

"Can't you go through your mail later?" Chris groused. "Jennifer and I have to leave. It's a long flight back.''

His father had effectively tuned Chris out. "When's your wedding, son?" Ted glanced up, eyebrows drawn together.

Chris named a date in late December—before Christmas. "I'll check on available military housing for you and Mom as soon as I get back. Jennifer made note of it. For Hope and Rolf, too. But we discussed this in Acapulco. What gives?"

Ted tapped the creamy square on a closed fist. "We're all being given presidential commendations. In the Oval Office, according to this invitation. If my calculations are right, it's the Friday before your wedding."

"Let me see that." Chris plucked the card from Ted's hand. "Phew," he whistled a minute later. "Hope, come see this. This is a big damn deal."

She peered around Chris's elbow, then helped herself to the envelope her father still held. "This only has Dad's and Mom's names on the front. Don't get your wings polished yet, brother. I imagine Dad's being honored because if he hadn't challenged the screwy stuff going on at the museum, the prez and his family would be grease spots by now."

"All of us played a part," Chris insisted. "From what I know of these presentations, they generally include relatives of recipients, too."

Hope stared at the engraving on the card. She was having a hard time breathing. If that were true, then both Ryder and she would receive one, as well.

"Count me out," she said, slicing through their chatter. "I've already arranged to fly to Maryland a day before the wedding. Anyway, they won't expect everyone to attend. Dad can pick up my certificate, or the government can mail it."

Ted looked aghast. "Not accept a presidential summons? That's nonsense."

Hope tossed the envelope on the dining table and hefted her duffel. She ignored the wilting balloon bouquet and the candy Ryder had given her. Almost in afterthought, she unzipped her bag and tossed in the stuffed dog. "My mind's made up. Chris, is it still okay if I hitch a ride to the airport? I'll rent a car there. Dad, if you hear any news on my convertible, call me, please." She hugged her parents, then headed out the door.

Chris and Jennifer lingered several minutes over their goodbyes. Hope guessed from the way they had their heads together that she was the topic of conversation. She didn't care, she thought as she tossed her bag into the open trunk. Wild horses couldn't drag her to D.C. or anywhere else Ryder McGrath would likely be.

She expected Chris to try to twist her arm on the short drive to Tucson. He didn't say a word, and Jennifer talked mostly about the upcoming wedding.

"Now that we've met, Hope, I'd love for you to take part in our ceremony."

"Something simple?" Hope dragged her attention back from daydreams about her own wedding, a wedding she'd never have.

"Trouble is, my maid of honor and bridesmaids have already been fitted for gowns." Jennifer's delicate forehead puckered. "My twin cousins are lighting candles. A close friend is handling the guest book. I've been so busy, Mother has managed most of the details, and I think she's probably attended to every last one."

Chris interrupted for the first time. "Micromanaged is more like it," he said dryly.

Hope curved a hand over the diamond tennis bracelet that circled her future sister-in-law's wrist. "It won't hurt my feelings to just be a guest, Jennifer. I'd hate to upset your mom. Especially if she learns what went on here when we should have thrown you parties. She'll brand Chris's family as out-laws rather than in-laws."

Jennifer inspected a diamond buried in red nail polish on one finger. "Mother…is…well, I wasn't going to tell her and Daddy." She sighed and edged closer to Chris. "Now, with the presidential commendation, I'll have to, I suppose."

"I know Chris says it's a big deal," Hope said. "But not to outsiders. Don't tell them."

"They'll know. Or maybe you aren't aware… Daddy is Senate majority leader."

Hope nearly swallowed her tongue. "Oh," she said meekly, but at least now she understood the micromanaged wedding. "So your wedding's huge?"

Jennifer again dashed a hesitant look toward her intended.

Chris responded with an explosive snort. "It keeps growing. I lost count at eighteen hundred. According to Jennifer's mom, those are her nearest and dearest friends."

Hope clammed up. What more was there to say? She was thankful they'd arrived at the airport. After parting from the happy couple, she made her way up a floor to a rental-car agency. Leaving the elevator, Hope couldn't help comparing her wedding plans to theirs. Once she'd intended to have a small, intimate church service. One attendant apiece. An ivory gown borrowed from Rolf's wife, and Ryder wearing his dress blues. That was six years ago. This time she would have settled for vows at the courthouse in front of a justice of the peace.

Stillwouldstillwouldstillwould. The litany rolled through her brain, and Hope forcefully blocked the silly phrase. *She wouldn't.* Where was her pride? Only a desperate fool would forgive him this slight. Anyway, it was immaterial. Ryder was gone for good.

HOPE'S NERVES almost shattered the day she returned to work, and she pulled from her mail bin a memo scheduling her for an upcoming IFF code-change class. A colonel she'd never heard of had been assigned to conduct it. She crumpled the page, round-filed it and sorted the rest of her mail. *Ah.* She, too, had received an expensive cream-colored envelope that bore the presidential seal. That she tucked unopened into her zoom bag, and threw the whole works into her locker.

The flight line still buzzed with talk of the arrests. Few in the squadron had liked Lance Denton. Hope's flight crew was only too happy to recount the sordid details for her benefit.

"But maybe a parts-smuggling ring sounds tame to you, Major Evans," her flight operations chief said. "Man, nothing but boring ever happens to me."

Hope grinned as she signed off on his clipboard with a flourish. "Frankly, I'm ready for boring."

Except, as she flew her scheduled missions over the next few weeks, Hope found her mind wandering too frequently to the escapade she'd shared with Ryder. She didn't want to think about him, but at thirty thousand feet, flying on instruments, there was little else to occupy her mind. Could it be something about having her head above the clouds that made her mellow toward him?

Time after time throughout November, Hope called Ryder's features to mind. Jet dark hair. Amber eyes. Crooked smile. *Where was he? What was he doing? Was he safe?*

She hadn't visited her parents since the day she left with Chris. Partly because work kept her busy, but also partly because she didn't want to face the memories. Hope decided she'd deal with where to spend Christmas later. She took care of Thanksgiving by volunteering for duty.

Two weeks before Chris's wedding, a week before the commendations were to be presented in D.C., Hope received the shock of her life—Ryder's unmistakably deep voice on her telephone message recorder. He sounded incredibly tired, but it seemed as if he expected Hope to be delighted to hear from him. He gave her a number in D.C. to call him back.

As if she would. Did the man think he could pop in and out of her life just like that?

Hope's mom had left a message on the same tape. She was all bubbly. Full of talk about Chris's wedding. At the end of her rambling, Dory hit Hope with both barrels. "Your father booked you a seat on our flight, dear. If you don't go and receive your honor pin, you'll really let him down. I've never asked much of you kids, but I'm asking this. Rolf is so proud, he's bringing Krista and the children. Be there," Dory said sternly, hurriedly leaving the date and time of the flight.

Hope stormed around her apartment. "I will not be blackmailed. I will not!" Nor did she answer her phone for the next few days.

Ryder left messages. A lot of messages. Hope couldn't believe he had the nerve to sound aggrieved by her continued silence. One night he called every hour on the hour. She unplugged the phone and the bedroom extension. But she didn't sleep. She sat up all night hugging that goofy-looking stuffed dog he'd given her and crying like an idiot.

Next day she felt like a zombie. The remarks of her flight crew underscored the obvious. "You look like hell, Major."

The crowning blow came when, just before checkout, her flight commander called her into his office.

"Sir!" Hope snapped off a salute.

He set her at ease and tilted back in his chair. "I've never had anyone in my squadron receive a presidential commendation before. It's come to my attention that you're intending to skip the ceremony."

"I... That's correct. I'd already requested leave for my brother's wedding."

"You'll attend the awards presentation, too. That's an order, Major."

"Yes, sir." Hope burned to ask if her meddlesome father had called and applied pressure, but the colonel kept her at attention while he lectured her on duty. Hope felt about an inch high by the time he dismissed her. All right, she'd go, darn it. It seemed she had no choice.

"Okay," she said that night into the phone. "You win, Mother. I'm going to fly to Washington with you and collect that damn award."

"Wonderful, dear. I told your father you'd do right in the end."

Hope gnashed her teeth, waiting for Dory to drop some bombshell like telling her she should let bygones be bygones and forgive Ryder. Hope had her speech all worked out. She would not, under any circumstances, see or speak to Colonel McGrath.

"This is our night to host our bridge group, Hope. So unless you have other questions, I'd better run. See you at the airport."

"Oh? I didn't mean to keep you," Hope mumbled. Her mom's apparent indifference rattled Hope. She did not, however, believe her sneaky mother didn't have an underlying agenda. Hope would keep her memorized speech handy.

She felt guilty when, the next morning at the airport, Dory said repeatedly how much they'd missed Hope's visits and how wonderful she looked. Once in the air, Dory donned her grandmotherly persona. All she could talk about was seeing Rolf and Krista's kids.

"I have to admit," Hope confided with a grin, "I almost bought out the toy section at the BX myself."

Dory patted Hope's knee. "Soon you'll have to quit being the world's most generous aunt and concentrate on spoiling your own baby."

Hope's flush was automatic. She gazed out the window at the swirling clouds, telling herself that her mother hadn't meant to be callous.

A moment later, Dory, who sat in the center seat between her husband and daughter, leaned toward Hope and whispered softly, "Oh, dear. Were you trying to keep it secret? But darling, you *are* pregnant. The glow is unmistakable."

Hope spun, struck her head on the window and let out a yelp.

Ted glanced up from the magazine he'd been reading. "Really, ladies," he admonished.

Frantically, Hope dredged her memory for the date of her last period. All she recalled was that one had ended the week before she'd called on Ryder. Helplessly, her fingers spread protectively over a belly that bulged only slightly over a snug seat belt. The wonder of the possibility left her smiling. Then, because her mother was still staring at her curiously, Hope managed to murmur, "It is possible."

Dory covered her lips with both hands. Tears sprang to her eyes. "So you haven't seen a doctor? Don't worry, we'll buy a home-test kit the minute we land."

"Mother." Hope gripped her arm. "Maybe you're

wrong. I've been eating like a horse and I haven't had a speck of nausea."

"Some women don't. I never did," Dory said.

They sat in silence for some miles. Then Hope roused. "Don't...don't tell a soul," she begged. "Not even if you're right. There's so much happening to our family this week." She gestured helplessly.

"But you'll tell Ryder."

Hope wanted to bolt. To hide. Dory's tone implied Ryder would be happy about the news. Hope had a sinking feeling that he'd run and never stop running. That, however, was his problem. He deserved to know if he'd fathered another child. A sigh wormed its way from Hope's lungs. "Yes, Mother. If the test is positive, I'll tell Ryder."

Smiling softly, Dory laid her seat back a notch and promptly closed her eyes.

RYDER SAT between Chris and Rolf Evans at the bar in the officers' club at Andrews Air Force Base. "You're positive she's coming to the awards presentation?"

Chris clapped Ryder on the back. "For the three-hundredth time in an hour, yes. Hope is definitely on the flight with Mom and Dad. Getting her to listen may be a horse of a different color. She can be one stubborn female. I don't envy you, man."

Rolf Evans ordered another round. "Most women would smother you with sympathy once they heard how you were injured bailing out of a plane shot down by guerrillas. Knowing my sister, though, she'll ask why it took you a month to hack your way through the Nicaraguan jungle."

Chris took Ryder's unfinished beer and thrust a new, full glass into his hand. "Yeah. Hope won't care that you tracked down that plane and held off rebels so your partner could fly it to safety. She'll never accept that you were under orders to tell no one.''

"Thanks. You guys know how to make a guy feel good.'' Ryder looked from one to the other of Hope's brothers. "Since you know she's so damn stubborn, help me come up with something spectacular. There must be a way to get her attention.''

Five minutes later, Rolf thumped Ryder so hard on the back he almost tumbled off the stool. "There is a way. Guaranteed. Might be too embarrassing for you, though.''

Ryder sat up straight. "Anything. I can't live without her. I'll walk over hot spikes barefoot from here to the White House if that's what it takes.''

"Well, it's not quite that drastic. Almost. Man, I couldn't do it.''

Chris reached around Ryder and punched his brother's arm. "I hate the way you're always so smug. Spit it out, big bro. Let Ryder decide.''

HOPE STOOD in the bathroom of the house Chris had arranged for them to rent while the family attended the awards ceremony and wedding. Tears of joy tracked down her cheeks, blocking her vision of the bright blue test strip she held. Her mother had been right. She was indeed pregnant with Ryder McGrath's child.

Dory, who'd been waiting in the bedroom, tapped twice on the door and finally stuck her head around the corner. "I heard sniffling. Are those yes sniffles or no sniffles? I can't stand the suspense. Put me out of my misery, Hope.''

"Yes, oh, yes!'' Hope flung her arms around her mom, and they cried together.

Dory pulled back first. "Are we happy?"

Hope nodded as she scrubbed away the tears. "If you only knew how I've longed for a child. With Chris getting married, I felt, well, that it'd never happen for me." She sobered instantly. "I'll have to give up flying. I'll put in for a change in flight status right away. They'll give me flack because I'm single, of course. It's mandatory to list a reason. But I'll never tell who the father is. Mom, you can't breathe a word to anyone. Especially not to Chris or Rolf. If word got out, it could ruin Ryder's career. Not that I reported to him at the time we made love, but...it could get sticky."

"Oh, Hope. You said you still love Ryder. After you tell him about the baby..."

"No." Hope brushed past her mother and stalked into the bedroom. "Now you see him, now you don't. Even if I could live like that, and I can't, think how harmful his vanishing act would be to a child. No, Mother. Ryder and I are through. I said I'd tell him about the baby and I will. I won't promise it'll be this weekend. I still have to get through Chris's wedding. I'm bound to fall apart, and Chris and Jennifer would probably rather I didn't look like a puffy-eyed bullfrog when I meet her family."

"It's your decision, of course, Hope. Please, all I ask is that if he tries to explain his absence, you'll listen with an open mind and heart. Every time he looked at you I saw a man so in love he hurt. For your child's sake, give him a chance to explain."

"All right. Although I can't imagine what he could say or do to change my mind after pulling a two-month disappearing act without so much as a word."

Dory opened the door. "A resourceful man could still pull a rabbit out of a hat."

"That's a magician, Mom. And Ryder's no magician.'' She yawned. ''It's late, and I'm tired from the flight. I believe I'll unpack, shower and go to bed.''

''But, dear. We're meeting Rolf, Krista and the children for dinner in an hour.''

''Go without me. Offer my excuses, please. Tell them I'll see them at the ceremony tomorrow. We're doing lunch afterward, right?''

''Yes, then shopping. Krista is dying to shop somewhere other than the BX.''

EVEN HOPE HAD to admit the next morning that there was an air of excitement surrounding the upcoming ceremony. She thought it was more than pulling into the circular driveway at the White House in a long black government limo. Her mother looked elegant in a seafoam-green, tea-length dress. Her father was handsome in one of his old uniforms. She and Rolf looked pretty spiffy in their dress blues, too. And Krista, with her pale golden hair, holding their cherubic infant, could pass as a real-life Madonna.

Chris, Jennifer and her distinguished parents got out of the next car, followed by the Fletchers and several others from Verde Vista. Not everyone came, of course. Hope had to admit she was disappointed after the last car unloaded. No Ryder. It was obvious no one had given him the lecture on duty.

Lined up behind a guide for the journey inside, Hope refused to let her joy in the day be dimmed. She, Major Hope Evans, had much to be thankful for. A loving family. A good job. And a new life growing inside her.

A hush fell over the crowd as they were directed into rows forming a semicircle around the awesome presidential seal that took up a fair portion of the floor. The vice president entered the room first through a side door.

Hope heard the door she and the others had used open and close again. She didn't turn, for in the next moment the president of the United States appeared. She didn't expect her knees to knock together, but they did. When the president cleared his throat, it was as if no one in the room breathed.

"I speak for myself and all of your fellow Americans when I say thank you for following what was in your hearts." He studied their faces somberly. "I applaud whatever led you to step beyond the chain of command to perform a feat above and beyond simple bravery." One by one he read their names. Those who were present stepped forward to shake his hand and receive a gold pin on their lapels. The vice president passed out certificates etched in gold leaf. Hope was reading hers when Ryder's name rang out. She thought she would faint when the crowd parted and he strode confidently to the front of the room. He wore a cocky grin—and an awkward, heavy cast on his right arm.

Hope's mouth went dry. Her stomach rolled and pitched. Her first thought was that the bullet wound had somehow become infected. But no—that was his left arm.

Their eyes met briefly. His smile sobered, even though the president repeatedly pumped Ryder's left hand.

"Colonel McGrath is the recipient of two awards today." In a few words, the president heralded Ryder's most recent daring feat in the jungles of Central America.

"Mr. President," Ryder said, tearing his gaze away from Hope. "With your permission and that of the vice president and our other honored guests, I'd like to make a presentation myself...if I may."

Appearing ruffled, the president glanced at his contingent of aides. They all shrugged. "Why not? A hero is allowed to deviate from protocol."

Ryder fumbled in his pants pocket. The moment stretched. Finally Chris stepped forward and relieved Ryder of his two certificates. The newly proclaimed hero at last wedged a small box from his pocket. Awkwardly, he went down on one knee in front of Hope.

Her eyes couldn't have opened any wider. Wanting to yank him to his feet, she felt a ripple of laughter from the people huddled close enough to witness the unexpected show.

Ryder popped the lid on the velvet box and extended it toward Hope. A two-carat delicate green diamond caught a shaft of light and made her blink. A collective sigh went up from the circle as everyone leaned around Hope for a glimpse of the gem that mirrored the sheen of her eyes.

"Hope Evans, before God and the elected officials charged with running our country, I apologize for any grief I've caused you as a result of doing my job. I'm not a hero. I'm a man trying to ensure that our nation's a little safer. I've asked to be relieved of that duty. My commander agreed. For I discovered my love for something that stands in the way of doing my job. Or rather, someone. *You, Hope.* You're a hard lady to catch, but now that I have your attention, please...will you marry me?"

A swell of applause started somewhere in the back of the room.

Hope stood frozen in place. Her heart galloped at a breakneck pace. The room and all the faces save Ryder's receded. *Would he want her if he knew about the baby?*

Behind Ryder, the president frowned. "Well, Major Evans? This may well be the first marriage proposal in the Oval Office. Please don't keep us in suspense. The vice president and I have a luncheon to attend in ten minutes for the young royal couple from Spain."

The tips of Ryder's ears turned bright red. He just kept looking at Hope.

Tongue stuck to the roof of her mouth, she nodded once and then twice. She should probably give back that medal for bravery. Hope would be darned, though, if she'd announce to the top boss of all that she and Ryder had gotten the cart before the horse. She finally did manage to stammer out a passable "Ye...e...s."

Somehow Ryder got to his feet. Neither he nor Hope paid attention to the barrage of handkerchiefs that were whipped out to dab away tears as he placed the sparkling ring on the third finger of her left hand and sealed his promise with a kiss. A kiss that went on so long the president and vice president threw up their hands, then slipped away. Attendants tried to usher the other guests out.

Chris succeeded in breaking the couple apart with his announcement. "Jennifer and I agree, you two have time to get a license and join us next Saturday in a double wedding. We won't take no for an answer."

Hope started to protest. "But...I don't have a dress. Ryder and I need time to talk over our plans."

Krista poked her. "We have a week to shop, and all these fabulous stores."

Jennifer's mother fanned herself furiously with her Gucci handbag. "But...but the seating for the reception is set. The caterer..."

Chris's fiancée winked at Hope and turned her entourage aside. "Mom, don't worry. It'll be okay. Call the caterer tomorrow. Order a few more cases of champagne."

"Champagne?" Hope said weakly.

"You don't have to drink any," Ryder promised. "You'll find a dress, Hope. A double wedding suits me. What more is there to discuss?"

"The baby." As Ryder gaped at her, Hope straightened and gathered his good hand to her breast. "I…you…we're pregnant. I intended to tell you soon. Not necessarily here in the Oval Office where the CIA tapes everything," she admitted in a hushed tone.

Shock darkened Ryder's eyes. Hope waited, and when he continued to look shell-shocked, she tried to remove the ring he'd painstakingly placed on her finger.

"Wait. Stop." He carried her fingers awkwardly to his lips. "I know what I said. About the risks of having a baby and all. But dammit, Hope, I don't want to live without you." He slid his hand to her belly and cupped it protectively. "Marry me Saturday and you'll make me the happiest man alive."

The babble of the last honorees to be led from the room drowned out Hope's shaky little "I will."

One thing they taught in Special Forces was lip reading. Ryder read hers.

So did Hope's family, who'd hovered near the door. Now they exchanged high-fives and let attendants shoo them out as Ryder locked Hope in another embrace.

Chris and Rolf sneaked peeks over their shoulders. "We done good, little brother," Rolf said, dusting the area of his heart with the tips of his fingers.

"Yeah, but the real credit goes to Dad. Or Mom for telling us year after year how great he was for proposing in front of his entire squadron."

"His position as the Evans Romeo has been severely compromised," Rolf mused, hooking a thumb toward his soon-to-be brother-in-law.

Their laughter rolled into the Oval Office.

Hope heard as she emerged from that last marathon kiss. "I recognize my brothers' evil laughter. They're planning somethin, I know. Let's elope, instead."

"We can't. I called my parents and my sister last night and invited them to the wedding."

"You knew what Chris and Jennifer had planned? What if I hadn't said yes?"

"At Rolf's suggestion, I was prepared to take my proposal a step higher. I'm really glad I didn't have to beg the commander in chief of all the armed forces to issue you a direct order. You have this attitude about taking orders, Hope."

"You got lucky, Colonel. Very lucky."

"Actually, Major, I like to think I'm resourceful. I had a few other rabbits in my hat."

"Um." *Rabbit in a hat?* "Was this, by chance, a family conspiracy, Ryder?" Her mother had used that term yesterday.

"Remember where we are, Hope. *Conspiracy* is not a word to toss out lightly in D.C.," he said, tugging at his tie.

Hope couldn't resist rising on tiptoe to kiss him again. A loud smack to which she added a few heated moans. Breaking away, she winked at the granite-faced attendant. After dusting her hands together, she led a flabbergasted Ryder past the man. "Let the CIA decode that, McGrath."

Grinning, Ryder got into the swing of things. "I guess it's a darned good thing I refused the CIA's recruitment offer," he said as he tagged after her down the silent corridor.

"Really?" She stopped. "You refused to join the CIA?"

"Yep. You have my word this time, Hope. I'm finished globe-trotting."

"Are you sure? What if you get bored?"

In the middle of the White House hallway, he scooped Hope against his chest with his one good arm. He deliberately circled his palm around and around her back until strong physical sensations traveled up both their spines. Tipping his head, Ryder caught her earlobe between his teeth. "I plan to spend every day of the rest of my life loving you, Hope. You and Junior and maybe a half-dozen more. I guarantee, *boring* won't be a word found in our vocabulary."

"Yes, Colonel…sir," she said, releasing a shaky breath.

IN UNIFORM

There's something special about a man in uniform. Maybe because he's a man who takes charge, a man you can count on, and yes, maybe even love....

Superromance presents *In Uniform*, an occasional series that features men who live up to your every fantasy—and then some!

Look for:

Mad About the Major
by Roz Denny Fox
Superromance #821
Coming in January 1999

An Officer and a Gentleman
by Elizabeth Ashtree
Superromance #828
Coming in March 1999

SEAL It with a Kiss
by Rogenna Brewer
Superromance #833
Coming in April 1999

Available wherever Harlequin books are sold.

HARLEQUIN®
Makes any time special ™

HARLEQUIN SUPERROMANCE®

From January to March 1999,
read about three women whose
New Millennium resolution is

By the Year 2000: *Marriage*

The Wedding Vow by Laura Abbot.
Available in January 1999.
Allison Sinclair knows *why* she wants
to get married, but she doesn't know *who*.
Until she meets Chris Naylor....

The Maine Man by Ellen James.
Available in February 1999.
Meg Danley seems to have lost sight of her
goal—to be married by the year 2000—until she
catches sight of *The Maine Man!*

A Man for Mom by Sherry Lewis.
Available in March 1999.
Sharon Lawrence isn't interested in remarriage—
but her teenage daughters think Gabe Malone
might be *A Man for Mom.*

Available wherever Harlequin books are sold.

HARLEQUIN®
Makes any time special ™

COMING NEXT MONTH

#822 THE MAINE MAN • Ellen James
By the Year 2000: Marriage
The last thing on Meg Danley's mind is marriage. For one
thing, there's no fiancé in sight; for another, her demanding
career leaves no time to plan a wedding. Both good reasons for
Meg to regret the vow she made ten years ago with her two
best friends—they'd all be married by the year 2000. Meg is
quite prepared to miss the deadline...until she meets
Jack Elliott. Suddenly marriage is a definite possibility.

#823 ARE YOU MY MOMMY? • Kay David
Count on a Cop
Ray Menendez is a cop. A good cop. He knows the standard
procedure for dealing with a lost kid—turn him over to the
proper authorities. When his ex-wife, Abbie, asks him to help
the little boy she found, he knows that *not* getting involved is
also the smart thing to do. But even though their marriage is
over, he doesn't want Abbie to get hurt. Sometimes the smart
thing isn't the *right* thing....

#824 WHAT A MAN'S GOT TO DO • Lynnette Kent
Home on the Ranch
Rancher Dex Hightower wants custody of his six-year-old
daughter. So he needs to hire the best lawyer in town. And that
means Claire Cavanaugh. But Claire grew up on a ranch and
she isn't convinced that kind of life is best for a little girl. But
Dex isn't like the cowboys she's known. Maybe life on a ranch
with *him* wouldn't be too bad—even for a grown woman.

#825 FIRST BORN SON • Muriel Jensen
The Delancey Brothers
Tate Delancey and his brothers have inherited a winery in
Oregon, and Tate sees it as the perfect opportunity to start a
new life. He never expected things to be easy, and that was
before he found out the winery came with a beautiful but
prickly field manager named Colette. She fights him at every
turn—but he soon realizes fighting's the last thing he wants to
do with her!